CLEO BROWNE

# August

*A Tombs Security + Devil's Rose MC Crossover*

# Contents

# Trigger Warning

This book deals with a badassery in all its forms.
Please be aware that in order for these characters to be badass,
this book contains content that some readers may find
disturbing, such as graphic descriptions of violence and
torture, R18 sex scenes, and hiking.

# Hey, readers!

This book goes out to YOU. All the wonderful folk who took a
chance on my first book, Rhodie.
Without you, this book wouldn't have happened. I would have
just faded away into obscurity never to be seen or heard from
again.
So, this book is your fault.
Enjoy.

# Chapter 1

Gus

"Oh Guuuuuuus,"

Shit, shit, shit. The rumble of my brother's footsteps gets closer and closer and I'm really not in the mood for their shit right now. I can either take it on the chin or hide. I push my chair out and slide to the floor.

"What are you doing?"

Over the top of my desk, my sister stares back at me. Her eyes large behind her thick-framed glasses.

"Jesus, Dayz! How long have you been there?"

"From when you said shit three times and then slithered to the floor."

"Who slithered to the floor?" Tav asks, playfully pulling on Tuesday's messy bun.

"Gus. He was going to hide from you and Jules."

"Why?"

"Probably because you're going to bust his balls about Ana." Shrugging, she takes a seat at the small conference table in my office. It's where we have our team meetings and where she always sits.

Tav pulls up the chair across from my desk, leaving the other for Jules. Who, speak of the Devil, saunters in just as I heave myself back into my chair. When I first came up with the idea for Tombs Security, there was no question that I would involve my siblings. Now, I regret that decision.

"Ok, say what you have to say and then get back to work. I've got shit to do."

My younger siblings all share a look. Well, Jules and Tav do, then they look toward Tuesday, or Dayz as we call her, who is, per usual, avoiding eye contact. She's on the spectrum, so we're used to this behavior. Tav clears his throat. As the easy going sibling, he's always the one tasked with getting the ball rolling on shitty topics.

"So, you have that meeting with Ana today."

"Yep."

"Aaaaand it's been, what? Two months since you last saw her?"

"It's been two months and 13 days since Ana came to the Devils Rose MC clubhouse to lockdown with us," Tuesday butts in.

As if I don't know how many days it's been since a short, curvy Kiwi whirlwind crashed into my life. Two and a half months ago, my sister tracked down the guy who murdered our parents. He was stalking a member of the local MC. Long story short, we ended up putting a stop to the skin trade in our part of the state, got rid of a Polish crime lord and somehow became allies with both the local Bratva and the Devils Rose MC. Oh, and my sister became an Ol Lady. In the middle of that messed-up ride, I met Ana. Best friends with the head of the Bratva; his secretary, and the most intriguing woman I'd ever met.

"We caught you holding hands-"

"- and that time we caught them kissing in the hall-"

"-Thank you, Dayz, I forgot about that. So you see Gus, we all thought you had the start of something good with Ana. And then nothing. What happened? Did she ghost you?"

Shaking my head, I take in my siblings. Jules and Tav are both staring at me across my desk. Well, Jules is giving me his RDF, Resting Dick Face. Tav is eagerly waiting to hear that Ana realized she was too good for me or some shit. Tuesday, as usual, is sitting with her laptop open on the table, tapping away whilst listening in.

"No, she didn't ghost me, dickhead. We just... lost touch."

Tav's eyebrow rises. "You...lost touch? Dude, how hard is it to text someone? Shit. There's no hope for you." He shakes his head in disgust.

"Look, we all had shit that we had to do after breaking up Kraykowski's trafficking ring. Ana is just as busy. She has to make sure the Bratva is running smoothly while Roman's away. We have business to attend to. That's what happens when you're an adult."

"An adult would learn that communicating openly and honestly with each other is the best way forward in a relationship. Trust me," Dayz says.

I roll my lips between my teeth and notice my brothers are smirking at her statement. Dayz has terrible communication skills, but obviously being with Rhodie is rubbing off on her. I wasn't sure that the enforcer for the local MC was going to be the best choice for my baby sister, but Rhodie is a pussycat as far as Dayz is concerned. He's patient and gentle with her and doesn't seem to have any problem with the fact that she is quite the violent interrogator.

"That is expert advice, Dayz, thank you. Rhodie been teaching you stuff again?"

"Yeah. I got the lecture on communication and consent when I surprised Rhodie by sticking the Dr Joel Power Probe Prostate massager in him without warning."

Absolute chaos breaks out over that little tidbit as Tav falls to the floor in a coughing fit and I watch Jules lean forward and thump him not so lightly on the back. I raise my voice to be heard over the two of them.

"Dayz, remember when we had that chat about too much information?"

"Of course. We've had it numerous times since I was 14. Wait, ok, soz, yup got it. Not something to share with brothers." Jules sits back, straightens his shirt, not a hair out of place, and watches Tav finally pull himself back into his chair, looking like absolute shit. His face red, cheeks wet from crying, either from the choking or the beating Jules just gave him.

"Fuck Dayz, too much." He gasps out.

"Ok brother, so what are you going to do?" Jules asks me, returning to their point.

"Roman wants a complete overhaul of security systems at his country house office. Since Ana is running the show at the moment, my meeting is with her."

"Aaaaaaand?" Tav prompts, waving his hands in a circular motion to keep me talking.

"And I'm not sure I have time for a relationship. I have this business and you fuckers to keep in line."
Tav's hand flies to his chest as he gasps, "What!? We do not need you to keep us in line, August. Last I checked, we are all old enough to take care of ourselves. Us looking out for you on

the other hand..." he waves his hand around, obviously hoping for Jules or Dayz to agree with him, but they both sit there with blank looks on their faces.

"You two are shit at backing a brother up," he snarks out before carrying on. "What we're trying to say, Gus, is that it's time you put yourself out there. I mean, you're a good-looking man now, but once those grays really come in and you get a gut, willing quality women will dry right up." Tav makes a weird slurping noise to illustrate his point, but all it illustrates is how much I want to punch him in his face. Which looks a hell of a lot like mine, just without the crooked nose from where I broke it playing football.

"Jesus, I'm 38, not 108."

"Male fertility reduces from around the age of 40, however, it is recommended you procreate before the age of 38. Less mutant sperm that way." Dayz very helpfully pipes up.

"Did you fall down a fertility hole, sis?" Tav asks, which is a fair question. Tuesday often has questions and then falls down the black hole of research.

"No, Rhodie and I were looking at the best time for us to procreate." The sound of Dayz's tapping on her laptop breaks through the silence that's descended. Jules slowly turns away from our baby sister until he's staring me in the eye.

"When are we killing him?" He asks in a low voice.

"No one is going to kill Rhodie. Because I love him and he loves me and you all love me and that means that he's exempt from killing." She squints up at us, a furrow in her brow, so Tav answers her.

"Yeah, Dayz, you know when you love someone, you don't want to do things that will upset them."

"And killing Rhodie will definitely upset me."

Tav leans forward and whispers to me and Jules, "Pops will kill him."

I can't help but agree with that deduction. However, this fleeting talk of Dayz procreating has led my mind to a place where I have a little boy who looks like my brothers but with Ana's bright green eyes. I shake my head at the thought. No time for that, I have shit that needs doing.

"Right. While you're all here, interrupting my work day, I need someone on the florist in town, Flora's Buds. They got broken into recently and want a full system. Jules, I'm sending you."

He nods and takes the initial contract paperwork I hand him.

"Dayz is working with that new accountant in town, so Tav, you're on monitoring our current clients for the meantime. All good?" They all nod, but no one seems to leave. Staring at my family, I take a deep breath and hold it for three beats before breathing out.

"Ok, now if you could all kindly see yourselves out so I can go to this consultation with Ana, that would be great."

"I haven't eaten since I started working on this job. I need sustenance." Tuesday speaks into the room, knowing full well her brothers will drop everything to go to lunch with her.

"Come on, Dayz, lunch is on me." Tav gets up, shoving the expensive, ergonomic guest chair with his foot. I make a note to kick the furniture in his office. I watch as he helps Dayz pack her shit up before he throws his arm over our little sister and they chat about potential food choices. Sitting across from me, Jules is busy giving me the stink eye.

"Is there something I can help you with?"

He stands and stretches. "Nope. Just don't fuck this up." And with those words of wisdom, he messes up the pens on my desk and walks out whistling, following after Tav and Tuesday. I love them, but Jesus they give me a headache. Checking the time, I realize if I don't move my ass, I'll be late.

## Ana

Shit, shit, shit. I have an hour before that handsome, bossy bastard August Tombs walks through my door and I'm not ready to see him yet. I have way too much work to get done. I love my job, but with my boss and best friend off gallivanting around Russia, it's left me in charge of the Bartashev Bratva. Shaking my head, I will myself not to snort at the absurdity of it all. I'm a 5'3, chonky woman from New Zealand. Only in Roman's world would it make sense to choose me to keep the Bratva ticking over in his absence.

"Miss? Ivan and Jenn are here to see you."

"Thanks, Igor, and please, I've been here for like five years. Can you call me Ana?"

"Of course, miss," I squint at him as he backs out of the doorway with a wry smile on his face. He's been doing that since he met me. He's soon replaced by Ivan, Roman's brigadier, and his very awesome wife, Jenn.

"Come in, come in! And sit down, Ivan." I usher them in and give them both a big squeeze. I've known them almost as long as I've known Roman and Sasha.

Taking my place behind Roman's monstrous desk, I look across the room at my friends who stand out like dog balls in this room. Both in their late 40s, dressed head to toe in black; Ivan and

Jenn look like grim reapers in the surprisingly jolly and yet horribly garish office. Although I suppose that's what you get when the decorator is a bisexual Pakhan with dubious taste and the money of Jeff Bezos. Only Roman's inner circle know the real Roman. The Roman the world sees is the cold, calculating head of the Bratva. His real friends know he loves trash reality TV and ugly furniture.

"So Ana, how are you?" Ivan asks in his accented English.

"Oh, all formal now that you're visiting me here at the office? Where were those manners when I was checking up on you at home, huh?"

"It's this office. It does something to me." He smirks back at me as I roll my eyes. "Whatever. Right, give me the update. How are you getting on?"

As a brigadier, Ivan's job is to oversee his own crew. However, as my friend, he protected me and August Tombs and got shot because of it. I owe this man my life.

"Ah, tis but a scratch, my dear."

A scoff escapes me at the reference. "Riiiight. Ok, scratch that. Jenn, how's he getting on?"

I ignore Ivan's cry of indignation and I take great glee at his discomfort when his wife spills exactly how well, or not well, he is getting on. We spend the next while going over Ivan's injury and his rehab. Jenn is a real ball buster, so I have a feeling that he's going to come out of rehab healthier and stronger than when he went in.

"Well, this was a good chat, but next time, maybe just call Jenn in. No one lets me talk." The big man broods in the plush purple armchair he's stuffed himself in. Ivan is at least 6'5 and he's about as wide as a fridge, so sulking doesn't look good on him.

"Don't be a baby! You know we love you." I say, waving a hand dismissively at him. Ivan's face lights up at this and as his wife playfully admonishes him too. I love these two. You can tell they've been together for a long time and think the world of each other. But nothing makes a girl feel more painfully single than having a happy couple up in her grill.

"Do you want to get that? That's the second time it's gone off,"

I've been willfully ignoring the sound of my phone vibrating on the top of the desk.

"No way! I'm in a very important meeting with my two favorite people."

"Lying isn't very becoming Ana. No one likes Ivan enough for him to be their favorite," Jenn says with a twinkle in her eye.

"Yeah, yeah. Right, we'll let you get back to it, kid. Give me a yell if you need anything. Anything at all." Ivan says, and I watch as he tries to haul himself out of the tiny chair he's sitting in.

"No way, big man. You're on leave until the doctor gives you a clean bill of health. Remember, if you need anything - more rehab, new equipment - anything, just let me know and I'll arrange it. Jenn, make sure you let me know, yeah?" Getting up, I make my way around the desk to hug my friends.

When I first arrived in America, the sheer size and scale of everything overwhelmed me. After growing up in foster care in small town New Zealand, with very few people to call family or friends, a sheer stroke of luck led me to Roman and his Bratva family.

"Will do, don't you worry. He'll be back to work in no time. I'm sick of him being at home.'' We both share a laugh while

Ivan glowers down at us.

"I'm right here," he huffs out.

"We know. You're hard to miss." I smirk up at him. He lunges to wrap his large arm around my neck, giving me a noogie that is going to do absolutely nothing for my hair, then dropping a kiss to the top of my head.

"You're doing a good job as underboss, girl. Roman left us in excellent hands."

Not being able to stop the snort that escapes me, I slap him on the shoulder. "Whatever. I'm just the secretary."

He shakes his head at me and wraps his arm over his wife's shoulder as they leave.

Running my hands through my hair, I twist it up with a claw clip, ignoring the jumping and bumping of my cell phone across the desk. The number is flashing as unknown and I don't think answering it will do me any favors, so I continue to ignore it. Note to self: ask Tuesday to trace the number or something.

"Miss? August Tombs is here,"

"Mr? Send him in, please." I watch Igors' white eyebrows fly up to meet his non-existent hairline before a small smirk drifts across his face.

"Certainly Miss," Igor backs out of the doorway, and in mere moments, August Tombs fills the space. He's every bit as broodingly beautiful as I remember. Damn it. I hoped that the stress of being threatened and then locked down at the MC clubhouse had somehow messed up my perception of things. But no. He's still thigh-clenchingly hot.

"Ana, it's good to see you again." Gus eats up the space between us with his long legs. For a moment there, I'm not sure whether to meet him halfway or what. I decide to walk around my desk as it's what I do with all the people I have meetings with. I extend my hand, but Gus has other ideas. He places his large hand on the small of my back. His soft, woodsy scent wraps around me as he leans in and brushes his lips against my cheek before releasing me. If I were a weaker woman, I'd follow him and perch my size 16 ass in his lap, but I'm made of tougher stuff, even if my vagina doesn't agree. I take a couple of breaths before returning to my chair.

"Gus, it's good to-"

"Ana, I'm sorry that-" we both stop and awkwardly wait for the other to speak. Gus clears his throat, opens his mouth, but before anything can come out, my phone vibrates its way toward him.

"Do you wanna get that?" Gus asks, that damn sexy eyebrow raised.

"Nope. It's fine. That's my personal cell. Let it go to voicemail."

He eyes it for a moment until it stops, and the light goes off.

"I was just wanting to say that I'm really sor-" he watches as my phone lights up once again, moving across the desk "You should get that."

"No, no need."

"Dammit, Ana, pick up the phone."

"No." I watch as his jaw clenches slightly "I don't answer personal calls when I'm in a meeting. Besides, it's an unknown number. I don't answer them." The light goes off on my phone and the vibrating stops once again. We both stare at it, waiting. I'm staring so hard it's almost like I'm daring the bloody thing to ring again. As if I willed it into existence, it lights up and starts vibrating once again.

"Fuck, that's it!" Gus snatches it up in his hand and I jump up, thinking he's going to throw the thing at the wall. Instead, he slides the call button before growling, "She's busy. What do you want?"

His head tilts for a moment, his perfect man-brows pulling together in a frown over his chocolate colored eyes. His dark hair is longer on the top, pushed back by him running his hands through it rather than artfully styling it. His light brown skin somehow glows under the crappy mood lighting Roman chose for this room. How unfair.

"Yes, that's fine. I'll let her know and she'll be in touch."

Shit, I missed all that. He regards me for a moment, squints, purses his lips and stares for even longer.

"So, who was it?"

"Immigration,"

"Immi– shit! Immigration?! What did they want?"

"They want you to know you haven't updated your working visa papers, and as your employer is currently in Russia, you will be escorted from the country in 30 days."

A squawk leaves my mouth and I'm temporarily stunned. What the absolute hell is going on?

"No, there must be some mistake. That isn't right. I'm allowed to live and work here for another three years. We just got my visa extended." This can't be happening. I love it here. My friends and my new chosen family are here.

I think better when I'm moving, so I kick off my heels and pace aggressively around the room.

"That is all correct, however with your employer out of the country for an unspecified amount of time and you taking over a new role, you are in the unusual position of being without your so-called 'work sponsor'."

"Shit a brick! There must be something I can do? Surely Roman has a contact in immigration?"

"If he did, this would never have been flagged."

"Surely they'll be understanding? I mean, my paperwork is done and he won't be out of the country forever. If I talk to them and explain the situation, they might go easy on me."

"The one thing this country doesn't 'go easy' on is immigration."

"Knowing how America was founded, I find that very ironic."

Gus huffs out a breath before his eyes travel the length of me. I feel it like a caress. Is it hot in here?

"There is one thing that could work."

"Hit me with it."

"Marry me."

# Chapter 2

Gus

I think I've broken her. As soon as the words came flying out of my mouth, Ana froze on the spot, a wheezing noise escaping her plump lips. I drink her in like a man dying of thirst. It's been just over two months since I was last in her orbit and my memory didn't do her justice. With her shoes halfway across the room, her little painted toes are on display. Her pencil skirt outlines her wide hips and lush thighs while her drapey blouse shows off her large tits and a hint of cleavage. My pulse picks up and I'm pretty certain it's centered directly in my cock. My gaze drifts up to take in her wide moss green eyes framed with thick black eyelashes. What I wouldn't give to see them looking up at me with my cock in her beautiful mouth. Speaking of her mouth, I watch as her pink tongue pushes through her plump lips and she wiggles it around, back and forth, side to side.

"What the hell are you doing?"

"I'm checking to make sure I haven't had a stroke." She says, as if it's obvious.

"What?! Shit, do you feel ok? Quick, have a seat, let me check." I'm on her in two strides, my large hands on her lush hips, pushing her down onto the ugliest couch I've ever seen.

"Wait, get off me!" She slaps at my hands while I try to grab them.

"Dammit, I can't tell if you've had a stroke if you keep hitting me!"

"I think I'm fine. My speech isn't slurred or anything. What about you?" I stare down at her in confusion.

"What about me?"

"How are you feeling?" She grabs my face in her small hands and starts moving my head around.

"Any slurring? Facial weakness? How's your mobility?" At this stage, we're just grabbing and moving each other's body parts around, and I'm not sure why. I take a step back and take a deep breath.

"Ok, what the fuck was that?"

"I thought one of us may have had a stroke."

"And you thought that because...?" I don't remember Ana being nuts, but I guess they were unprecedented times and all.

"Well, I'm pretty certain you asked me to marry you. So I figured either I had a stroke, or you did."

"I did ask you to marry me."

"Why would you do that?" She frowns up at me.

"To stop you from being forced out of the country. Think about it, we get married and you get a spousal visa. It doesn't matter how long Roman is away, or what job you do, you'll still be able to live here."

I watch as she hops up off the couch and starts pacing again. I noticed she did this when we were at the MC. It was after we found out that both she and my sister, along with Roman's ex wife and daughter, were all set to be kidnapped and auctioned. It's a stress tell.

I follow her with my eyes as she stomps across the room from one side to the other. This has to be the ugliest room I've ever had the pleasure of being in. Roman's house is as you'd expect from the Pakhan of the Bartashev Bratva. Huge, with a lot of marble and gold accents. But this room, his home office, this room looks like the furniture came from an Elton John yard sale.

I go back to watching Ana pace, drinking in the sight of her ass as it jiggles away from me before she turns and I get to enjoy the sight of her tits jiggling toward me. She stops directly in front of me, toe to toe, looks up at me, frowns, and then stomps off again. I can hear her muttering to herself and I'm not sure if it's all in English or not.

"What ethnicity are you?" She spins to look at me.

"What?"

"I know you're from New Zealand, but what ethnicity are you? You aren't white, but you're not black either. Do they have black people in New Zealand? Anyway, it's just that I'm certain you don't always speak English." A flicker of uncertainty passes over her face before a small smile teases at her lips.

"I don't know what I am. I got left at the hospital a day or so after I was born. I was born addicted to whatever my mother was on, so no one wanted to adopt me. I spent my time in different foster care homes. But my mum, or the woman I call Mum, is Maori, indigenous to Aotearoa, New Zealand. When she gets frustrated or mad or whatever, she rants in Maori. I must have picked up the habit." She shrugs and smiles to herself as she goes back to pacing.

I realize with those words that there is actually very little I know about this woman. Does that make me want to take back my proposal? Fuck no.

When I walked into this ostentatiously ugly office today and I saw her, I knew I wanted her. By whatever means. Not just her body, though that is a fucking bonus. I love a woman with meat on her bones. I'm not a small man and I like to know that the woman I'm with can take a good, hard fuck. Aside from that, I like the way I feel around her. My chest feels warm and I feel lighter than I have in a while. I enjoy orbiting around her, and if I want a chance to really get to know this woman and all she offers, I need to convince her my idea will work.

"Look, I know I was an ass and didn't get in touch. I didn't ghost you–"

"– I dunno, I felt pretty haunted–"

I blow out a breath, eyes on the swirly patterned rug. "I'm sorry. Shit just got busy running damage control and making sure all known threats had been taken care of and then I realized I'd left it too long."

She lets out a little sigh before looking up at me. "Gus, I get it. I had a phone too, you know. I could have contacted you. But you're right, shit got busy, and we left it too long. So why this now? If marriage is the best way for me to stay, then I can find someone else. You don't have to sacrifice yourself on my behalf."

A pain shoots through my jaw due to how tightly I've clenched it thinking of Ana with someone else. No fucking way is that happening.

"Look, it makes sense. I like you, I'm sure you like me," I watch as a beautiful blush stains her cheeks. "We know we have good chemistry –" fucking good chemistry, from what the few kisses we shared told me. "– I know your friends. You know my whole family. It will be easy to show immigration that we are the real deal."

She's chewing on her plump bottom lip and I really want to reach over and pull it from her teeth, but I keep charging ahead. "We stay married for two years, then after that, if you want a divorce, I'll give you one. That should be long enough for you to have permanent residency."

"And that's it? That's the plan?" She asks, and I can tell she's not convinced.

"Look, I'll give you 24 hours to think about it. In the mean-time, let's look at this security plan, yeah?" Her shoulders slump in relief and she walks behind the biggest desk in the world, her business persona wrapped around her once more, showing how in control she is. She's fucking breathtaking and I really hope she'll be mine.


## Ana


"He WHAT!?" Roman screeches at me from my computer screen. His gorgeous big blonde husband cringing at the sheer volume. I'm tucked up in my PJs on the Elton John couch with a glass of wine, a box of chocolates, and my two best friends on the screen.

"She said he proposed to her Roman. But you may not have heard her over your obnoxiously loud popcorn chewing," Sasha says drily.

Just over five years ago, I was backpacking around Texas and stopped at a gas station. A few men that can only be described as 'fucking shifty' came in and I got the hell outta there. Growing up in foster care, you get a sixth sense of when bad stuff is gonna go down. Hearing muffled yells coming from a car in the forecourt, I popped the trunk only to come face to face with a big, blonde hottie. Said big blonde hottie happened to be the husband of the head of the Russian mafia. Sasha took me home with him to keep me safe in case of any blowback from the failed kidnappers.

When he first introduced me to Roman, I thought he was the coldest, most calculating person I had ever met. But I realized quickly that it is the mafia mask he puts on. In reality, around his close friends and family, Roman is a teddy bear. And quite the screecher.

"Turns out when my employer decides to leave for over 2 months, immigration gets all funny about it."

"We'll come home straight away, won't we, babe?" Sasha says, but I can tell by the look on Roman's face he's scheming.

"I don't know Sash, I have a lot of work to do. I really am needed here." Sasha gives his husband the most offensive side-eye I've ever seen.

"Think about it. Ana marrying August gives her permanent residency. I think you should do it. While you're at it, make sure you do ALL your wifely duties."

I feel my eyebrows hit my hairline and I choke on the Ferrero Rocher I've just popped into my mouth. I'm in a precarious sitch where I don't know whether to spit or swallow, (heh, that's what she said) so I decide to spit, chocolate goop going all over my front. My eyes are watering and I'm hacking like a cat with a fur ball. By the time I get myself under control by chugging half a glass of wine to wash down the rest of the death ball, both Roman and Sasha are staring at me in horror.

"On second thought, maybe leave the poor man alone."

"I hate you sometimes." I manage to wheeze out.

"No, you don't, you love me."

I sigh because I know it's true. "Yeah, you're right. I love you and miss you both." I say to the two men on the screen. "Can I confess something?"

"Shoot," Roman says around a mouthful of popcorn.

"I think I like him. And I think I might want to marry him." I whisper out before I quickly cover my eyes with my hands, my legs coming up as I curl into myself. My mortification at my confession only abates when I hear sniggering. Peeking through my fingers, I look at the screen.

"Babe, the chemistry between you two was so hot that even Tuesday picked up on it, and that woman is oblivious to anything that isn't murdery or Rhodie," Sasha says.

"Look, Ana. As your best friend and your boss, marry the man. It solves your residency problem and means that you stay indefinitely. That paperwork we have to file for your working visa is a total ball ache."

"What do you mean 'we'? I fill that paperwork out! You just sign it, you lazy *zasranets*!" I flip him the bird and watch as he runs a finger beneath each eye as if wiping away tears.

"She's calling me an asshole in my mother tongue. She truly loves me," Roman sniffles out.

"Yeah, yeah." I chew on my lip for a moment. "So, do you think I should do it?" Roman stares at me for a moment, his face softening

"I've seen the way he looks at you. I've seen the way he treats his genius sister. I've seen the way he treats his family. He's a good man, Ana. He'll treat you well and keep you safe when I cannot. Give him a chance." He gives me a soft smile before it turns shark-like. This is the Roman the public sees.

"And if he hurts you, I'll kill him."

* * *

Lying in bed after three full hours of Googling everything I could possibly think of that would help my immigration case, it would seem smarty pants August Tombs is right. The best way to get out of this is to marry him. I mean, what's the worst that can happen? You fall in love with the man and he realizes you're not worth it. Then he leaves just like everyone else you loved when you were a kid. That's what. Ugh. Damn my childhood trauma and fear of abandonment, which, let's be honest, is a totally valid fear to have if you were dumped as a baby.

Thinking back on my childhood, it wasn't all bad. Yes, there were crappy foster homes. Too many kids. Super strict and sometimes abusive parents. But there were also happy homes too. When I was 8, they placed me in the home of Michael and Deborah Taylor, and it felt like all my Christmases had come at once. Almost too good to be true. Michael and Deborah, or Mick and Debs as they liked to be called, fought a long hard battle to gain my trust, but once they did, they became my first proper family. So much so that I started calling them Mum and Dad after a year.

We spent every weekend and holiday in the outdoors, camping and tramping. We'd take the caravan out on a road trip, never quite knowing where we would end up. Once we were wherever we wanted to stop, Mum would set up camp while Dad and I would tramp and fish and do outdoorsy stuff. Dad taught me everything I know about surviving in the bush. It was on one of our tramping trips that Dad told me about his dream of traveling to America. Somewhere along the way, Dad's dream became my dream. We'd talk about the things we'd eat and what we'd do.

Life was the best I had ever had it. Until the day I was called to the school office and told I had to get home quickly. When I got there, Mum was a mess. Dad had had a heart attack at work and there was nothing they could do. The weeks that followed were awful, me and Mum were in a daze. Then Child Services arrived. Without Dad, they didn't allow Mum to keep me as her foster daughter. Another family took me in, but I hated it so much that I ran away. For the next two years, until I aged out of the system, social workers would find me at Mick and Debs and drag me home. But it wasn't my home.

Once I was old enough to leave the system, I went back to live at home with Mum, working my arse off in terrible jobs, trying to save enough money to travel to America and live all of Dad's dreams. Never in my life would I have thought that would lead me to managing the Bratva in Roman's absence. Mum always laughs about that little twist of fate. I wonder what she'd think of me marrying a man for a visa? Knowing Mum, she'd take one look at August Tombs and tell me to "let that man bang you like a screen door in the wind". I would be lying if I said I hadn't thought about it. In fact, I've thought about it so much, I had to get a new B.O.B because I wore mine out.

Could I do this? Could I marry him and convince everyone we are a couple without getting hurt at the end of two years? Could I have August Tombs as my husband? Or should I go home to Mum? The thoughts bounce around before settling on an answer. Gus is coming by tomorrow at 11am, but I don't need the extra time to think. Reaching for my bedside table, I feel around for the rubbery lilac case of my cell phone. Phone in hand, I pull up Gus's contact. I type one word and hit send.

Yes.

# Chapter 3

Gus

"Are you sure you're ok with this?" I squeeze Ana's much smaller hand with my giant, rough mitt. We're standing outside my cabin, looking towards my Pops' house where he and my siblings have gathered for our usual Wednesday dinner. We can't do Sundays because that's Pops "self care day". That means he spends the day doing all sorts of old-fashioned man grooming with products that probably contain lead or arsenic before he heads to Rosie's Diner to try to pick her up.

Looking down at the tiny brunette beside me, I admit I was shocked when she texted last night with her answer. I was slightly concerned that maybe she hadn't thought it through enough. But, I've since learned that once this woman decides to do something, she does it and she doesn't fuck around. I called into her office at 11 am to find her in a cream-colored pants thing. The pants that are attached to the top, whatever you call them. I call them a gift from God because this thing showed off her tits perfectly, the deep V exposed tanned flesh with enough cleavage to be sexy, but keeping enough covered to have me wanting more. If I thought that was a sight, watching her walk purposefully ahead of me into the courthouse almost had me buckling at the knees. Her big, round ass jiggling its way up the courthouse steps level with my eyes is something that is burned into my memories forever.

A gentle squeeze of my hand snaps me out of my thoughts.

"Yup. Dinner with your family is the best time to tell them. Get it all over with at once." Her green eyes bore into mine before she decisively nods her head. I take a deep breath and gently squeeze her hand back.

"Here we go."

* * *

"You got married? Wait, didn't she hate your guts like two days ago?" Tav says, his face screwed up in utter confusion.

"Yup, she hates him," Dayz agrees, eyes on her fork separating her peas from her potatoes.

"I don't hate August,"

"Ah, yes you do. I remember you clearly stating when we were on lockdown, 'August Tombs is a bossy asshole. I hate him'," Tuesday states matter-of-factly.

"I said 'I hate his alpha bullshit'," Ana corrects gently. As if that makes it better. Although, I concede, I was a bossy asshole trying to keep everyone safe and I don't regret a minute of it.

"Um, I think I would remember that."

"I'm not sure you would, because if I remember correctly halfway through my sentence Rhodie stuck his tongue in your mouth and you lost all train of thought.”

I watch as Tuesday’s eyes narrow slightly. She tilts her head for a moment and then nods.

“Yeah, actually, I could see how that could happen.” Rhodie takes a big bite of his bread roll, smiles widely, and looks at my sister as if she invented Harley Davidson, beer, and strippers.

“Well, I called it at the clubhouse. I saw this happening from a mile away. So, welcome to the family girl.” Pops says and starts digging into his roast.

“Wait, how come she gets a welcome? You call me names and shoot at me!” Rhodie drops his roll in outrage.

“She -” Pops points over the table “isn’t trying to stick anything into my grandson.”

“That you KNOW of,” Tuesday helpfully points out, making the table groan collectively.

“Anyway, we got married and Ana has agreed to take my name.”

Jules’s eyes flick back and forth between the two of us. “So, what’s really going on?”

“What do you mean? Are you deaf, kid? They got married. She’s probably pregnant. Are you pregnant?”

I see a red blush taking over Ana’s face as her mouth opens and closes, but nothing comes out. This, however, does not deter my grandfather.

“You don’t look pregnant. Has your, ah, bust gotten larger?” Pops asks as he gestures with his fork in a big circle around his chest. My eyes roll toward the ceiling and I’m silently willing Pops to stop, but he just keeps going.

“I remember your grandmother, God rest her. As soon as she got pregnant, her tits got huge. It was a fun nine months.” I can feel something rising inside of me. I’m not sure if it’s bile or my blood pressure, but I really want to put my hands over my ears and take a few deep breaths. Instead, I pinch the bridge of my nose and count to seven.

"Ana is being investigated by immigration and I offered to marry her. So, no, we are not pregnant."

My family stares at me for a beat before they all start talking over each other about how this makes so much more sense. I look at Ana and she's wide-eyed, taking in the chaos that is my family.

I like to keep a tight rein on things. Myself, my siblings, and my Pops. They're all my responsibility, but it can be a Herculean task sometimes. I wouldn't have them any other way, though. I know what it's like to lose the people you love in the blink of an eye, so anything I can do to make sure who I have left is safe and happy, I'll do it. I reach under the table and gently place my hand on Ana's smaller one, resting in her lap. I give it a little squeeze and she turns her face to me. Every time I look into her bright green eyes, I feel calm. She smiles up at me and gives my hand a squeeze before letting it go and starting in on her meal.

"So, how is this whole thing going to work, exactly?" Tav asks, gesturing between me and Ana with his fork.

"You'll have to ask Gus. It's his plan." Ana shrugs before going back to her meal. God, I'm glad she enjoys her food and isn't into eating only three salad leaves with no dressing. I swallow my mouthful, giving myself a little extra time because if I'm being honest, I didn't think she'd agree, let alone that we'd get this far.

"Well, for starters, we have to live together. Thankfully, Ana has agreed to move in with me."

"Sweet! We can be neighbors!" Dayz says with more

enthusiasm than I would expect from her.

Following the murder of our parents in a home invasion, Pops came to live with Dayz and Tav, who were only 13 and 16. The problem was, none of them wanted to live in what Dayz had dubbed "the murder house". So Pops moved them all into a caravan on site while they demolished the old house and built a smaller farm-style one. After college, both Jules and I decided we would rather be home in Rose Grove with our family than in the big city. Thankfully, all the houses in this area are built on enormous land blocks, so me and Jules had small two-bedroom cabins built near the back of the section. After Tav and Dayz finished college, they returned home and did the same thing. I live on one side of Dayz, Tav on the other side of her, and Jules next to him. We can see each other from our porches. It may seem weird that my family lives this way, but it works for us.

"Yeah, totally neighbors. We could sit on the porch drinking wine and stuff." Ana offers, however, Dayz is shaking her head emphatically.

"That's a nice offer, but I can't do wine. Tequila is fine, though."

Tav frowns her way. "Why can't you drink wine?"

"It makes me slutty."

Ana chokes a little, and it feels natural for me to reach behind her and rub her back until she settles.

"Now what have I told you, baby girl? There's no such thing as being slutty. There's only being a strong woman who is comfortable with herself and her sexuality and if she so wishes, she can share that with whom she chooses." Pops nods to himself and I can see Ana's lips twitching.

Fucking hell, I knew that someone must have given Dayz all

the information that young women get, but I just kinda figured that happened at school. Or maybe Pops gave her a book or something. Now I'm wondering just what Pops' parenting actually entailed.

"I like when you drink wine," Rhodie growls before dropping a kiss on my sister's neck. Suddenly, he flinches back from her,

"What the hell was that?"

"Horny dog training tool." Pops sprays Rhodie with water from a spray bottle I hadn't even noticed sitting next to him on the table. A sweet chuckling sound washes over me and I glance down to see Ana bright-eyed watching the shit show that is Tombs family dinner.

"Jules, you found a good woman yet, like your brother?" Since Dayz settled down, Pops has been on our cases to think about 'hitching our wagon' to one woman. Which is going to be fucking hard for Jules, given he seems to only entertain women in groups.

"Nope. Don't need a good one, just a willing one. Or two." He smirks at Pops with a glint in his eye. Pops just sighs before turning his beady eye onto Tav.

"What about you, boy? Any females?"

"Well, Pops, they tend to not like being called that. But nothing serious on my end. I've been out a couple of times with a nice woman, but she's hesitant."

"Lemme guess," Jules butts in, "She's at least 10 years older than you and needs to take it slow for the kids?" Tav gives him the stink eye, but given that Jules was born with the stinkiest eye in our family, it's a losing battle.

"No! She's only 5 years older than me." Tav mumbles out.

I check on Ana and am pleasantly surprised to see her eyes pinging back and forth over the table, bouncing between my siblings and grandfather. It's not like she doesn't know them. They were all locked down with us at Devils' Rose MC. But there were lots of people there, the MC brothers and their families. Roman and his family. They all sort of ran interference for my family, I guess. Now, she's getting the full, uncut version and I'm surprised by how relieved I feel at her enjoying herself and not running for the hills. I lean down, taking a sneaky sniff of her scent, before whispering in her ear,

"You doing ok there babe?" She turns her face to me, eyes glittering, a broad smile across her face.

"Your family is fucking whackadoodle. I love it."


## Ana


It's been an entire week of married life and all my meager belongings are now settled in Gus's cabin. It made sense to move in with him seeing how the past five years I've lived in the guest wing of Roman's house. I didn't think Gus would appreciate living in the Bratva compound, not that there's anything wrong with it, but I felt like it could get a little too testosterone-y once Roman and Sasha return.

When Gus told me he lived in a cabin, I have to say I was a little surprised, given how NOT outdoorsy he was when we fled into the woods after a group of men stormed Roman's house with guns. My first impression of Gus, aside from him being ridiculously hot, was he was incredibly bossy. And shit at being outdoors. He may be stealthy and formidable in his urban environment, but out in the wild, he was like a bull in a china shop. You can't go into the woods thinking you can control it. You have to work with the landscape and use natural camouflage. Maybe even try to keep quiet when stalking or being stalked. I mean, sure, not everyone spent time with a dad like mine, but surely the man has seen at least one of those survival shows.

Anyway, I may not have expected August Tombs to live in a cabin, but looking around, it's decorated exactly how I imagined. Stereotypical functional man decor - brown leather couch, giant TV, and a coffee table in the lounge area. Brown leather and wood bar stools pushed in under the island. A small wooden dining table with a tidy, little pile of junk mail, coupons and newspapers, that doesn't look like they've been touched at all.

The bedrooms are even more bland. Or perhaps that's just the small guest room I'm currently in that also houses a treadmill and some boxes of spy-looking stuff. It's a necessity, though. We both agreed that at this point it's best to keep separate bedrooms, which is fine with me because being this close to Gus is seriously messing with my head. The smell of him everywhere in the house is playing havoc on my hormones. Seeing him on the first morning I stayed over, shirtless, in gray sweatpants, drove me to a lukewarm shower and a little one-on-one time with his very fancy, removable shower head.

"Babe? Are you home?" That's another thing, he's started calling me babe, and it makes my stomach flip every time I hear it. I've always found him attractive, and when we were in lockdown, it felt like we had the beginnings of something. But with a little time apart, I can see that diving into something more than we did would have been a big mistake. Even now, I'm not sure what I want out of this thing with Gus. He has the ability to break my heart without meaning to, so I want to tread carefully.

"Yup, I'm here." I walk out and find him leaning on the kitchen counter on his elbows, his head in his hands. His firm ass is right in front of me and I have the biggest urge to slap it to see how hard it really is. He spins around and my eyes shoot to his face. I don't want him to catch me creeping on him.

"Gus? Everything ok?" His frown suggests everything is not ok. His eyebrows are dark slashes over those chocolaty eyes and there are deep lines above that slightly crooked nose that looks like it's been broken before.

"Well, immigration called, and they thanked us for sending through our marriage certificate and wished us well for the future."

I breathe out a long, relieved breath. "Well, that's nice of them. Is that why you have that face?"

"Ah, no. I have this face because they would like us to see a couple's counselor of their choice."

"Wait, what? What the hell for?"

"Apparently, it'll help strengthen our case if we can show our counselor how well matched we are." He pushes away from the bench and runs his hands through his hair a few times. Gus is tightly wound on a normal day. Presented with this type of shit and he looks fit to burst. We need to settle down and get control of the situation.

I take a breath and let it out. "Shit. Ok, no, we're ok. We know each other fairly well. We get on. You said it yourself, we're attracted to each other. Your family likes me, my besties like you. We've got this, Gus," I tell him with an emphatic nod. "When's our first counseling session?"

He looks at me, and I can't tell if it's with fear or regret. "Today, in about an hour."

"What the actual fuck!?" Now I'm leaning on the bar with my head in my hands.

"I think it's a ploy. Get us when we're stressed. See if we show any weaknesses or gaps in our relationship. But you're right babe, we're ok. We've got this. Hey, hey, look at me." His warm hands grip my shoulders and he gently turns me to look at him.

"We've got this."

How the hell did we go from me trying to calm him to him calming me? See what I mean? He's way too potent.

"Yeah, you're right. Let's show this counselor how bloody happily married we are. We've got this."

* * *

Ok, I'm not sure we've got this. I was feeling good when we first walked into the couples' counseling office. It was all really welcoming, a lovely jolly receptionist, flowers, calm prints on the wall, and relaxing elevator music piped through the speakers. We held hands as we waited. Smiled at each other. Had witty banter with the aforementioned jolly receptionist. But that was the ruse to lure us in. Now Gus and I are sitting entirely too close on the smallest loveseat I've ever seen in my life, being interrogated by a woman whose resting bitch face could rival Jules.

"So, how is your sex life?"

"Our what now?" I can't help myself, that just popped out. We went from talking about how we met (minus the illegal details, of course) to sex. I would have at least thought she would have warmed us up for the sex question. Perhaps bought us a drink, told us we look pretty, that sort of stuff.

"Your sex life? You're newlyweds?" She adjusts her small wire-framed glasses to read her notes. "Yes, you're newlywed, so I'm expecting you're having a lot of sex."

Gus coughs to clear his throat, and I wait for him to answer and yet nothing comes out. Bastard.

"Um, yes. Totally. We have sex. All the sex. All the ways you can do it, we are having it." I squeak out. I swear if I had a narrator in my life, the voiceover would say, "In fact, they were not having sex. None of the sex. All the ways you can do it, they were not having it."

I'm sure my vagina is lamenting over being married to the hottest guy alive and there has been no P in V action. For good reason, I tell myself.

"Hmmm. As I expected." What the hell? I shoot a panicked look at Gus, who throws his arm around me and rubs my arm with his rough hand.

"Would you say you have had some challenging times in your relationship?"

A flashback of how we met, running from armed men to the foiled human trafficking auction, flick through my mind.

"Not really. We've been pretty lucky, haven't we, babe?" Gus asks as he drops a kiss on the top of my head.

"Yeah, very lucky."

"Hmmm. That's not quite ideal. We like to know our couples have what it takes to weather any storm." She looks up from her notes. "August, is there something Ana loves doing that you dislike?"

He gives me a small smile. "Yeah. She loves camping. I'm not as comfortable as her in the great outdoors."

I snort because that is one hell of an understatement. The

hand that has been stroking my arm gently pinches me, and I glare up at his smirking face.

"Perfect! Before our next session, which I will schedule for next Wednesday, I would like you two to go on a camping trip. Maybe this coming weekend. The weather is meant to be nice."

"Oh, yeah. That sounds like it could be fun," Gus says through his teeth, but Marta, our counselor, ignores him and carries on.

"Next Wednesday, 5.30pm. I'll see you then." Without saying a word, she stands and walks to the door, holds it open for us, and waits as we struggle to unwedge ourselves from her couch. We walk past, saying our thank you's, and head down to Gus's SUV.

"Holy shit, what was that?!?" Gus grumbles under his breath.

"I don't know! All I know is that I'm going camping this weekend and so are you!" I squeal a little and I can feel my excitement building. This is exactly what I need. Whenever I'm overwhelmed or confused, a tramp or an overnighter in nature centers me. Usually, I just take my tent and bits and pieces to Roman's woodland retreat, but this weekend I'll be able to find us a nice campground to stay in.

"Hey babe, don't look now, but did you notice that car earlier?" Gus's posture is ramrod straight. He's facing me, but he's looking out of the corner of his eye.

"Blue sedan, tinted windows, paint scrape on the front bumper?"

A smile plays on his lips. "Exactly."

"Yup, noticed them not long after we left your house."

"Our house," he murmurs.

"Our house."

He nods and then opens my door, keeping an eye out on our

surroundings. Helping me in, because his car doesn't have running boards, he waits until I'm settled before buckling my seatbelt. Usually, I'd be pissed by this display of manliness, but obviously, I lost my feminism somewhere because I'm quite liking the treatment. Although I have to keep telling myself not to get used to this. It's just for a visa. I'm jarred out of my thoughts when Gus slams my door and I check the rearview mirrors to watch his back, not wanting anything to happen to him, and to note their license plate. He gets in on his side, shutting the door behind him.

"Got the license plate,"

"Good girl." My stomach clenches at the endearment. I never thought I'd like that sort of thing, but in Gus's gravelly voice aimed at me? Holy Fuckamoley, it's panty drenchingly hot.

"We'll get Tuesday on to it." I nod my head at this and make a note to call Ivan to see if he's heard anything on the streets. With Roman in Russia, the Bartashev Bratva runs a genuine risk of someone wanting to make a run for Pakhan, and they won't care if I'm in the way. Shit a brick.

# Chapter 4

Gus

Pulling into the Devil's Rose MC clubhouse, I take in the industrial looking main building. When Dayz first stumbled upon these guys, I did my research on them. I mean, I know Dayz can handle herself, but no big brother would ever let his sister hang with a biker club without doing their research. What I found was a group of men, some ex-military, some looking for a family of sorts, but all good men. Who sometimes do bad things. The perfect place for my sister.

Parking up, I wave out to the brothers busy working in one of the MC's garages, unhooking a car from the back of a tow truck. Rose Grove is what you'd call small town Texas, or maybe big small town Texas. There's a large enough population to have two high schools and enough business to keep the three garages and tow service the MC own booked up.

Stepping out of my SUV, I leave the keys inside because no one is stupid enough to steal a car from an MC compound. I look around and marvel at how it was only a handful of months ago that we were busy hunting underworld scumbags and my sister was torturing information out of them. It still blows my mind how someone so sweet can be so nonchalant about maiming people for justice. What was interesting was that Ana was also totally ok with it.

Shoving through the front door, I come to a stop when I see Jules parked up at the bar with Fox and Nitro. Raising my brow at him, I walk past, headed for Marx's office. Since the proverbial shit hit the fan, Marx and I have cultivated a friendship. I like the man. He also knows what it's like herding cats into a box, except our cats keep tipping the fucking thing over and shitting everywhere but in their litter tray.

Rapping twice on the door, I wait for the gruff "Enter" before stepping in. Marx's eyes flick up and I see the big man visibly relax.

"Oh, thank fuck it's you. Quick, shut the door before any of those assholes think to put more shit on my plate." Kicking the door shut with my foot, I shake Marx's hand before sinking into the leather chair.

"So, I hear congratulations are in order." The big man's beard twitches and his white teeth peek through.

"Ha, thanks. Who would have thought that was gonna happen?"

Marx huffs out a laugh. "Hate to break it to you man, but I think 90% of us thought it. Even Tuesday saw it, and she hadn't even figured out Rhodie was into her. And that man was not subtle." Shaking my head, I chuckle at that. God, watching my baby sister falling in love was an absolute trip.

"So, I'm guessing you're not here for congrats."

I shake my head at his shit-eating grin. "I'm sure you know about our tail? Wondering if you've heard anything. We aren't heading for another clusterfuck, are we?"

A frown crosses Marx's face before he picks up the bottle of whiskey on his desk, tipping it towards me. "Nah, I'm good, thanks, man."

I've got shit to do, like stop off at the store to buy sweet treats for me and Ana to take on our camping trip. It's been enlightening these past few days watching her lit up in a way that I've never seen her before. Even though camping is really not something I want to do, it's something I will do every single fucking day if it brings her the amount of joy I saw in her last night. When I asked her if there was anything she needed me to pick up on my way home tonight she just told me to trust her and then patted my ass, making my cock spring to attention, before bustling off to finish baking the protein bars she was working on.

That's another thing I've learned about her since we've been married. The girl can fucking cook! Holy shit! I'm not sure where she finds the time, because we're both working, but every night I've come home to a delicious meal and my gorgeous little wife waiting for me. Fuck, I love calling her that. I've noticed she blushes every time I call her 'Wife', so I know she enjoys it. I also know she enjoys the little touches I give her. She's an enigma, though. She has a backbone of steel and isn't afraid to argue with me about things she cares about. She is in control but adaptable. She doesn't sweat the small stuff like I do. But, she also always seems to have one foot out the door, and that's something I plan on remedying this weekend. I don't think she's realized that for me, this is it. She's mine.

I watch Marx pour his drink, take a sip, and then plonk it back down.

"I have no fucking clue who's tailing you. Things have been eerily quiet around here since we shut down Kraykowski and his auction. Roman, for better or worse, has Kraykowski's boss Kovalev by the short and curlys, so they haven't caused a problem. Yet."

I nod because I agree entirely with what he's saying. We were all braced for the blow back, but somehow we tied things up so neatly that there hasn't even been a whisper of trouble, which is worrying in itself.

"What I can tell you is that something may be coming our way. Savage has been having trouble in his town. With that being only two towns over and us as allies, we're bound to feel the ripple effect. Ana heard anything?"

Running my hand over my face, I let out a sigh before answering, "She's meeting with her friend Ivan, Roman's brigadier today. If I hear anything that could affect us, I'll let you know." Marx lets out a grunt before pouring himself another drink. "I still think it has something to do with the Bratva, but until we can get more info, we're just gonna have to watch our backs."

"What? Your genius little sister not been able to come up with anything?" I grin at him, because we both know Dayz is like a dog with a bone where there's a mystery to be solved.

"Oh no, she traced the plates to an out-of-state car rental place. The dude who rented the car used a fake ID. Tony Manero."

Marx's eyebrows furrow. "Why does that name sound familiar?"

"John Travolta's character in Saturday Night Fever."

He clicks his fingers and points at me. "Fuck yes! That's it. Shit film."

I wholeheartedly agree. Not only is it a shit film, but it collectively scarred me and my siblings one year when Jules and I came home for the holidays. Pops somehow had a copy of it and developed a fascination for the dance moves in that infernal movie. Me and my siblings had to not only watch Pop's hip movements but also listen to him wax lyrical over how those said hip movements got him all the ladies. Rubbing my hand down my face, I try to dispel the images in my head.

"Shit Gus, clean plates and a fake ID are not a lot to go on." Marx says, a frown creasing his dark brow.

"Nope. I'm sure it'll all come to a head. I just hope it's not this weekend. I have a romantic getaway planned with the wife." I can feel the broad smile on my face and I don't give a shit, although judging by Marx's smirk, I know he's going to be an asshole.

"I heard you were going camping? Last I remember, you weren't that comfortable in the great outdoors."

"Yeah, yeah, fuck you too. One day you'll find a woman you'll do stupid shit for, mark my words."

Marx's eyes widen and he shakes his head back and forth. "The last thing I need is a woman to try to keep under wraps with the assholes I've surrounded myself with."

Laughing, I get up, ready to leave, but then freeze in my tracks with Marx's next words.

"Yo, while you're here, can you tell Pops to stop blowing shit up in our yard?"

Slowly turning to face Marx to see if he's fucking with me, his dead serious look has me hustling out the door and through the clubhouse on a mission to find my wayward grandfather. I come to an abrupt stop when I see not only Pops, but all my siblings sprawled around the common room.

"What the fuck? If you're all here, who the hell is in the office?" Everyone with the Tombs surname looks toward me and two of them talk over each other.

"Listen here, boy! I can be wherever the fuck I want to be," Pops barks out at the same time Tav yells.

"I had to bring Pops in the van. He needed help to unload some of his tools for Rider. And Jules is organizing an orgy!"

"I could lie, but we all know that's what I'm doing," Jules says in a bored voice. I pinch the bridge of my nose because I know Dayz is going to tell the absolute truth when I ask,

"Dayz?"

"I came to have sex with Rhodie during my lunch break. I'm eating the sandwich he made me, then I'll be heading back to the office." I mean, it's not as bad as I thought it was going to be. At least she's planning on doing her job at some stage.

"Thank you, Dayz. The rest of you get back to the office sometime today, please? I'm on leave from now. I want to get home and help Ana pack for camping."

"She's done. I saw her earlier." I turn slowly to look at Jules.

"Have you been at work at all today?"

He shrugs. "I'm good at multitasking."

I bet you are; I think to myself. I could stand here and get on their cases, but I can't be assed. I have a woman to get home to.

"Do you want us to shadow you on your trip?"

Earlier in the week, Dayz ran surveillance on both our and Ana's offices and saw the same man in different cars watching us. If it was just the one time at the counselor's office, I'd shrug it off, but we've seen him three times now and I'm not really keen on putting my wife in danger. If this was a client, I'd be all for organizing a shadow. But this is me and Ana and I don't really want to have my siblings watching us.

"If you want, we can keep an eye out for badly named creeps

watching you and our new sister-in-law?" Tav presses on, purposely avoiding He Who Shall Not Be Named. Pops wasn't in the meeting where He was mentioned, and we don't want to kick off a disco relapse. Looking at my family, there is only one answer.

"Fuck no! I don't want any of you near me. No offense Dayz."

"None taken Gus. I don't want any of you near me when I'm with Rhodie, either."

"What about your safety? Are you sure you don't need eyes on?" Tav is like a dog with a bone sometimes, and I get it. As much as we like to mess with each other, we love and protect each other fiercely.

"Between me and Ana, I'm sure we'll be fine. But just to be safe, do you want to make sure my tracker is all working and up to date?"

Our business is security of all kinds. The simple kind that homeowners and business owners may need, right up to government-level security. Dayz is a hacker that sometimes outsources to the FBI and we often get called in to help with delicate cases. Because this can occasionally be dangerous, we all agreed to have biometric trackers implanted. Any of us can see where each other is by checking our app. This came in handy when all the shit hit the fan with Devils Rose MC and the Russians. Pops decided he was sick of waiting for the bad guys to come to us, so he went and got himself kidnapped. Being able to track his health and whereabouts took the stress off all of us. Well, that and knowing for a fact that Pops is by far more dangerous than most criminals out there.

"Yup, you're all good. Ana gave us the coordinates for your campsite. It's only 2 hours from here, so any trouble we're there." Tav says, Jules and Dayz nodding their agreement.

"You have the MC too, Gus. The camp site sits in both DRMC and Death Riders territories. Shit hits the fan, sing out." Marx states, clapping a meaty hand on my shoulder. I'm not a small man, but Jesus, Marx is huge. Nodding my thanks to him and his brothers, I blow out a breath and try one last time to organize the Tombs clusterfuck.

"Ok. Pops, stop blowing shit up. Tav, Jules, and Dayz get back to the office. I'll see you all on Sunday." I walk through the common room, stopping to slap both my brothers harder than I need to before wandering over and dropping a kiss on the top of Dayz's head.

"Have a good time Gus and don't die," she says whilst patting me on the back

"Thanks Dayz. Will do."


Tav


I wait for my big brother to leave the compound before I gently freak out

"We're seriously not letting him go alone, are we?" Looking at my siblings dotted around the common room, they look surprisingly relaxed about this whole thing.

"He said he didn't want us to keep an eye on him," Dayz says, Rhodie at her back, rubbing her shoulders, because that sappy bastard can't keep his hands off her.

"How often do we actually listen to what he says, though?"

A snort sounds to the left of me and I spin around to see Marx covering a smirk with his hand before clearing his throat. "Maybe if you guys listened to him more, I'd have less shit going down in my clubhouse." He raises an eyebrow at me, but I wave that off. I have an older brother to worry about. Some nefarious people could be after him.

"So we aren't going to do anything? Just let him out into the wilderness with only a tiny foreign woman to protect him from the elements and Tony Manero -"

"What the hell has John Travolta got to do with this?" Pops asks the room.

"- and we're all gonna sit here and do nothing?"

Jules rolls his eyes whilst Dayz has a frown on her face, head tilted to the side like when you confuse a dog.

"You do know that he can take care of himself, right?" Jules says in his bored voice.

"Jules, you know as well as I do, Gus is a badass with a gun in the right environment. But in a campground with families nearby, he isn't going to go all Rambo and have a shootout, is he? He's far too responsible for that shit."

"Tav's right Jules. Gus won't compromise innocent people around him, and his hand-to-hand combat is the weakest of the three of you," my favorite sister in the entire world points out.

"Exactly! So, what's the plan? When are we leaving?" I look around the room and note that none of my siblings are moving.

"Wanna take a breath, kid?" Marx raises an eyebrow at me. Before I can answer him, he carries on. "Tuesday came to me to organize a tail when she noticed the guy watching Gus and Ana. If any of you go after him, he'll know. None of you fuckers can be quiet when it comes to butting into each other's lives. I've got Wire and Remy on it."

Huh? Wire and who? My eyebrows pull down while I try to remember which club girl that could be, but I'm drawing a blank.

"Remy? Who the hell is Remy?" I look around the room and my eyes land on a cute, librarian looking woman with glasses waving at me.

"Um, hi. I'm Remy" She has such a quiet voice I have to strain to hear her. I wave back because I don't want to scare the poor woman who looks completely out of place in an MC clubhouse.

"Tav, Remy, Remy, Tav. Remy's father is a Death Rider." Marx grunts out like that answers everything.

"Remy is a junior hacker. She's going to learn all the tricks of the trade from Wire and me," Dayz helpfully explains.

I feel a confused squint coming on. "Like an exchange student?" I ask into the room. It's a weird set up but I guess I can see how it could work.

"Pretty much," she whispers into the room. Jeez, I have no idea how the hell this woman has come from an MC because she has to be one of the most timid people I've ever met. But, that's not my concern at the moment.

"Um, ok. So you're sending the two geeks - no offense-"

"None taken" Remy whispers while Wire calls me a 'Fucker'.

"-To the wilderness to watch my brother? Are you feeling alright, Marx? In whose world does that make sense?"

"First off, Octavius, this is my MC and I can send, or not send, whoever the fuck I want. Second, Gus and Ana don't know Remy, so it'll be easier for her to get close to them without causing suspicion. Wire needs to get some sunlight and he has no trouble shooting anyone if need be. Is that ok with you?" He growls out at me, and I feel my asshole clench a little.

"Ah yup, sounds wonderful. Thanks for that, Marx. Much appreciated."

I hear a snort and I look over to see Jules with a shit-eating grin on his face.

"We'll have eyes on at all times and me and Remy will check in with Dayz every hour on the hour. She'll forward the alerts to you guys. If anything looks off, you'll have more than enough time to get there," Wire says helpfully, lowering my blood pressure.

"I don't know what the fuss is about. Trust me, that boy has my genes in there. He'll not only be fine in the woods, he'll thrive and take out anyone who needs to be taken out." Pops says and I have no idea who the hell he thinks he's talking about, but it's most definitely not Gus. Gus is a thinker and a planner. Gus will not thrive in nature and he sure as hell ain't taking anyone out. That's what Dayz is for.

Which she proves when she says, "All he has to do is incapacitate the guy and transport him back here. I'll take care of the rest."

"Yes, you will, baby," Rhodie says before sucking her face off.

"Do you have to do that in front of us?" Jules growls out at the same time Pops pulls his spray bottle out from wherever the hell he hid it and squirts Rhodie, to the amusement of the MC brothers.

"Argh! Stop fucking doing that, old man!"

"Get off my grandbaby then, fucker!"

An ear-piercing whistle breaks through the ruckus and we turn to look at a growling Marx.

"That's it! Tombs family, get back to the goddamn office and please, for the love of fucking God, take Pops with you!"

"Aw come on Skid Marx, you know I'm growing on you," Pops says through a smirk before standing, clapping Rider on the back, and whispering that he'll be back tomorrow so they can finish working on... whatever the hell secret project they have going.

"Ok, ok, we're going. Dayz, need a ride?" I don't care about Jules, he can get his bastard self back to the office.

"No, Rhodie is going to drop me off in a half hour or so," I frown at her empty plate.

"But you've finished your sandwich?"

"Oh, that was for energy. We're going to fuck again and then I'll be back."

All hell breaks loose with Pops' spray bottle, Jules' growling, and Rider's high-pitched laughter. Wire and Remy are watching the chaos and from the corner of my eye, I see Marx back down the hallway and into his office, slamming the door shut.

# Chapter 5

Ana

I go over my checklist one last time to make sure I have everything packed and ready to go when I hear the crunching of gravel outside the cabin. Looking through the lounge window, my smile grows as I rush to the door and throw it open.

"Ivan! Looking good, bud!" Ivan's large body lumbers toward me and I give him a side hug, glad to see that my friend is looking even better than the last time I saw him. I lean back to say something and then hear what suspiciously sounds a lot like a gun being cocked.

"Get your fucking mitts off my grandbaby-in-law," a rough voice growls, and I can't keep the smirk off my face. Ivan very slowly turns his large body, his arm coming up behind him before I feel him jerk.

"Don't even think of reaching for your weapon, you big fucker. Take your hands off her and step away."

Ivan's head angles my way and a snort of laughter escapes when he raises a thick, dark brow at me. He holds his hands up in a placating manner and takes one big side step away from me before we both turn to look at Pops. He has his usual uniform on - pressed chinos pulled just a fraction too high, navy short-sleeved shirt tucked into said high pants, beige socks, and his navy blue Skechers. Oh, and also, one hell of a frown marking his deeply tanned face.

"I don't know how you commies behave around married women, but here we keep our hands to ourselves," he huffs out. Once again, Ivan slowly swings his gaze toward me.

"Did he just call me a-"

"Yup. He did,"

"I'm old. I can call you whatever the hell I want," Pops barks out before lowering his weapon.

"You keep your big ass out here, got me?" He stares Ivan down before looking toward me, his gaze softening.

"Stay on your porch girl, I'll be right over there on mine keeping eyes on. I don't trust any of the Bratva fuckers. Apart from you and Lexi girl." He nods to himself then stalks off to go sit in his rocking chair on his porch, facing us.

"Wow. So that's what you married into, huh?" Ivan cracks a huge smile before a chuckle rumbles through his big body. Letting out a sigh, I gesture for him to have a seat, but instead, he leans on the porch railing while I have a seat.

"So, I'm sure you didn't come here to be held at gunpoint and called a 'Commie'."

He rumbles once more. "No, that wasn't on my bingo card for today. Although I have ticked off 'punch someone' and 'threaten 5 people' already, so I'm doing well."

We both have a small chuckle at that.

"How's Jenn? Happy you're back at work?"

"That woman is loving it. She's redecorated our master

bedroom now that I'm not lying in it anymore." He rolls his eyes, but I can see by the look on his face he doesn't mind this at all. He loves Jenn completely and I wonder what it would be like to have that for myself with Gus. I shake off the thought and get back into my business brain.

"So, what brings you here today?"

Ivan must see the change in me because he nods once and then straightens, "There's been murmurs on the streets that something is coming."

"Damn it," I whisper under my breath.

"Not sure what, though. What I can tell you is that it's not coming from the inside." His hard gaze holds mine and I understand that he's done whatever he needed to do to make sure not only myself, but the Bartashev bratva is safe.

"Thank you, my friend" I reach out and pat his hand.

"Eh, no touching!" Barked across the yard. I flip Pops the bird and hear his wheezy laughter follow.

"Do you think whatever it is has anything to do with whatever Roman is dealing with in Russia?"

"It's hard to say, but at this point, I don't think so. Nothing I've heard or seen so far points to that. It could be something completely different, but still dangerous. So stay safe little underboss, ok? And if you need me, I'll be there." With this, he nods at me and looks towards Pops while I stand to walk him to his car. Following him down the steps, I watch him open his car door. He looks back at Pops, flips the bird, and then pulls me into a side hug.

"Remember, if you need me, I'm there."

I smile up at my large friend and nod while listening to Pops grumble from his porch.

"Thanks Ivan. You're the best. And the same goes for you,

mate. You need me, I'm there."

He winks at me as he climbs into his car, starts her up and drives away down the Tombs' long drive. Pops mean mugging him on his way past.

Heading back inside, I shake off Ivan's words and take them as they are. No one in the Bratva is running a takeover and whoever has been watching me and Gus hasn't approached us yet, so we may as well get on with life until the shit hits the fan.

My phone vibrating on the table grabs my attention and I see Gus' face lighting up the screen. His far too handsome face, with his sharp jaw and his slightly crooked nose.

"Hey Gus,"

"Hey babe. Just wondering if you need me to pick up anything on the way home?" His voice is somehow hotter over the phone, causing my sex starved vagina to clench.

"Um, no, I don't think so. I think we're all set."

"Ok, babe, I'm on my way home now. I'll see you soon."

He hangs up and I throw myself face down onto the leather couch, and then think better of it because it's leather and belongs to a man and I'm not sure if said man has sat bare arsed on it. And then the image of Gus's perky, hard ass materializes in my brain, and I'm really fighting hard against my attraction to the man. Gus was very gentlemanly when he suggested we sleep separately, seeing as our wedding was so whirlwind and at the time, I agreed wholeheartedly. However, that was before the counselor ordered us on a camping trip. Now all my traitorous vagina can think about is how she'll be spending two nights in a tent with Gus's peen and how she wants to ride him into the sunset.

Scrunching my eyes closed, I tap my phone against my forehead whilst reciting, "No Peen in Vajeen action. Your vagina will stay empty the whole weekend. You can do this. You are a bad bitch with the self-control of a thin, blonde vegan health and fitness influencer."

"Who are you talking to?" My eyes fly open and I let out a scream, throwing my phone toward whoever just busted me in the middle of my "no sex" mantra.

Hearing a grunt, I look up to see that my well-aimed cell phone throw has hit Gus directly in the penis that will not be entering me.

"Shit a brick! Are you ok?!"

He most definitely is not ok. Gus is hunched over, and the sound coming out of his mouth is identical to the slow release of air from a balloon when you pull on the blowy up part. He stumbles a little and then keels over sideways, landing on the floor. He's gagging slightly, and he has sweat beading on his forehead. I slowly drop to my knees on the floor beside his head, and speaking in hushed, even tones, as you would with a rescue dog, I gently ask,

"Gus, um, are you ok?"

His watery eyes are staring at me like I've just asked him if I could line up him and his brothers and run a train on them. Clearing his throat, he tries to answer, his voice coming out quite a bit higher than usual before he coughs and tries again.

"Babe, I'm gonna need an ice pack and then I'm going to lie here for a little bit, ok?"

Nodding my head, I jump up and find an ice pack in his very well organized freezer. I've noticed before that Gus likes to be tidy and in control of things, but the man's fridge and freezer are so well organized it borders on serial killer. Dropping back down to the floor, I move his hands from his junk and then gently place the ice pack where it needs to be. He closes his eyes in relief and rolls gingerly onto his back. I decide to join him on the floor, and when he feels me moving to lie next to him, he rolls his head in my direction, cracking an eyelid open.

"Babe, what are you doing?"

"Lying next to my husband until he's ready to move."

His full lips quirk up slightly before he opens his other eye, dark chocolate eyes staring into mine.

"You don't have to, babe. I'll be fine in a bit. Gimme a minute and then I'll help you with the last of the stuff and we can hit the road."

"Gus, do you trust me?" I quirk my brow at him, waiting for an answer. I'm interested to see what he says. I know he trusts his family and the MC to an extent, but will he trust me enough to know I have this taken care of, or will he want to make sure himself? He opens his mouth, then closes it, before looking me in the eye.

"Yes, I do. But I would still feel better if you let me double-check everything." His brow furrows, and he looks a little shy at his admission. I don't mind. It's a big enough thing for him to trust me, and if he has to double-check everything for his peace of mind, then I'm ok with that.

"That's cool. I'll let you double-check so you don't stress out. But just know, I've got you, Gus."

His smile lights up his entire face, the frown and stress lines he usually has marring his handsome face are gone. He slides his hand toward me until he bumps my hand, then he twines his long fingers around mine and we lay there. Looking at each other and smiling goofily.

"What the fuck are you doing just lying there?" A gruff voice breaks through the moment.

"They're having a romantic moment, Pops. These things

happen in unusual places, at unusual times," Tuesday answers him in a not-whisper. That is one thing I've learned about the quirky woman. For the life of her, she cannot whisper.

"But why? They're meant to be getting on the road for their camping weekend."

From my position on the floor, where I can't see either Pops or Tuesday, I can damn well hear the amusement in Pop's voice. The whole family has been giving Gus shit for the last few days about us camping, knowing full well that the man hates the great outdoors.

"Is there any specific reason you two are here, in my home, interrupting my moment with my wife?" Gus grits out before sighing and moving to a sitting position, bringing me with him.

"No. Just wanted to wish you luck and tell you I survived three months in the Vietnam jungle and my genes didn't produce a pussy that can't survive in rough conditions. So suck it up and make that campsite your bitch," Pops says before giving a single decisive head nod and leaving without saying goodbye. Tuesday just shrugs before saying "What he said," and trailing her grandfather out.

"Well, on that note, shall we get this show on the road?" I stand, offering my hand to Gus, who takes it in his large, rough hand.

"Just let me vomit quickly and we'll be on our way."


## Gus


"I swear to God, Gus if you don't get your hand off the Jesus handle, I'll pull over, kick your big ass out, and leave you on the side of the road," Ana growls at me through clenched teeth.

"If you had let me drive, we could have avoided this."

Turning her head horror movie slowly, her green eyes wild, she makes a feral growling noise causing me to drop my hand and shrink back. Watching her ample chest rise and fall as she takes deep breaths has me thickening in my pants, which, even though it's not the best time, still has me rejoicing after that shot to the dick I got earlier.

"August, this is my car. I know where we're going, you don't. It makes no sense for you to drive other than the fact that you're a control freak."

I don't disagree with her. I am a control freak. I have no idea if I was always like that or if I became like that because I'm the eldest in a family with no parents. I don't think Pops counts. He's basically one of the kids.

"Ok, ok. Just, we're being followed." Taking a quick glance in the rearview, I can see the silver car that's been following us for a while now. Different from the last one that tailed us.

"I know. I clocked them three miles back."

"I clocked them when we left the gas station." Ana slowly turns toward me again, a scowl marring her face. Jesus, she's beautiful when she's pissed.

"Yeah, three miles back. Are we having a competition?"

I decide to push her buttons. This could be a terrible idea, but aside from the first night we met when she hit me with her sass, she hasn't really pulled it out again. I want to know what makes this woman tick. What pisses her off? What excites her? What would she sound like as I push into her tight pussy? Jesus, and there goes my cock again.

"No, no competition. Just wanting to make you aware."

"Oh, well, thank you. I would never have known, even though

I have perfectly working eyes and noticed the car at the same time as your superior man eyes did."

She blows out a breath and I'm pretty certain she calls me an egg. Whatever that means. I watch her from the corner of my eye and I can't help the smirk growing on my face. I see her bright green eyes side-eye me and her lips twitch before she huffs out a breath and hits me playfully in the arm.

"You're an asshole, you know that?"

Snorting out a laugh, I take in how quickly her annoyance at me has subsided. "Yeah, I've been told once or twice." My eyes flick to the mirror and I see hers reflected.

"So, Mr. Tombs, the all-knowing, all-seeing master of the universe. How do we want to play this?"

That is the million dollar question. Thus far, the car has kept a good distance from us. Could it be a coincidence? The weather is fine at the moment, and we are headed to a popular campsite. It could be nothing. But then Ana and I helped foil an organized crime ring, so it could very well be something. Although Ivan's information makes me feel a little bit better. The last thing I want to do is take on the Russian mafia in my new hiking boots and walk shorts. The outfit hardly screams "badass".

"I think we just carry on with our plans, but we keep our ears and eyes open. If the car turns into the campsite, then we get set up and get eyes on them first. My brothers and sister have your car on their tracking system and I have my implant, so they'll know immediately if anything is wrong."

"I agree. I also have Ivan on speed dial."

"Then I think that's all we can do. Let's hit nature and show Marta that we can most definitely and successfully do shit that you love and that I absolutely hate."

At this, Ana throws her head back and laughs, her eyes

sparkling.

"Gus, I have every faith that with me at your side and with all the stuff I have packed and planned, you will love camping." I roll my eyes at her and love the warm feeling in my chest as she snorts at me.

We drive for a while longer in comfortable silence, and it intrigues me how Ana can be so happy to enjoy each other's company without having to hash out every detail. Thinking back to the night we met when I saw her standing in Roman's office with a scowl on her beautiful face, I thought I was going to be in for a hell of a time with an awful bitch.

When security alerted us we were surrounded and to flee into the woods that back onto the property, I was sure that she was going to lose her shit and I'd have to keep us both safe. However, that isn't what happened. What happened was she calmly noted what was on the security cameras, slipped off her heels, replaced them with tramping boots, and took off out the door with me following close behind. Once we hit the treeline, it was like watching Rambo from those old movies. She blended in with the surroundings, and I was left following in her wake like a bull in a china shop. I mean, sure, I pissed her off a couple of times with my lack of outdoorsy-ness, but after sarcastically admonishing me, she was straight back to her usual self, never holding a grudge or questioning things too much. Not even when Marx's men picked us up and told her she was coming back to the clubhouse to lock down for her safety.

"How are you always so chill?" I see her eyebrows pinch, but she doesn't take her eyes off the road.

"Huh? What do you mean?"

Taking a breath, I try to get my thoughts into words. "You're just so, adaptable, I guess is the word. When we met, you didn't argue once when you were told what was happening. Well, not until I got a little bossy there." I see her eyebrow raise and a small smirk on her face.

"A little?"

"Well, you know." She glances at me before she rolls her eyes. "So? How can you just take everything in stride?" She concentrates on the road for a moment, her lips pinching and I watch as she moves them side to side, chewing the inside of her cheek.

"I don't always take everything in stride. But, I try to. You know I grew up in care, right?" I nod, not wanting to interrupt her too much. "I guess, when you never know where you're going to be from day to day, you either struggle with the changes and end up a ball of anxiety and nerves, which I saw happen to a lot of kids, or, you just let it go." Shrugging she side-eyes me before her gaze returns to the road ahead.

"You just let it go?"

"Yeah. I mean, as a kid, you have little control over anything. So, I learned that the things you can't control you just let go of and concentrate on what you can control. Do I most likely have some weird childhood trauma that needs addressing? Probably. Do things piss me off? Of course, they do. Did it piss me off when you'd try to take over and tell me what to do? Yes, but that was more because you didn't think I could handle myself. I think I proved to both of us at that moment that I could."

Thinking back on what went down, I guess once we got to the clubhouse I was overbearing, but that wasn't what she thought it was.

"I knew you could handle yourself. I wasn't an ass because I thought you were some delicate woman."

"Ok. Then why?" Shit, now I'm going to have to tell her the truth. She has been honest with me and a piece of her childhood. The least I can do is to be honest with her.

"I, um, I liked you. From the moment I saw you. And then we ended up in the clubhouse with all those big, handsome fuckers and I guess I was marking my territory." I cringe after saying that because it makes me sound like an absolute asshole, but it's the truth. "And also, because I'm a man, and sometimes we can be really stupid."

A smile splits her face, and she throws her head back and laughs. "Hey, you said it!"

I hold my hands up and hum my agreement.

"I liked it." She says so quietly I almost miss it.

"You liked what?" I whisper back.

"I liked you claiming me. And I liked you when I first met you, too. Although it might have wavered when I realized you don't like being outside." Her lips twitch before she laughs at her joke.

"Yeah, yeah. Just get us there already and I'll see what I can do about digging deep and activating those jungle genes Pops has given me."

# Chapter 6

Ana

I can feel the frustration bubbling up and I'm either going to kick the man, or I'm going to go on a long walk in the woods and leave him to it. I take a couple of breaths and tell myself that he's only trying to help.

"Hey Gus, do you want to leave this to me, and maybe go get eyes on that car that followed us in?"

"Are you sure? I mean, this is quite a large looking tent. You might need the help-"

"Nope! I'll be fine! I've done this before. I'll be all good. Remember, we want eyes on, may as well do that now while they're distracted putting up their own tent." I snatch the tent pole that he's been waving around out of his hand and try to bodily shove him in the direction of, well, any direction other than where I am. I'm pushing against his stupidly big, hard body, and I finally look up when I feel it vibrating.

"Ok, I get it, babe. I'll get out of your hair," he chuckles as he walks away and I thank all and any gods that may be out there that I didn't have to murder my husband of less than a month.

I get to work setting out all my tent bits and pieces. I find this task always calms my mind, like meditation, if you will. It reminds me of laying out all the pieces for my dad when I was a kid and we'd put the tent up while Mum got our outdoor kitchen stuff set up. She'd have our lunch waiting for us after we were done.

It's also a good time for me to sort through things in my mind. Gus's question about how I'm so chilled out has me looking at him in a different light. I know Gus well enough to figure that, well, for want of a better word, he's got a stick up his butt about most things. I've seen it in some of the kids I had been fostered with, the need to be in control. Knowing Gus's family background, I can see clearly how it affected him. He lost both parents to a violent act in the blink of an eye, his baby sister the only one at home that night, assaulted by the men that did it. He then grew up to be the head of his family. He went into security, to keep others safe. He lives on the same land as his siblings. He rules the roost so as not to be caught off guard or surprised. The man is a planner, which is why it baffles me slightly that in the space of 2 minutes, he decided we should get married.

Buzzing in my pocket has me putting down what I've been doing and wrestling my phone out of my denim cut-offs. My mum's face is lighting up the screen so I swipe to answer.

"Hey Mum. What's up?" I sit in the camp chair that I'd set up outside our tent and settle in for a good ole mother daughter chat.

"What? A person can't call their newly married daughter to ask how their day was?" Shit shit shit! In the whirlwind that was my wedding, I totally forgot to tell Mum. Fuck nuggets!

"Oh, you know about that, huh?"

Hearing a snort on the other side of the line has my lips tipping up. "Well, you see I was chatting to Roman-"

"-since when do you and Roman chat?"

"-since my daughter got married to, and I quote, 'a broody hunk of man meat' and forgot to tell me." I groan a little. Damn Roman.

"So, I need all the deets, *kotiro*. I have popcorn and a glass of wine. Hit me with it."

I should have known she would be fine with it. Mum has always been supportive of my choices. Her reasoning being "You want your life story to be the type of book that would be banned in Florida."

"Ok. Did Roman tell you how we met?"

"Mmmhmmm,"

"Right. Well, Gus found out I was having visa issues and offered to marry me. We talked it over, came to an agreement, and got married."

"Aaaaaand?"

"And nothing. He's helping me out."

I hear a huff over the line and some muttering, "Do you want to jump that man? Ride him like a cowgirl breaking in a stallion? Have his beautiful little babies and grow old with him?" I inhale a breath so quickly I end up giving myself a coughing fit. "Welllllll?"

Clearing my throat, I look around to make sure no one can see or hear me. Even though I'm alone, I'm never sure when Gus or his siblings will pop up.

"Yes. Yes. And maybe?" I can hear a high-pitched squeal and frantic clapping over the phone.

"Clear a space baby girl. I've already booked my tickets. I arrive in two weeks to meet my new son-in-law. Don't run from that man before then. I want to meet him."

Letting out a not-so-delicate snort, I'm offended at Mum for even thinking I'd run.

"What?! I don't run from anything. What are you talking about, woman?" If we were on a video call, I'm sure she would have rolled her eyes at me.

"You don't run from anything apart from people who may end up loving you more than you think you deserve. Don't argue. You know it's true. You did it for a full year before you accepted me and your dad. You did it for two years before you realized that Roman, Sasha and Ivan were there for you. You, my sweet girl, always have one foot out the door."

Pulling my lips between my teeth, I realize she may be right. I may have been holding back from Gus. Not because I don't like him, but because I've been in enough situations to know that sooner or later people will move on. I could voice exactly how I'm feeling, and trust my mum with all of it, but instead, I choose to very maturely grumble, "Do not."

Her laughter on the other side does nothing for my spiraling mood.

"Do you have more truth bombs to drop on me or are you done now?"

"I'm done. Zipping my lips right now. Have fun camping baby and I'll see you on the 9th. And trust that man!" With this, she hangs up without telling me she loves me. Rude.

I get back to my task, setting up our bedding and the inside of the tent while Mum's words bounce around in my mind. Shockingly, I do trust Gus. Not only do I trust him, but I feel safe with him, and I've only had that feeling twice before in my life. The first was when I met my mum and dad, and the second was when I met my Bratva family, Sasha, Roman, and Ivan.

Huh. Weighing up all my options, I decide to just let this whole thing play out. If we become more than friends, then that's great. If not, then that's great too. Gus has been an awesome friend so far, even if he is too bloody hot for words.

"Whoa! Look at how much you got done once I left." A grin spreads across my face as I crawl out of our tent, only to come to a halt at Gus's feet, where he's standing just outside the doorway. My eyes travel from his brand spanking new hiking boots, which still have the plastic price tag holder thing attached, up his very shapely light brown calves, to the bottom of his brand spanking new hiking shorts, up his torso sheathed in a navy blue Henley, to his handsome face. His chocolate-colored eyes are flashing down at me with heat. He reaches out, cupping my face in his large palm, his thumb gently grazing the apple of my cheek, back and forth.

He swallows before rasping out, "Good job, babe."

Shit, he's so hot and this position is making me think about all sorts of things. I can feel my pussy throbbing from the sheer need to have this man inside me.

"Well, howdy neighbors!" A far too cheery voice cuts through the intense stare down Gus and I are having. A small "eep" sound leaves my lips and I thank the kooky health teacher in high school who taught us girls that pelvic floor exercises are a woman's best friend. Without her, I would have peed myself in fright.

Gus spins to greet the newcomer and I very inelegantly get to my feet. I mean, I'm not a small girl. I'm still partially in the doorway of our tent and Gus is standing in the way. If I wanted to, I could get a face full of his ass, but that's not really appropriate at a public campground.

"Hey there!" Gus fakes a cheery greeting back. Now that

I'm standing at his side, I notice his eyes are darting to our surroundings. He's in security man mode and it's kinda hot.

"Hey, I'm Craig, and this is my wife, Mandy. Our campsite is right there, making us neighbors. Thought I better come and welcome you to the neighborhood." Craig is far too pasty to be out in the sun without sunscreen, and he also looks like he has never camped a day in his life. Actually, neither does his wife, judging by the fact they are dressed almost identically to Gus, in outdoor clothes that still have the sheen of newness reflecting off them.

"Nice to meet you both. I'm Gus, and this is my wife Ana."

"Wow, you folks make a beautiful couple, so exotic," Craig says, giving us both the once-over. In a move that was not choreographed, Gus and I side-eye each other.

"Anyhoo, we couldn't help but notice your impressive setup, and well, it's our first time doing this, so we were wondering if you would like to join us for a few drinks later on?" Craig says nervously, before looking at his wife, who nods up at him. He then turns back to Gus and me before winking. What the heck? Gus throws his arm around my shoulders and we look at each other before turning back to Craig and Mandy.

"Ah, yeah, sure man, why not?" Gus answers, and we smile back at the couple.

"Great! Awesome! Yeah, ok, we'll see you a bit later then. Cool!" They smile at each other before wandering back to their campsite setup.

Gus and I look at each other, baffled. "That was a little weird, right?"

"I think they're probably harmless, but I'm going to send their picture and plates through to Dayz to run background."

"Good thinking. What about the silver car?" I ask him,

ducking out from under his arm so I can get our outdoor kitchen set up.

"They're on the other side of the camp. I think it might be a coincidence. I didn't get a good look at the guy, but the girl is like me."

"A bossy bastard?" I helpfully offer as Gus rolls his eyes.

"No. She's not wilderness friendly. Boyfriend did all the tent building while she slathered on sunscreen, a hat, sunnies, and pulled her book out. By the looks of them, they're just a normal couple like us."

"But?"

This earns me a smirk. "But to be safe, I've sent their plates through to my sister as well."

"I wouldn't expect anything less from August Tombs."

## Gus

Stretching my legs out in front of me in the very comfortable camp chair Ana set up, I take a long pull of my beer and think about my wife. Fuck, she's phenomenal. After we had everything set up, she told me about a trail she had heard about that led to a waterfall. So we made the hour-long trek to see it. Jesus, that was an exercise in restraint. She's thick in all the right places and she's fit as hell. She led the way, and I followed along, watching the muscles in her shapely legs flexing in her short denim cutoffs. I was hard enough to pound nails most of the way, but I've resigned myself to the fact that I'll be painfully hard this whole weekend with no possibility for release. I've spent the whole time we've been married, fucking my fist every time I've had a shower. I'm surprised that she's never noticed how often I wash.

But, as painful as the walk was, it was nice. We told each other stories about our childhoods. She laughed until she snorted when I told her about Pops' shenanigans, and I was glad to hear that even with Ana's rough start, she had a lot of happy memories. Her parents sound amazing and I'm looking forward to meeting the woman who raised her.

Once settled back at camp, Ana got on to cooking our dinner, letting me know in no uncertain terms that she didn't need my help. She somehow managed to cook a delicious pasta meal on the grill as if she wasn't already impressive enough. We dug into that, topped it off with the dessert I picked up, and now I'm relaxing with a beer while I wait for her to return from the communal bathrooms.

I've given her a time limit before I come looking for her, but I'm not too worried. Dayz got back to me with the details on the young couple, as well as Craig and Mandy, and both pairs are normal, possibly slightly boring but with no criminal or Bratva ties. I take another pull of my beer before something out of the corner of my eye catches my attention. My wife is storming toward me, her face red, her short legs working double time. I put my beer down, stand, and rush toward her when she hisses, "There's naked people everywhere!" Wait, what?

"What?"

"Naked people. On this side of the campground, there's naked folk."

I can't quite figure out what she's talking about. There are two sides to the campground. When I went to recon the silver car couple, I had to cross a footbridge. The communal bathrooms sit between the two sides. Still, I have no idea what the hell she is talking about. Placing my hands on her heaving shoulders, I apply pressure in the hopes it'll help calm her. It's what we do to Dayz when she's overwhelmed.

"Ok, take a breath, and tell me what you mean by naked people."

She nods, takes a breath, and starts again. "Ok, I was in the bathroom, which was all fine, and then on my walk back here I saw, like, three naked couples."

"Ok. And what were they doing?"

"Just hanging out." She waves her hand around like it makes sense.

"Well, howdy neighbors!  Want to come over for those drinks?"

Both our heads whip in Craig's direction as he's standing there smiling at us. He's wearing some type of patterned skirt thing that you sometimes see Samoan men wear on the islands. I rub my hands up and down Ana's arms and she calms a little.

"Do you want to go over there, or do you want to just chill here?"

She gulps before eyeing Craig, then turns back to me. "No, the naked people were weird, but Craig and Mandy seem nice, so let's just forget what I saw and have a pleasant night with a friendly couple. You said yourself they're harmless."

I give her a chin lift before calling out to Craig, "Hey Craig, we'll just grab our drinks and we'll be there in a bit,"

"Sure thing, neighbor!" He ducks back into his tent, and I grab a couple of drinks for Ana and me.

"I mean, they're weird, but they're probably very nice people. Hey!  They can be our first married couple friends!"  Ana giggles.

"What about Roman and Sasha?"

She rolls her eyes. "They haven't been here since we got married, so I've demoted them. It's now Craig and Mandy in the top spot." She snorts a laugh and I let her lead the way.

Standing outside Craig and Mandy's tent, Ana softly calls "knock knock" before she pulls open the door flap with one hand and moves inside. I'm following behind her when she stops abruptly and I accidentally bump into her back, sending her careening forward with a squeal. I try to grab her hips before she tumbles to the ground, but I'm too late. Ana throws her hand out to catch herself and it's then I realize Craig is sitting naked on a camp chair inside their tent with his cock in Mandy's mouth and my wife has just landed on her knees next to her, with her hand in Mandy's hair from where she tried to catch herself.

"Sorry neighbor, I just got so hard thinking about you two coming over I just couldn't wait," Craig huffs out whilst pumping into Mandy's mouth. Ana screeches and falls back onto the ground, crab-walking back until she bumps into my legs, causing me to jolt from the shock of it all.

"What the actual fuck!?" I whisper out because nothing could have prepared me for this. Grabbing Ana's hand, I pull her up and back against me, staring at the sight. Mandy comes off of Craig's actually quite impressive length, wipes her hand across her mouth before turning to us, topless, tits shaking everywhere.

"Aren't you two going to get naked and join us? Gus, I cannot wait to ride what's in your pants. Craig loves to watch me being filled up, don't you, baby?"

My mouth drops open and no words come out, but they don't have to because my spitfire wife yells, "No one is riding his dick apart from me! It's mine!" Her cheeks redden once she realizes what she's said and I can't think of anything other than getting back to our own tent and having her ride me.

"Wait, I thought you two were up for this?" Craig asks nervously, pulling his Samoan man skirt thing on.

"*Lavalava*," I hear whispered at me by Ana.

"What?"

"His Samoan man skirt is called a *Lavalava*" I hadn't even known I'd said that out loud, and to be fair, there are bigger things at play here than being linguistically and culturally correct.

"Up for what?" Ana asks, trying really hard not to make eye contact with Craig's dick or Mandy's tits, which are still out for the world to see.

"Wait, you know that this side of the campground is for swingers, right?"

"What!??" I yell and I'm sure I can hear Ana whisper "The naked people" as realization dawns on her.

"Um, no. We didn't know that this side of the campground was for swingers."

Mandy scrambles to put something on and both she and Craig look a little mortified. I don't know what to say, but Ana pulls herself together.

"Oh my gosh, we are so sorry! No, we just thought that the campsite we booked looked nice and secluded. Please, um, forgive us for getting our wires crossed, and, um, we hope you find a friendly couple to spend the evening with. Ok, goodnight," and with that she scurries through the tent flap.

I give them both a quick wave and follow close behind my wife, chasing her down as I feel the giggles bubble up in my throat. I watch her dive through the tent flap and curl up on top of the air bed, groaning as if in agony. I crawl onto the bed next to her and pull her hands off her scrunched-up face.

"I can't believe I've booked us into a swinger campground!" She hisses out before covering her face again and I can't help it. I burst into laughter. She takes her hands from her face and squints at me before she slaps me on the shoulder.

"It's not funny! Those poor people! Holy shit, I can't believe that just happened!" She looks at me with wild eyes before she, too, starts guffawing. We lean into each other. Her scent surrounds me as does the pure joy of just being here with her.

As my laughter dies down, I look into her sparkling eyes and I just can't hold back any longer. I lean in, pressing my mouth to her soft, plush lips, and gently take a sip. I pull back and her arms come up over my shoulders, her tiny hands playing with the hair at my nape. I lean forward, this time with more urgency, and kiss her like my life depends on it. She tastes like sunshine and oranges and when I let out a groan, my little minx sweeps her tongue into my mouth, tasting me as I taste her. She sucks my tongue into her mouth and I move over her lush body. Her legs part, giving me the space I need to grind my hard length over her denim clad core. She kisses me in earnest, her hips moving, undulating under me. I break free of her lips, kissing down the column of her throat, tugging on the neck of her tee to gently bite her collarbone.

"Ah Gus! Yes, yes" she breathes out. I run my hands down her soft sides, and under her to cup her ass, holding her tighter to me as I grind down on her. I clamp my lips on her neck and suck gently, her bucking getting erratic before she slowly moans my name and shudders.

*"Awww yeah, that's it, she likes her ass being licked like that."* Ana and I freeze and look at each other, eyes wide.

*"That's right baby, I know you do. Dirk, stick a finger in there,*

*while your wife sucks my big dick,"*

I roll off Ana and we lie next to each other, chests rising and falling as we catch our breath.

"You didn't get to cum, Gus. Do you want me to -"

*"That's it, Dirk, get that ass ready for me,"*

I close my eyes and shake my head.  "Nope babe, I'm all good."

*"Mandy, ride her face while I suck off Dirk,"*

Silence falls in our tent and I'm trying to think of something, anything, to ease the awkwardness of hearing our neighbors fucking when Ana pipes up with, "Well, I guess I'm happy they found a couple that shares their same tastes."

We look at each other and then both burst into laughter.

"Shhhh! They'll think we're laughing at them. They might get a complex!" Ana slaps me.

For the next hour, we snort, cry, and not so silently laugh as we try to get through the trauma of listening to Craig talk Dirk through fucking his wife.

# Chapter 7

Ana

Waking up with a start, I realize both Gus and I are cuddled together on top of the bed, neither of us in our sleeping bags. We must have drifted off listening to the fuckfest that was happening in the tent next door. By the sounds of it, Mandy is one lucky lady. Craig lasted a lot longer than I expected. Checking the time on my phone, I realize it's a little after 1 am, but I need to pee again, so I decide now should be a good time. Surely all the naked people have tucked themselves up in their tents, or some other couples' tents by now.

"Gus," I murmur lowly. I also gently lay a hand on his arm and press a little, to rouse him without waking him fully. "Gus,"

"Mmmm?"

"I'm just going to the bathroom. I'll be back," I whisper gently in his ear. He lets out another grunt and nods. Taking that as my cue, I slip on my flip-flops, crawl out of the tent, turn on my cell phone torch, and hot foot it across the campground, as fast as my flip-flops will take me.

I'm glad the campground has good lighting around the bathroom area. I take a quick look around for creepers and find none, so I slip inside, coming to a halt when I bump into a woman slightly taller than me with glasses and a lovely face. She kind of reminds me of Miss Honey from Matilda; the book, not the movie. This woman has blonde hair in a bob cut and is very pale. However, you can tell from her face that she is incredibly sweet and kind, hence Miss Honey.

"Shit! Sorry, I didn't see you there,"

"Oh, no problem. It happens all the time." She has the quietest voice and I have to strain to hear her over a kid using the Dyson Airblade before they leave with their mum.

"Then, honey, you need to make yourself known. As my mum would say, 'Pull back those shoulders, let the world see you, then take it by the balls and make it your bitch'." A shy smile breaks out across her face and her eyes light up as a small giggle escapes.

"Ok, I'll, I'll try. Thanks," she gifts me with another sweet smile before she shuffles out the door.

I take another quick look around before I choose the last cubicle, lock myself in, and do my business. Over the sound of my high-pressure pee flow, I can hear murmurs on the other side of the door. What? Is that a man? And I'm bloody certain I heard him mention mine and Gus's names. I finish up my business, pull up my shorts, and close the lid of the toilet. I feel bad about not flushing, but I don't want to draw any attention to myself. I chose this cubicle purely because it was the furthest from the door and it had a larger window than the others. Both factors make this the A+ cubicle of choice for crappers, but it's a blessing. Hopefully, he'll now think I'm in here pooping, which gives me a little bit of time.

Looking at the window, I'm pretty sure with a bit of a wiggle, I'll fit through it. I take off my flip-flops, cursing the grossness of toilet floors but needs must. Climbing onto the closed toilet lid, I send up a quick thank you to whoever decided that the toilet doors needed to go almost to the ceiling. Quietly unlatching the window, I push it out as far as it can go, looking down and making sure no one is out there waiting for me.

Once I make sure it's safe, I pull myself through the window, cursing my wide hips when they wedge slightly. I have to twist a little and use my hands to free one saddle bag at a time before I can fully pull myself out of the window, landing inelegantly in a heap on the hard ground. I don't even dust myself off before I'm sprinting back toward our tent, or at least what a woman of my size and weight would call sprinting. If I'm honest, I'm impressed with my speed and stamina. I dive through the doorway, landing on Gus, who wakes up alert and ready for a fight.

"Gus! It's me!" I hiss out.

He blinks twice before growling, "What's wrong?" His sleep roughened voice has heat pooling between my thighs, so it's not until he grips my shoulders and asks again that I answer him.

"I was in the bathroom." I huff out, "A man came in and was talking to someone. He was murmuring low, but I'm certain I heard our names. I climbed out the window and came straight back here to warn you. I made sure he didn't follow me, but I think it would be safer for us to ditch the tent till morning. We don't want to be sitting ducks and at least this way we can monitor anyone coming our way."

Gus blinks at me once before nodding and putting on his

boots. I give the bottom of my feet a quick wipe with baby wipes because even certain death isn't gonna have me putting my shoes on with toilet feet, then I shove my feet into my boots. Grabbing my emergency camp bag, I silently leave the tent, Gus following close behind.

"So, babe, what's the plan?" Gus whispers in my ear, causing goosebumps to break out on my skin.

"The plan is to set up camp in the trees. I packed two pairs of your infrared goggles, and one of those wee cameras you guys have that can send alerts to our phones. I know you hate it out here, but I think it's the best option." Gus stares at me for a long moment before he places his hand on the back of my head and pulls me in for a hard kiss.

He pulls back and rests his forehead against mine. "Fuck, babe, the plan is exactly what I would have done. We stay in the tent, we're sitting ducks with only one way in, and one way out. This way, we have the upper hand. Tell me what you need me to do."

This is huge. I know Gus enjoys calling the shots. Yeah, he can cooperate with others, as long as he's one of the decision makers. When the shit hit the fan and he, Marx, and Roman had to work together, all three alphas would have had to compromise for the best outcomes. But for Gus to defer to me in this case? To trust my judgment and let me call the shots? It means the world to me. He sees me as his equal, someone that he can trust to keep us both safe. I will not let my husband down.

## Gus

I follow my wife into the treeline and this time, instead of barreling along like I did the last time we were in this situation, I follow her lead. Last time I was in protection mode. I mean, it's my job and my default setting. This time I know that the little woman in front of me can take care of herself, so I'm willing to fall back. In some ways, it's actually kind of nice to not have to be in charge. To be able just to let someone else call the shots for a change.

When my parents were killed, I was 21 years old and studying architecture. In one night, the course I had mapped out for my life changed and instead, I went into the security business. Jules joined me first, then Tav, and lastly Tuesday. I can't speak for my brothers and sister, but I take pride in knowing that we have helped people. We've helped small mom and pop businesses from losing money because of petty crime. We've kept family homes safe with our surveillance, and we've protected some pretty high-profile names when on tour. We have even helped the MC rescue victims of trafficking and get them back home to their families. Together, Tombs Security all works as one. Even if it does take all the people skills I have to juggle my sibling's personalities. But running the business, managing my staff, and looking at every scenario and outcome can take a toll on a person.

I look around at where Ana has stopped in a well-wooded area close to the campsite. She has her head tipped back, looking up into the trees. The moonlight is dappled and if I was a sappy bastard, I'd be waxing lyrical over how it's casting a wondrous glow on her face. And it would all be true. Ana is fucking beautiful. But even if she wasn't, I would still feel it in my bones that this woman is my perfect counterpart. Now I just have to get her to see it. I'm not sure of her feelings for me exactly. I know she wants my cock. I've seen the way she looks at me sometimes, but anything more than that, I have no idea.

"I think this would be a good spot for us to place the camera. It should cover our tent and most of the angles that anyone could come at it. What do you think?" She turns her face to look up at me, eyes shining brightly with intelligence. Taking a quick look around, I note that she's correct, although the tree two over looks like a better spot, so I point it out. She creeps over silently, sizes it up, and nods.

"Yep, you're right. Good spotting big guy," she murmurs out. Just like that, no arguing that her spot was better. She sets off climbing up the trunk like it's something she does every day. I've seen people in the Pacific islands scaling trees for coconuts and things; do they do the same in New Zealand? I should really find this shit out. Marta, the marriage counselor, strikes me as the type of person who would ask that shit to catch us out.

Ana places the camera and makes her way back down. I reach up and wrap my large hands around her soft hips, helping her down the last couple of feet. With her back plastered against my front, I slide my hand around to rest on her soft stomach as I rock into her slightly before placing my lips next to her ear.

"How the fuck do you know how to climb like that?" The apple of her cheek plumps up as she smiles.

"Misspent youth" She pats my hand and walks off looking for something. I'm not sure what. She leads me a little further into the woods, finds what she is looking for, and then from her pack pulls out some plastic sheeting. I watch her plump ass wiggling in the air while she lines the ground under an overhanging rock formation I hadn't even noticed. She crawls under and gestures for me to join her. It's not the comfiest, but it is big enough for both of us to fit and it will shelter us from the weather. Sitting leaning against the rock, I wrap my arm over her shoulders and she rests her head against me.

"So, little Miss Bear Grylls, does every kid in New Zealand learn this stuff?"

"Nah. I mean, we go to a lot of school camps and learn some of this camping stuff, but it was mostly stuff my dad taught me. Before going to live with Mick and Debs, I was angry. Pissed off at everything and everyone. Adults all sucked, so did school, and it's hard to make friends when you don't know how long you're going to be staying in one place. If I made any friends in the homes I was staying in, it wasn't long before they got adopted or moved on. So by the time I landed with Mick and Debs, I was a pissed off kid with no hobbies and nothing I enjoyed doing." I nod, not wanting to ruin her flow. She snuggles closer before continuing. "That first year was hard on all of us. I'd been let down so often that I didn't want to get my hopes up. I needed to keep the space between us so it wouldn't be so hard when I had to leave. I didn't make it easy for them to love me. But after a while, things changed. We went on trips away and slowly I began to think that maybe I wasn't going to be moved on. On those trips, Mick would take me tramping and fishing. He taught me how to make shelters so that when I got bored with fishing, I could make a little hut to hang out in." Glancing down at her resting against my shoulder, I see the smile on her face. "Somehow, Mick or Debs, or both, figured out that being out in the bush, the Kiwi wilderness, was my happy place. It was where I liked to think about things. Where I was the most relaxed. It still relaxes me now." She looks up at me and pokes me in the shoulder.

"So, August Tombs, what did you get up to as a kid?" I let my head roll on the cool rock as I think.

"For the first 5 years of my life, it was just me and Jules. He's only a year younger, so I can't remember a time when I didn't have him. He's always been grumpy and surly, and we spent a lot of time hitting each other with stuff, hence the crooked nose." She lets out a snort and I carry on. "When I was 5, Tav was born and then for my 8th birthday, I got Tuesday. I was so excited to finally have a sister because my 8-year-old self was so sick of having to share everything with my little brothers. The whole family was excited to get a 'little princess'. We got Dayz." Ana chuckles softly at this, humming her agreement that Tuesday Tombs is most definitely not a princess. "We had a lot of good times. Mom and Dad were great. They were both only children. They wanted to have a big family, so we would always have someone on our side. As the oldest, it was always my job to help Mom with the younger ones, and when I would act out, Dad would always remind me I had brothers and a sister who looked up to me, so I had to remember to set a good example."

"So you've always been responsible?"

"Fuck no! College was a wild ride of sex, drugs, and minor illegal activities. I thought I was a real badass."

"Oh, yeah?"

"Yeah. But then one night a mugger attacked my best friend and me. Jeremy was stabbed in the altercation. No matter how badass I thought I was, I was fucking useless at stopping the attack. I remember sitting in the police station giving a statement, with Jeremy's blood on me while he was in the hospital getting stitched up. All I wanted was to be back home. With my family. My safe place. Sitting there, shaking, in that station felt like the worst moment of my life. I didn't think things could get any worse. Then my phone rang and Pops told me that Mom and Dad had been killed. That one night changed my life. I realized I have so much to lose and so much to protect that I needed to keep my head at all times."

"That's why you hardly ever drink alcohol?" I give a quick nod. It's not worth it. I need to have all my wits about me. One slip up and who knows what could happen.

"I'm not too sure how this marriage is going to work in the long term, if we'll stay together for the whole two years or whatever. But so that you know, I've got your back, Gus. Anytime, anywhere you need me, I'll be there." I look down at her upturned face. I can see the sincerity in her eyes as she stares up at me, filling me with her truth. She may not think this is forever. Shit, after her childhood she may not even trust that I'll hang around, but she's willing to pledge her support to me, and that means more to me than I can ever put into words.

Swallowing down the lump in my throat, I whisper, "Thank you. I –" I feel vibrating on my thigh and realize that both mine and Ana's phones are sending us camera alerts.

"Looks like we've picked up something," Ana murmurs. Pulling up the live footage on my phone, we both lean forward, heads resting against each other as we peer at the tiny screen.

"What the fuck, Miss Honey?" Ana whisper shouts.

"Do you know them?" She shakes her head, not taking her eyes off the screen.

"I bumped into that woman in the toilets. I thought she was the loveliest person I'd ever had the chance to meet. That sneaky bitch!"

She crawls out of our little shelter and starts silently pacing. I really need to find out how she can move so quietly. I'd be able to use it against my siblings. Looking at the footage playing out, the woman's face comes into better focus.

"Fuck! That's the couple from the silver car! That's the woman I saw when I went to recon them. Dayz said they weren't a threat. Obviously, she was wrong." Rubbing a hand down my face, I look up when Ana comes to a stop in front of me

"What do you want to do?" She asks in a low voice. I quickly run through all the options in my mind and there's not a lot.

"We can't take them out because we're in a camping ground surrounded by families and horny fuckers. The only real thing we can do is neutralize them and then load them up in the trunk. Take them back to the MC and see if Rhodie or Dayz can get anything out of them." Ana stares me down for a moment before nodding her head.

"I agree. You take him, I'll take her. I'm going to kick her ass for fooling me."

A smile grows on my face as I follow my wife into the fray. The woman is inside the tent, her partner outside keeping watch. Sizing him up, I feel good about what I'm about to do. We're fairly evenly matched, which will make taking him out a little easier. Sneaking in from the side, his pulled up hoodie gives me the element of surprise when I give him a quick jab to his blind side. He swings toward me a lot quicker than I thought he would. I block the blow, get in close enough to wrap my arm around his neck, and then hit the deck, wrestling him onto the ground. I hear a squeak and when I look up, Ana is pulling the woman out of the tent by the hair. The guy I'm wrestling with taps my forearm that's wrapped around his throat before rasping out,

"Gus! It's me, Wire! Fuck, it's me!"

Looking down in shock, I see Wire staring back at me, wide eyed. I let him go before scrambling up to stand. Swinging my head around, I see Ana also has the woman in a headlock.

"Shit, Ana! It's ok, let her go."

The next thing I know, a glaring light comes on, blinding me.

"Neighbors! Are you ok? We heard a ruckus!" Craig's voice breaks through the night and I blink my eyes to help them adjust. And then I wish I never had, because standing there in all his pasty glory is a pants-less, long cocked Craig.

"Ah, yup, no, we're ok, thanks, man. We thought these guys were robbing us, but we've got it under control," I wave out to him. He squints at me for a moment before addressing Ana.

"Ana, are you ok? If you would feel safer, you can come and wait for Gus in our tent if you like?" I growl a little before reining myself in. I mean, it is a nice thing for Craig to offer. I look at my wife, who is looking anywhere but Craig.

"Um, no thanks, Craig. Thank you for the offer, but um, I think I'll be ok."

Our naked neighbor lets out a sigh. "Too soon?"

"Yes Craig, way too soon."

"Ok, well, you can't blame me for trying" We watch his glow-in-the-dark ass bend slightly as he goes back into his tent.

"What in the fuck was that all about?" Wire rasps out before coughing.

"W-was that guy naked? I didn't imagine that, did I?" a very quiet voice asks.

Staring at the slightly worse for wear Wire and the librarian-looking lady, I can't help but feel annoyance bubbling up.

"Who the hell are you? Actually, why the fuck are you two snooping around us in the first fucking place? Please tell me you weren't in the women's toilets earlier, Wire?"

I watch his eyes dart around and I swear to God I'd see a blush on the computer man's brown cheeks if the light was better.

"Fuck. Marx sent us to keep an eye on you. Make sure you're both safe. We noticed you left the tent in a hurry and never came back. I sent out a message to your sister and then me and Remy decided we'd check it out."

"Hi. I'm Remy." I can see how Ana would have been fooled by this woman. She exudes gentle energy, the opposite of almost everyone I know.

"Hi. Um, sorry for pulling your hair." Ana gently pats Remy's hair into place.

"Oh, that's ok. You didn't know we weren't a threat." Remy smiles and waves her off.

How the hell did this woman end up here with Wire? Whatever, it doesn't matter. I'm still pretty pissed. I mean, what the fuck? I get everyone is trying to keep us safe, but we have this shit under control. I could have spent the last hour tucked up in bed with my wife. I clench my hands at my side while I try to settle down. I feel a small, soft hand slip into mine and, as if by magic, my blood pressure lowers. I look down at Ana, whose lips are twitching.

"You're going to laugh, aren't you?" I frown down at her.

"Well, I mean, it is kinda funny. We're both hypervigilant and neither of us recognized Wire. Or that we are camping in the middle of a bunch of swingers."

"Whoa, whoa, whoa, hold the fuck up. These guys are swingers?" Wire asks, looking around at the tents surrounding us.

"Yup."

"Your neighbor had quite an impressive penis. I wonder if

he knows how to use it?"

Ana and I share a look before we both burst into laughter.

"What? Did I say something wrong?" Remy quietly asks, but I'm a goner. All the stress of the past hour, broken sleep, squatting under a rock in the woods, and Craig's cock has sent me over the edge, taking Ana with it.

"Oooook. Well, nothing around here is out of the ordinary. Remy and I have been keeping tabs and running backgrounds on everyone in the campground. Although none of that picked up their bedroom activities. I'll cancel the alert I sent your siblings and we'll leave you to get some sleep."

"Um, it was lovely to meet you. Good night," Remy quietly calls, but it's lost in the noise of our laughter.

# Chapter 8

Ana

"So, you went camping on the weekend. How did that go for you both?" Marta stares us down as Gus and I sit almost on top of each other in the tiny loveseat across from her.

"It went well. We went on a couple of nature walks and met some nice people," Gus answers with a straight face, and I have to hold in a snort when Craig and Mandy pop into my mind.

"Right. And what about any conflict?" She asks, her eyes on her notepad, before staring at us over the top of her thin-rimmed glasses.

"We had a little tiff in the car, as I was driving, and again when I was setting up the tent. But other than that, we managed to work things out. I think Gus and I are old enough and ugly enough to sort out any disagreements we have, like grown-ups."

"That's an interesting turn of phrase you used. Is that common in New Zealand or are you alluding to you not finding Gus or yourself attractive?" Wait, what? I blink at Marta a couple of times and I swear she has a smirk on her face, like she has me on the ropes.

"You're kidding, right? I mean, you have eyes, and you're a woman. You know as well I do, Gus is damn hot. He's like an Adonis come to life. Seriously, I have to stop myself from jumping his bones every two seconds." Whilst my mouth is running away from me, I can feel my face growing hotter and hotter.

Gus and I haven't messed around since I got myself off rubbing up against him like a cat in heat. For some reason, we've drawn a very shaky line in the sand. I don't know if it's because Gus is unsure or if it's me, but the sexual tension is killing me. The problem is that we have both been flat out at work. Tombs Security got called in to help the FBI the Sunday evening we got back from Swingersville. This is the first time I've seen him for more than a few moments since then. It's now Wednesday.

And it's not as if I've been sitting at home twiddling my thumbs either. I've been trying to put out the small fires that keep popping up. When Roman left town, I was to keep an eye on stuff here, but he'd still be in charge. He's been gone for months and it feels like I've taken on more and more. We've had a few of our Bratva shipments messed with. They left port in Russia perfectly fine, so somewhere between there and here, shit's gone down. I've got men on the job and Ivan keeping me updated. Even so, it hasn't lessened my work any. Roman and I have been video calling a few times a day to come up with plans, but ultimately with the time difference and the distance, it's up to me to call the shots and I really don't want to. I'm a secretary, for God's sake!

"Well, yes, I can appreciate that Gus is an attractive man." I give her a quick nod, afraid that if I don't shut up, I'll pledge my undying love to him or something.

"Gus, how do you feel about Ana?  Do you find her as attractive as she apparently finds you?" I can feel my temper rising. This woman is cruising for a bruising. Why the hell is she asking shit like that? I mean, I like myself. I like my body and I'm happy with my face. But you can't ask Gus that.

"What the hell, lady? Ana is fucking gorgeous. I'm a damn lucky man that she married me." I slowly turn to look at Gus and find his dark eyes boring into mine. Not caring that Marta is talking to us, he leans forward and kisses me gently on the lips. He pulls back and I stare up at him for a moment, the spell breaking when he winks at me. Oh, right. It's for show. I can do this.

"Right then, I can see that things seem to be going very well. You survived a stressful situation for you Gus -" I cover my snort with a cough. This woman has no fucking idea how stressful camping was, "- and you're both very attracted to each other.  I feel happy that you two are getting on well. However, I won't sign you off just yet. I want to see you both again in a fortnight, same day and time, ok with you?"

Gus and I look at each other before plastering fake smiles on our faces and nodding our agreement. Marta stands, and as per usual, walks us out. As we're walking into the underground carpark Gus gently takes my hand in his and laces our fingers together.

"I've missed you the past couple of days, Wife."

Pulling him to a stop with the hand I'm holding, I look at the differences in the size. His large hand, with a light dusting of hair, mine smaller with the short, blunt blue nails I'm rocking at the moment.

"I missed you too. I mean, I know this isn't real –"

"– It's real, Ana."

My head snaps up, my eyes locking with his intense dark gaze. I swallow loudly before murmuring like an idiot, "Oh. Ok." I'm not sure what to do. I want to whoop and dance around, but I also don't want to get my hopes up. Never in my life did I imagine someone like Gus would want someone like me. But how long for?

6 months. 6 months is how long good things last before they get taken from me. Only my parents, Roman, Sasha and Ivan, have lasted longer than that, and it took me years to find and trust them to keep my heart safe. I can't hope that I'm lucky enough for another good thing to hang around, can I? Gus snaps me out of my thoughts when he runs his large finger gently down the side of my cheek, causing my stomach to flip and my pussy to clench. The things this man can do to me with one touch are dangerous.

"So, I want to take you out on a date, little wife. But, Marx has asked us to call by the clubhouse. You all good with that?" Gus' soft, lush lips press against the back of my hand that he's holding.

"Shit. If we've been summoned, that means something is going down."

Gus lets out a sigh. "Yup. It will either be something dangerous or something to do with my family,"

"Which, if Pops or Tuesday are involved, could be both," I smirk up at him.

"Ugh, you know them so well. Let's call past home first, drop your car off and we can go in mine. Afterward, I'm taking my wife out for dinner."

"Race you there" I shove him away from me and run in my

heels toward my car, clicking the remote start button on my key fob. A weird click sounds out and then I hit a brick wall, the wind rushing out of me as I land on the ground and a loud POP! echoes through the parking garage.

My breath comes rushing back to me and my fuzzy brain registers that the brick wall looks, feels, and smells a lot like Gus. Blinking my eyes, I watch as Gus checks me over, patting me down, his jaw clenched tight, eyes wild. Reaching up, I cup his face in my hands.

"Hey, hey, Gus, look at me." I force his face up to mine, so he's looking at me. "I'm fine. I'm ok. Take a breath, big guy." I stare into his eyes and feel his big body deflate. He sits back and I take the extra space to sit up, him straddling my legs. He grabs me and crushes me to his body.

"Thank fuck you're ok," He growls out before he has his angry face back on, glaring in the direction of my car.

"Back up dude, I need to see what the fuck that was." I push him gently back so I can get my shaky feet under me.

What the hell was that? I mean, I'm no expert, but in the movies that is the sound a car makes before the whole bloody thing blows up. Whatever that pop sound was is not something usually portrayed in the films. Gus gives me his hand and pulls me to stand. We gingerly walk toward my car, Gus's arm around me, holding me tight to him. I see the interior and windows are covered in some weird goop. It's a mixture of red and beige-looking stuff, and if I didn't know any better, I'd think it was some type of animal brains.

"What in the actual fuck?" I turn to look at Gus, but he's already on his phone, barking out orders. I take a few deep breaths and categorize all the aches and pains I now have thanks to my big, strong husband landing on me. Not that

I'm complaining. I'd rather be bruised and alive any day of the week.

"Babe, Marx is going to send one of the guys with the tow truck. We'll take your car back to the garage at the clubhouse and have the guys go over it. My brothers are already there. They can comb your car for a trigger or check to see if anyone has tampered with it. Ok?"

"Fuck yes, that's ok."

He gives me a quick nod, then wraps his arm over my shoulders and leads me to his SUV. Helping me inside, his hands linger on my waist, before making sure I'm settled in enough for him to put on my seatbelt.

"I can do that, you know," I tease. His eyes shoot up to mine and I can see the strain in them. He's barely holding it together. I lean forward and kiss him. This is the first time I've initiated a kiss, and I know I've taken him by surprise. When I pull back, his frown is gone and a small smile plays on his lips.

"Thank you, baby. I needed that."

He slams my car door, then walks around the front to get in, his large body still stiff with anger. Gus is on a mission and even though I haven't admitted to myself exactly how frightening that was, it makes me feel better knowing I have this man by my side. I just hope I can hold on to him.

## Gus

Fuck, I need to get a grip on myself.

Whatever the fuck that was scared the hell out of me. It may not have been a bomb, but my adrenaline doesn't know that.

Once we got to the MC clubhouse, I led Ana inside, left her with Remy and some of the brothers, and came out to the gym. I had client meetings earlier, so I was in my finery. Not that it matters now, as I've just tossed my suit jacket onto the nearest lifting bench. My tie is who the fuck knows where and I was too rough unbuttoning the top buttons of my shirt, so they're also strewn somewhere. I'm bashing the hell out of the boxing bag, and the tear of my knuckles against the aged leather feels good. My brain knows Ana is safe, but it's almost as if my body needs the pain to remind me we are here, alive and well. The slam of the gym door echoes through the space and heavy footsteps come my way.

"You all good, man?" Resting my forehead on the bag, I take a deep breath before turning to see Rhodie and Marx side by side. It's funny because I never really noticed how similar the two truly look. I mean, it makes sense. My brothers and I all look the same, just different fonts. Where Marx is dark, Rhodie is lighter. His hair is less black, more dark blonde.

"Yeah, I'm good. Just scared me, you know?"

"You feel like your gut has dropped out of your ass, right?" Rhodie asks with a smirk. I swallow, thinking about how eloquent he is.

"Yeah, actually, it does."

He nods once, and I'm sure I see sympathy in his eyes. "That's how I felt when Chewy ran off and I wasn't there to keep her safe. One day I will put a ring on your sister and we'll be brothers. But until then, don't think you aren't already part of the family."

He slaps me on the shoulder and turns to head off, leaving me with Marx.

"You may not wear a patch, but we've got your back. Mainly

because I don't want to be stuck with your family if you die."
I flip him the bird while he chuckles. "Wanna see what we
found?"

I tip my chin and follow Marx through the clubhouse, gesturing to Ana to come with. She will have my balls if I leave
her out of this. We reach the garage and I'm not surprised to
see a few of the MC brothers and my brothers gathered around.
Alarmingly up front and center are Pops and Chewy, both of
whom have on biohazard suits and goggles. Chewy's are fogged
up, and I have no idea how Rhodie finds that attractive, but
he's all over her like a rash.

"Oh good, you're here. The stuff all through your car is, wait
for it, dum dum dum dum dum duuuuuuuuuum," Pops starts
drum rolling and I'm going to kill at least one of them if they
don't hurry up.

"CABBAGE!" they both yell in unison

"What the fuck?" Marx grumbles.

"Who the fuck would explode cabbage in your car, and why?"
I ask out loud, fucking baffled by the situation. Dayz brings
over a small dish with weird ass looking stuff in it and Ana
peers at it.

"Kimchi? Oh. Ooooohhhhhhhh" She looks up at me and I can
see a blush climbing up her throat, coloring her cheeks.

I watch as she looks sheepishly around the room, everyone
on tenterhooks to find out first, why the hell she has Kimchi,
and second, why it's all over her interior.

"What's that ooooohhhh for? You know why it's in your car,
don't you?" Chewy says, staring through her foggy goggles at
my wife.

"Um, yeah. I forgot I had it. One of the Boytsev gave it to
me." We all stand there staring at her. I feel a rumble in my

chest and I can't stop myself.

"Who, or what the fuck, is the Boytsev?"

Ana's brow pulls down low until she's scowling at me. "Don't bark at me, August Tombs! Boytsev is a foot soldier in the Bratva. The Bratva that I am reluctantly running and have meetings with. Is that ok with you?" She turns away from me and I'm certain I hear her call me a "fucking caveman." Call me suitably put in my place. I didn't mean to growl, but fuck. She's mine.

"Ok, so a footsoldier gave it to you. What the fuck for?" Marx asks, and it's a good fucking question. Like, who the hell gives someone cabbage?

"Oh, it was a gift. He makes Kimchi in his spare time. I forgot it was in the back seat and I guess the heat of the car made it get all ferment-y and it exploded." She shrugs her shoulders like it's nothing.

"Why is a Bratva foot soldier making fermented Korean cabbage?" Rider asks no one in particular.

"It's his hobby. He pickles things and makes some pretty amazing jellies as well. He usually hands them out for gifts."

The MC brothers and my family all look around at each other. Who the hell ever heard of a mobster Martha Stewart? Ana must sense everyone's confusion because I can see annoyance cross her face. She has a really expressive face which is helpful to me because it's easy to tell if I've pissed her off or not.

"What? Bratva can't have hobbies?"

"Fuck no! They're meant to be out shaking people down for protection money and killing people and shit. What is the world coming to when the gangsters are pussies?" Pops throws his goggles down on the ground in disgust.

"This may be a fucked up question, but if it was just Kimchi in the car, what was up with the clicking sound you heard?" Rider breaks in.

We wait on Tav to tell us, as he's the auto tech guy, but he says nothing. Until now, he's been busy texting on his phone. Jules had said he's been distracted lately. I really need to catch up with him. Since Ana and I got married, I don't feel like I've been spending enough time with my siblings, and that has to change.

"I can answer that." Jules says, stepping forward. He holds Ana's key fob up and presses the button, the car making that clicking sound again.

"Remote lock is fritzing. That's the sound you heard. It was just a coincidence that your Bratva Kimchi exploded straight after that."

Me and Ana turn to look at each other. Like what the actual fuck? That's it? Some forgotten cabbage and a fucked up remote lock? I run my hand through my hair and blow out a breath. It surely can't be that easy, can it? Fuck, maybe my work and the past few months have made me paranoid or something. I'm pulled out of my thoughts by Marx's phone going off and the big man yelling at whoever is on the other line.

"What the fuck?" Marx yells at his phone before his head snaps up, looking around at us.

"Death Riders coming in hot, ETA 5. They may need cover." Everyone in the garage nods and from the corner of my eye I see Chewy take off, most likely to Wire's "Command Center." Shit. Looking at Ana, I just know she'll want to get involved.

"Got a gun on you, babe?"

She stares up at for me a beat. "You do know that New Zealand isn't really a gun carrying place, don't you? I'm from

New Zealand, ergo no, I don't have a gun on me." I feel my eyebrows pulling down into a frown.

"Wait, you've been running the Bratva and you haven't been carrying protection? What the hell, babe?"

"I'm just the secretary. Usually I'm in the office and we have security," she shrugs. She fucking shrugs at me. I can feel my blood pressure rising, but I really don't want to be an overbearing ass and piss her off while we have drama going on.

"Can you use a gun at least?"

"Well, yeah, I used to go hunting with my dad. Trust me, big guy, I got this."

"Ok. Good, take mine. I'll grab one of Pop's spares." I pull mine out of my holster, check it over, place it in her hand, and press a quick kiss to her lips.

"I need you in the clubhouse, yeah? Keep an eye on Dayz?" From the look on her face, I can tell she would rather be in on the action. Running my gaze down her body, I pointedly stare at her high heels before locking my gaze with hers. She looks down at her feet for a moment.

"I have my boots in the backseat of my car."

"Covered in kimchi?"

She huffs a breath at me. "Ugh, fine" She gives me a none too impressed look before she nods her head and struts off toward the clubhouse, gun in hand. I turn to see my brothers and Pops waiting for me, checking their own weapons. Pops handing me his spare. To this day, I still don't know how many weapons that man carries.

"We'll flank the sides of the clubhouse, Jules and Pops, you on the north side. We'll take the South." They both nod and we split up, Tav and I sprinting to the other side of the compound.

The roar of motorcycles cuts the early evening air and I'm

glad we still have light. There's nothing worse than running security in the dark. I watch as the two prospects manually swing the gates open wide enough for the first of the Death Riders to come screaming through. The first rider screeches to a halt, booting down the kickstand. Four more follow closely behind, one of them comes in hot and lays their bike down. The distant roaring of incoming bikes almost drowns out the yells of the five Death Riders that are now inside the compound, the Prospects racing to shut the gates.

Tav and I are in position at the farthest front corner of the main building, and from where I crouch, I can clearly see through the chain-link fence a row of bikes bearing down on us. None of the riders seem to wear a distinguishable cut that I can recognize. As soon as they are close enough, they fire errant bullets, trying to cause as much damage as possible. The DRMC and Death Riders have taken a couple of the riders down, but killing them won't help us any. We need to know who the fuck these guys are.

With this in mind, I take a knee and line up my shot with a rider who isn't quite in formation. He may be young or new at this, but I don't give a shit, not when he's putting my friends and family in danger. I take a breath, block out the surrounding noise, exhale, and gently squeeze the trigger. My target's right shoulder jerks backwards before he falls from his bike, hitting the road and rolling a couple of times as his friends ride past us, into the distance.

"Fuck, we need help! Flack's been hit!"

My head spins toward the yells for help. The Death Riders are gathered around whoever came off their bike. I've not had much to do with them, other than meeting their Pres Savage and their SAA Dex. From what I know, they used to be 1 percenters, but Savage has been trying to go legit.

Movement catches the corner of my eye, distracting me from the injured Death Rider. I watch the guy I shot crawling towards his downed bike while the MC is distracted.

"Wanna come pick up some trash with me?" Tav follows my line of sight for a beat before turning to grin at me.

"Yeah, I'm a big environmentalist, let's go,"

# Chapter 9

Ana

I can't believe that big, bossy bastard has sidelined me. I storm through the common room headed to Wire's "Control center" as he calls his very impressive set up.

The clacking of computer keys drifts down the hall and I take a hard right into his room, watching for a moment as Wire and Dayz tap away at their keyboards, Remy intensely watching the CCTV video feeds dotted around Rose Grove township and on the main road to the club.

"Hey Ana, you been relegated to keeping an eye on the sedentary, huh?" Wire asks, his eyes not leaving his screen.

"How did you know?"

This time, Dayz answers. "We have amazing powers of deduction, duh," She gestures at another rolly computer chair by the door. "May as well pull up a seat. If anything goes down in the rest of the clubhouse, you'll be our first line of defense."

She finally turns to look at me, her eyes running down my seated body until they stop at my heels, and I can't help but feel a little judged by yet another Tombs regarding my footwear.

But you know what? These are my favorite shoes, so they can both suck it.

"Might wanna change shoes if you need to kick ass though,"

"Thanks, I'll bear that in mind."

"Riders incoming, ETA 1 minute. By the looks of it, four, no, five Death Riders. Followed by a large group of unknowns," Wire calls out, his eyes darting from one screen to another and another.

"That will be the five council members. Since Savage has been going legit, the only people on important runs are the five of them until he can rebuild the club with men he can trust," Remy softly states.

I watch as Wire tips his head to look at her, a slight frown on his face. I get his interest in what she said. From what Dayz has told me about being an Ol Lady and the MC, club business is club business and not something you speak about with family members. Although Death Rider rules could be different.

"How much do you know about the Death Riders, Remy?" Wire asks casually, eyes back on his screen. She shrugs her shoulders and blows her bangs out of her eyes, her blonde bob swaying a little at the movement.

"Me and my sister grew up there, we've seen all sorts of - oh no!" she gasps out, her eyes glued to the screen.

Mine shoot up and I see a Death Rider lying on the ground beside his downed bike. He doesn't seem to be moving and there is chaos around him as both Death Riders and DRMC brothers have their guns drawn, firing at the group of riders that chased Savage and his men into the safety of our gates. My eyes scan the screens for Gus, hoping he's ok but before I can find him, Remy jumps up.

"I have to get out there! That's my dad's bike! That's my

dad!" She makes a move for the door, but I'm already up, blocking the doorway. I grab her biceps, holding her still as she fights me to get to her dad. The girl is a hell of a lot tougher and stronger than I gave her credit for, not to mention she's taller than me by a good inch or two.

"Remy! Listen, it's bloody nuts out there! Just wait until Devil's Rose MC gets it under control." I all but shout in her face, trying to get her to listen to me. As soon as her eyes snap to mine, I soften my voice. "It won't be long and then you can get to your dad. Just wait a moment, a few minutes until it dies down, ok? Your dad will want to know you're safe," I stare into her big, brown eyes, the fear in them breaking my heart.

I know what it's like to lose your dad suddenly, and I can only hope that he's ok. He rode to safety, so I know he has fight in him.

Remy's body slumps a little, softening against my hard grip on her arms, and she nods her head, whispering, "Thank you".

God, this woman constantly has me wanting to give her a hug. I help guide her back to her seat, between Dayz and Wire. He gives me a nod of thanks before he reaches over, covering her much smaller pale hand with his larger, dark one. She lets out a breath, pulls her shoulders back and goes back to watching the feeds, although I see her eyes darting back to the one that her father is on now and then. He seems to be breathing, so that's a bloody good sign.

I still haven't seen any sign of Gus on the compound feeds. I know in my mind he can handle this, but that doesn't seem to settle my nerves.

As if she can read my mind, Dayz turns to look at me, well, my nose, "He'll be fine. He's done stuff like this a million times before. It's his job to protect people." I give her a thin smile and watch her turn back to her screen.

If I'm being honest, I have no idea what the hell her or Wire, or shit, even Remy are doing, but I'm sure it's important. It's only me at a loose end and Gus can damn well bet that next time, if there is a next time, I will not be sitting with my finger up my arse waiting for the men to sort shit out.

I've not taken my eyes off the screen and there seems to be a lull now. The other riders have long since left our screens, screaming off down the main road out of town.

I watch as the big ginger DRMC brother Switch races over to Remy's dad. He's an ex army medic, so I know the biker is in expert hands. Hospital is not an option if you live a touch on the wrong side of the law. Hell, Ivan's right-hand man used to be a doctor here at the local hospital before he realized working for the Bratva was less stress and more money.

Grunts and hollering from the common room make their way down the hall and Remy turns to me with a questioning look. I give her a nod and follow her as she rushes toward the noise. When I reach the common room, it's in chaos. The injured man has been placed on one of the main tables and about half a dozen men have congregated, the adrenaline running high, some shouting, one punching the wall.

From the last feed I saw, Savage and Marx were still outside with some men doing something or other, which explains why its fucking nuts in here. In the middle of the chaos, Remy sits at the table, her forehead resting against her dads, whispering to him while Switch tries his best to work in the middle of these less than perfect conditions. I can see the frustration on his face, so I move to stand next to him. Placing my hand over his hand, covering what looks to be a bullet wound in the top right-hand side of the man's chest. I wait for his eyes to meet mine.

"Is there somewhere better you can do this, without all this -" I glance around the room "- going on around you?"

"I have rooms at the back of the clubhouse, sterile, with all my shit. He's stable enough to move, I just have to get him there and these fuckers outta my space," I give him a nod, place two fingers in my mouth and let out an ear-piercing whistle, the noise stopping immediately, men looking in my direction.

"Listen up, Switch needs this guy -" "Flack" Switch grunts at me "- Flack, moved to his rooms. I need four strong brothers to move him, following all of Switch's instructions. Then you need to leave immediately so he can do his job. Got me?" Silently four guys move toward Switch and Flack, followings the Dr.'s orders to get him settled before "fucking off". Remy is still sitting at the table, staring at a little bit of blood that's on her hands.

"Hey, he's tough, and he's going to be ok" I grab one bloodstained hand and give it a squeeze. "Go wash that off and head on back, Switch won't mind," she nods at me, stands, and turns toward the hall her father was carried down. She stops, turns back and throws her arms around me, clinging to me.

"Thank you Ana. For everything." She releases me before heading after her dad, leaving me to my thoughts. Men trickle in, including the two Pres's, Jules and Pops, but no sign of Gus or Tav yet.

Feeling someone beside me, I turn and look up to see Dex, the SAA of the Death Riders. He gently taps twice on the table, "Nice work Bratva boss lady,"

I let out a snort and wave a hand at him. "Please. I'm just the secretary,"

"Still, thank you for helping Flack." He taps once more and I watch as he wanders off toward the bar.

Sick of waiting here twiddling my thumbs, I figure I may as well check the feeds once more. Walking into Wire's room, I see Wire and Dayz both eating popcorn, eyes glued to the screen.

"Where the hell did you get popcorn? And what the hell are you watching?"

Wire taps some keys and that somehow beams whatever they're watching onto the biggest screen he has, so big in fact that I have to take a step back to see it properly. On the black and white footage are Gus and Tav, with some other guy. They look like they're wrestling one of those floppy things that stand outside car dealerships. Either that or they're remaking "Weekend at Bernies".

"What are they doing?" I tip my head to the side as I watch all three of them land on the ground, before Gus jumps up, yells something and then kicks Tav in the leg before heaving the random man up once again. We all watch as they slowly get him inside the compound gates, through the lot and into the club.

"Showtime ladies" Wire says, standing with a smile, picking up his bowl of popcorn and laptop before exiting the room with me and Dayz in his wake.

## Gus

Walking over to the piece of shit that is still trying to crawl down the road after his so-called friends, Tav and I stand over him, taking him in. He's younger than us, probably in his twenties, and he looks like crap. But that could be because I shot him.

"Hey man, need a hand?" Tav smiles down at the guy, and you can see him visibly breathe out, looking relieved. I mean, we are big fuckers, but with me in my disheveled suit, and Tav in chinos and a tee, we look fairly normal. And more importantly, not MC. He nods up at us and I almost feel sorry for him. But not quite. You can't expect to shoot up a place, a place where my wife, siblings, grandfather, and friends are, and not expect consequences.

"Come on dude, let's get you up" Tav gives him a hand and pulls him up to stand. He's a little shaky on his feet, so I grab one arm, throwing it over my shoulders, while Tav does the same on the other side and we shuffle toward the MC gates.

"Oh hey, no, we don't wanna go in there. That's the local MC." He swings his head, looking around. "Where's your car at?"

"Oh, we parked in there. At the compound you and your dickbag friends shot at." His eyes widen and he tries to get out of our grasp. We wrestle him for a moment, but between his thrashing and Tav somehow not supporting his weight properly, we all end up in a heap on the road. Jumping up, full of frustration, I kick Tav while he's down.

"Fuck's sake Tav! Keep it together!" He rolls his eyes at me, calling me a "bossy fucker" under his breath and we heave this guy up again. Although he's not making it easy on us, giving that he's gone all floppy.

"Dude, quit it before I drop you. You'll be fine. Our sister is in there. She'll take care of you" Tav shoots the guy a wide smile and I really want to laugh. Unfortunately, he doesn't stop squirming, so in the end Tav and I have to wrestle him through the gate, drag him through the lot, and by the time we make it to the front door, I'm about done.

Tav kicks it open with his foot, before yelling out, "Oh Maaaaaaarx, we got you a present."

Both Marx and Savage spin toward us. Savage stares while Marx barks out, "Where the fuck did you get him from?"

"Oh, this? It's just a little something I picked up," Tav digs his toe into the ground, swinging from side to side looking all coy. Savage snorts as Marx rolls his eyes.

"You know where to take him. Drop him off then meet us in the main room, shits about to hit the fan."

By the time we get back, men are scattered around the common room. Savage, Dex and two other Death Riders are sitting at the main table, looking pissed. I'm guessing their other member is still being patched up by Switch. Ana has nestled her little ass on the couch next to Dayz, so I stomp in that direction, pick my wife up under her arms, take her seat, and set her on my knee. I see her roll her eyes at Dayz before she settles back against my chest. She just feels right, like she's where she's meant to be.

"Right fuckers, we have some shit going down. Death Riders were hit just before riding into our territory," Marx's voice booms through the room.

"We were coming back from a gun run. Usual, run of the mill, nothing should have been out of the ordinary," Savage says in a voice only slightly less booming than Marx's. I'm seriously wondering if riding bikes causes industrial deafness. I mean, why the hell else would all these bikers talk so goddamn loud?

"But?" My sister pipes up. She's looking far too excited about this.

"But shit didn't feel right from the moment we made the drop. Dex was getting antsy and Flack was acting super fucking paranoid."

"Flack? The guy that got shot? Remy's dad?"

"Yeah, he's been on edge lately, hence why Remy is here. Well, one of the reasons,"

"You wanted her here to learn shit from Wire and Chewy. What the fuck other reasons are there?" Marx says with a raised brow.

Savage opens his mouth, but before he can say anything, Rhodie jumps in, "The other reason better not have put my Ol lady at risk, otherwise I will fucking shoot you," he seethes. It's odd seeing him this way and remembering he is the Enforcer to the MC. I only ever see him as the love sick puppy that follows my sister around.

"Look, since we got rid of Hammer, our last Pres, Flack, has been on edge. Seeing ghosts and shadows where there are none."

"Until today at least," Jules blandly points out to him, earning him a scowl, but Jules' is far more powerful.

"Yeah, OK. Until today. He's been like this since Hammer was put out. Got worse when those three men you warned me about turned on us."

Our first time dealing with the Death Riders was back when Rhodie and Dayz first started dating and three of Savage's men crashed their date. Turns out they were moonlighting for Kraykowski, helping with the skin trade.

"And now?" Marx scowls, staring down Savage, who runs a hand down his face, his shoulders drooping.

"And now he's worried Remy is in danger. It's why he was pushing for her to come here."

Looking around the room, all the Devil's Rose men look slightly confused.

"Why does he think that?" Wire asks, looking up from his ever-present laptop.

"I don't know.  It doesn't make any sense.  Remy is a sweetheart.  But it has to have something to do with her specifically, because Sunny, his other daughter, is still with us.  Sending Remy to you was meant to achieve two things. First, she'll be well trained enough to keep an eye on things back home, and second, it keeps her out of whatever line of fire Flack thinks is coming."

"Well, kid, given that he got his ass lit up, I'd say he's probably on to something," Pops butts in. Dex frowns at Pops for a moment, but that just makes Pops smile wide.

"What do you know about Dex?" Ana whispers in my ear, her soft puffs of breath causing a shiver down my spine.

"Grew up in the area. Both parents are still alive, has an older half-brother that seems to be a ghost, hasn't seen or heard from him in about 20 years. Why's that?" She wriggles a little in my lap, causing my dick to stir.  Before he can get carried away, she tucks her head under my chin.

"He just reminds me of someone. Can't quite put my finger on it" I jump when I hear a palm hit the table, and then my sister stands to her full height of 5'1.

"Well, if you have no more information for us, may I suggest we adjourn to the Rev Room?"

"Jesus Chewy, we are not going to call the shed that," Marx grumbles as he runs a hand down his face.

"Aw come on! You hate everything I call it! You didn't like Smack Shack, Blood Shed, or Pound Town. And you have to admit, the Rev Room is good.  It's like that sex room in that movie. But we have motorcycles and our torture isn't sexy."

"You know what? Fuck it. I don't care anymore. Let's just

get this done," Marx shakes his head and then leads the way out to the shed. I twine my fingers through Ana's as we follow everyone.

"I wonder what new weird and wonderful tricks Dayz has up her sleeve this time?" Ana murmurs under her breath.

"Whatever it is, it's gonna suck to be that dude."

Following the brothers into the Rev Room, I see that it's had a makeover from the last time I was here. Instead of being dingy and dark, it now has a calming sage color on the walls and ambient lighting. The metal chair still sits in the middle of the room, above the drain, however, it is now a cheery yellow. There's a shadow board with all of Dayz's girly looking tools lined up, and Rhodie's sits on the wall opposite. There are even motivational posters on the walls and, is that a framed Live, Laugh, Love cross stitch?

"What the fuck happened in here?" I whisper to myself.

"Chewy happened in here." I turn to look at Marx, who has a resigned look on his face. "Look, I let her do whatever she likes in here because let's face it, I've somehow ended up with two Enforcers. If Rhodie can't get shit outta them, then Chewy most definitely can."

"Well, I mean when you put it like that, it makes sense to let them do whatever weird, freaky shit they get up to."

I watch as Dayz and Rhodie do paper, scissors, rock. Dayz wins and Rhodie drops a kiss on her lips before patting her on the ass.

"Um, what the hell is going on?" A Death Rider with a patch that says "Bones" asks the room.

"My sister is about to torture information outta that guy," Tav says, smiling proudly at our baby sister. Sometimes I wonder if it's entirely healthy that we let her do this. But she seems happy enough, and at present, she's the only person in our family in a normal, healthy relationship; so it's obviously not doing her any harm.

"You let the Ol' ladies do that?" Bones asks again.

Ana shakes her head and tuts at him. "You just watch and learn."

I pull her to me; her back to my front, and wrap my arms around her as we watch Dayz pull on fresh coveralls, this time leaving her goggles off. Pops does the same and they lean their heads together, pointing at different body parts while their victim sits there wide-eyed while the crotch of his pants darkens with urine.

"Babe? Put on my soundtrack please," Dayz sweetly asks. Rhodie smiles indulgently before pulling up the app and pressing play.

The first few bars of the song play through some type of hidden surround sound speakers, and LED lights I didn't initially notice run along the bottom of the wall start flashing to the beat of the music.

"What is that?"

*Everybody*

"Oh, fuck no,"

*Rock your body right*

"Is that –"

*Backstreet's back alright!*

Staring straight ahead, I try to avoid the shocked stares of the Death Riders. From the corner of my eye, I watch as Marx's head tips forward, his chin resting on his chest. Ana shakes in my arms from her silent laughter and I drop my lips to the top of her head to cover my own. A little snort slips out when I hear Savage's incredulous whisper, "What the actual fuck?"

Over the next hour, the four Death Riders are treated to the Tombs Show. They watch in awe and maybe a little fear as Dayz and Pops slice, dice, cut off, freeze, and burn various body parts to the soundtrack of Now That's What I Call Music 3.

# Chapter 10

Ana

"Well, I'm going to be processing that for some time to come," Savage grumbles to one of his men as we head back into the common room. Dayz is going to brief everyone on what she found after she cleans up a bit.

I feel a little weird not having Gus by my side. Every time we've come to the clubhouse, he's always with me, by my side, holding my hand, claiming me in front of the brothers. This time, I'm on my own as he helps his brothers clean up after Dayz. Although I have to admit she is one tidy torturer.

I take a seat up at the bar and order a cosmopolitan from the prospect, turning back into the room as Pops slams his machete down on the bar and joins me.

"Something hinky is going on, girl," I take a sip, letting the sweet concoction sit in my mouth for a moment before swallowing it down. Nodding, I place my drink on the bar top and turn to look at Pops.

"You can feel it too?"

He bobs his head and gruffly orders a beer. "Yeah. Something isn't right, but I don't know what. Although not to worry, we'll figure it out." He takes a pull of his beer and Dayz walks through the door with her brothers flanking her.

I take a peek at Pops and then back at the Tombs'. They really are a beautiful family. Deep tanned skin, dark brown, almost black hair. Gus's peppered with gray at the temples making him look sexy as hell. That along with his slightly crooked nose? He's a woman's walking wet dream.

"Goddamn, I passed on some good genes, huh?" he nudges me with his elbow, waggling his eyebrows.

"Shit, Pops, don't say shit like that. The last thing I want is to be married to a girl version of you!" Rhodie yells out with a twinkle in his eye. I'm sure these two like winding each other up just so they can fight.

"Marry someone else, then! My baby girl is too good for your sorry ass, anyway." He turns his back to Rhodie, and a smirk pulls up the side of his leathery cheek.

"Pops, if Rhodie married someone else, I would be so heartbroken I'd go mad with grief and remove his balls. Then I'd be arrested and rot in jail."

"Hate to break it to you, Chewy, but you've done way worse than take a man's balls and you're still here, free as a bird," Rider says, smiling down at her.

"Good point" She shrugs and walks over to Rhodie, plopping herself down in his lap.

"This place is seriously messed up," One of the Death Riders says under his breath, and I watch Dex nod in agreement.

There's something about this guy that I really can't quite figure out. Nothing bad, I'm not getting bad vibes outta him, he just seems really familiar and yet not. I mean, I had met him before in our previous dealing, and back then I had felt the same thing. He looks like someone I know but doesn't at the same time. I can't explain it.

"Still trying to figure it out?" Gus asks as he drops a kiss on my head and leans against the bar.

"Yeah, it's annoying. Like, he just really reminds me of someone and I can't quite put my finger on who. It'll come to me."

Clapping draws my attention as Dayz yells out, "Gather around men. Let me tell ye a story."

"Just get to the point, Chewy, yeah?" Marx barks out and I watch as she rolls her eyes at a man twice her size, completely unfazed.

"Fine. Dude in there was recruited for a new MC. They're currently nomad, but judging by the routes they've been taking, I would presume they follow your runs, Savage."

"Fuck. They've been watching us."

"Yup," she says, popping the 'p'. "They also know the ins and outs of your MC. What businesses you now own, who works them, who lives at the compound full time,"

"Mother fucker!" Dex stands and walks behind his chair and I brace myself for him to throw it. However, he just grips the back, his knuckles turning white as he stares down at them.

"It's my job to keep the MC safe. How the fuck am I meant to do that if I don't know who our enemy is?"

"How many patched brothers are there?" Dayz asks the room.

"12. We were 25 strong, but some of Hammer's loyal brothers left not long after him,"

I watch as Dayz squishes her bottom lip between her fingers. I know this is the stim she uses when she's thinking.

"And five of you went on the run today. I'm guessing they're the ones you feel safest with?" Savage nods at her. Her brow crinkles and she taps her fingers, one at a time, against each other. "Wait, earlier you said 'when Hammer was put out' not 'put down'. You let him walk?"

Savage frowns as he regards her question. "Look, Hammer was a good Pres, just got reckless near the end. Was making mistakes and the rest of the brothers were paying for them. The first move we voted on was to strip him of his colors and let him walk. We were trying to go legit, and I didn't think we could do that with Hammer's death hanging over us."

Dayz stares at him as she says, "Hmm. Might come to regret that, big man."

"Wait, do you think Hammer has something to do with this?"

Dayz bobs her head from side to side. "It makes sense in my brain. You said yourself he was leading the MC down the wrong path. Instead of following, you lot overthrew him as Pres. I would imagine that would piss a man like Hammer off. You let him live? He's definitely going to be plotting your downfall." I watch as Rhodie drops a kiss to Dayz's neck.

That relationship shouldn't really work and yet it totally does. I mean, in no world would you imagine a hardass Enforcer acting like the big softy and making sure his girlfriend is not only well looked after but also at ease in social situations. I've seen Rhodie talk Tuesday through interactions, what certain expressions mean, and I've seen her thrive through all of that. I really want that type of relationship and I feel like that's something I can have with Gus if I was open and ready for it.

I can feel the full length of his body pressed against my side, his hand resting on my hip like it was always meant to. I frown down at his knuckles, ripped to shreds. Picking up his hand from my hip, I bring it to my lips and gently kiss the grazed skin, before placing his hand back where it belongs. I glance up at him and I see the heat in his eyes. The hunger, the need. Heat pools between my legs and I really need us to get the hell outta here. I've heard enough of the drama. I know it sounds harsh, but this seems like a Death Rider problem.

"Right, we'll keep Flack here with Remy for a bit, you head on back to your MC and make sure everything is all good," Marx says to Savage, the other man's shoulders sagging in relief.

"Thanks, Marx. We'll get outta your hair. Let us know when Flack is good to ride and we'll be back to pick him up."

Marx gives a grunt that I'm guessing Savage took as his agreement

"Chewy, it was nice seeing you again. Even if it was slightly terrifying," Savage says as he waves to Dayz on Rhodie's knee.

"Yo, you gave us quite a few techniques we can use," Dex follows up.

"Hey man, no worries. You need anything, give me a ca-" The rest of her sentence is muffled by Rhodie clapping his hand over her mouth.

"You're mine. Those fuckers can find their own women," Rhodie growls out and I chuckle as I watch her try to get his giant hand off her face.

"You ready to head out for some dinner, wife?" A shiver goes through my body as Gus's deep voice washes over me. Spinning to look at him, I realize I don't think I have it in me to go out tonight. It's been a hell of a day so far.

"Can we just get takeout and go home?"

A smile spreads across his face. "Fuck yeah, that sounds perfect, baby. Let's go."

As usual, he laces his fingers through mine and we wave

goodbye to our friends and family, heading out to the car. Gus helps me in, buckles me up, and then pulls himself in.

"Ok babe, what are we in the mood for?" I tap my chin in thought.

"I have Dragon Palace on speed dial. Lemme call in an order and we can swing by and pick it up on our way home." Gus's large hand drops to my thigh and he gently squeezes.

"That sounds fucking perfect. Can you get me a kung pow chicken and some crab rangoons?"

"On it." I make the order and within 10 minutes we've picked it up and are on the way home.

"Babe, do you think our jobs have made us way too fucking paranoid?"

I let out a little snort before turning to look at him. "You think? Shit, we thought we had a car bomb on our hands and it was a jar of Kimchi."

We look at each other and crack up, giggling on and off as we wind through the streets. I watch as the town I've come to call home rushes past my window. Pulling into the drive, I take off my seatbelt and go to gather the food, turning when the sound of my car door opens.

"I'll take that thank you very much, my lady," Gus says with a terrible English accent, collecting the food bags in one hand. I shake my head as I slide down out of his SUV, lamenting that my car is out of action until it's been cleaned up.

"I can't believe we got all worked up over a stupid remote lock," I snort out as Gus chuckles. "I mean, could it be that the dude watching us is just a coincidence and the rest of this stuff is all random?" Gus unlocks the door, entering our house and dropping the food on the counter before looking at me.

"I don't know, babe. It seems too frequent to be a coincidence. We've both done some crazy shit for work and shut down some pretty bad guys." I nod my head in agreement because he's not wrong. I mean, I know that what I do isn't fully legal, but the people I work with are friends, and they're not the worst people I've come into contact with in my life.

"I agree. Maybe we should stay alert, but not so alert that we freak each other out."

"Deal. Now go get into some comfy clothes and I'll plate up"

Smiling big, I rush to my room to get out of this stupid pencil skirt and blouse. Do they make me look hot? Fuck yes. Are they comfortable? Fuck no. I decide if I'm going comfy I'll go all the way comfy. So I take off my bra, letting my big boobs drop down an inch or so, and I take off my Spanx underpants. Pulling on my oversized New Zealand Warriors rugby league tee and some soft shorts, I throw my hair up in a messy bun and head back to the kitchen.

I watch as Gus's eyes travel down my body, feeling like a caress.

He smirks at me, "Ok, I'm gonna go get into my comfy clothes, too. Be back in a moment."

A giggle slips out, hearing Gus say comfy. He's usually so wound up that I find him goddamn cute when he relaxes. I pick up a shrimp and go to put it in my mouth, coming to a dead stop when I see him walk through the door in a soft, almost threadbare t-shirt that pulls tight across his pecs, and low-slung gray sweat pants that really highlight how long and thick his cock is. I've seen him dressed like this before, but in this lighting and my libido, the way it is? Well, all I can say is there goes my appetite for food.

Gus stands in the doorway, the overhead lighting beaming down on him, making him look like an angel. If that angel was fucking hot and straight from Pornhub. Even my pussy is singing hallelujah at the sight of him. I let my eyes travel from the top of his head down to his toes. Shit, he even has attractive feet. My eyes begin their journey back up his body, stopping at the bulge that's thickening in his sweats. Taking a deep breath, I realize it's either now or never. We're married. We are both consenting adults and we are attracted to each other. Could this be dangerous and break my heart in the long run? Yes. But could this also become something else, something... more?

Locking eyes with Gus, I decide to trust in him, take a leap of faith, and see if he'll catch me. I put my chopsticks down on the counter. I stand from my stool and take measured steps toward him. I watch as his eyes drop to my tits, jiggling free in my soft tee before I come toe to toe with him. I reach up, placing my hand behind his head, bringing him closer to my level before slamming my lips to his.

## Gus

I let Ana lead the kiss, her gentle lips working against mine, her soft tongue exploring my mouth, but it's not enough. Cradling her face in my hand, I angle her head slightly to deepen the kiss. I want to devour this woman. I want everything she has to give me and more. My hands stroke down her back to her plump ass that I can't get enough of. Gripping her cheeks in my hands, I massage the soft globes, drawing her to me so I can rub my hard cock against her soft stomach. Despite that, it's not enough. I need her. I need her on my tongue and on my cock. Gripping her ass tight, I hoist her up, breaking the kiss.

She squeals and wriggles on my hard length.

"Shit, Gus, put me down! I'm too heavy!"

"You're fucking perfect.  Now give me that mouth."  She squirms a little more then holds on for dear life, as if I'd ever drop her. She'll fucking learn.

I carry her into my room and drop her on the bed, her messy bun coming undone, her hair spilling across my duvet cover. Fuck, she's a goddess. My eyes eat up the sight of her on my bed, her legs splayed out, and that's when I get a look up her short baggy shorts at her glistening pussy.

"Fuck baby, are you wearing panties?" She smiles coyly up at me, bending her knees, putting both feet on the bed, and opening and closing her legs slowly.

"Maybe, maybe not" She lets out a yelp when I grab her by the ankle and pull her to the edge of the bed, then I rip her tiny shorts from her, down her thick thighs, letting out a groan when the smell of her pussy hits me.

"Fuuuuuck baby, you smell so good." I lean in and rub my nose against the landing strip of black curls. Her pussy glistens in the low lighting, and I don't know whether to dive right in or start at those amazing tits of hers.

"Gus," she groans low, her hips moving gently on the bed. My little wife is hurting for me, and I'm not one to deny her anything.

Licking two fingers, I run them down the seam of her plump pussy lips, before spreading them open for me, revealing her swollen clit that is begging for attention from my tongue. But she's going to have to wait. Instead, I blow softly on the bud and then gently suck one pussy lip into my mouth, then the other.

"Holy shit, Gus please," she whispers out. I drop a kiss to

her mound before raising my head.

"You're going to have to wait, sweet wife. This is punishment for coming to dinner in those little shorts with no panties on. How am I meant to concentrate on my dinner, knowing your pretty little cunt is right there, teasing me?" I gently stroke my two fingers down either side of her pussy, then give her a little slap. She's so fucking wet that when I pull my hand back to slap her again, I see the fine thread of her juices on my fingers. I slap her once more, a whimper coming from her lips.

I'm so fucking hard and leaking that when I look down, I see a dark spot growing on my gray sweats. I pull them down my legs, releasing my angry-looking cock. I fist him a couple of times to help relieve him, but I know that there will be no relief until I'm buried deep in the prettiest pussy I have ever seen.

"Gusssss" Ana whimpers out. It almost sounds painful and at this point, I'm torturing both of us.

I place my hands on her knees, pressing, letting her know I want her spread, so she's open fully for me. Gazing up her body, she has her top pulled up, her hands squeezing those magnificent tits, tugging at the dark pink nipples. She's fucking stunning.

I stare at her pussy, wide open, waiting for my tongue, my fingers, my cock; and I'm done holding back. I bury my face into her sweet cunt and feast on her like a starving man, holding her open so I don't miss a drop of her sweet honey. I look up the length of her body, her soft belly sucking in and out as her breaths come faster and faster. She's so fucking responsive and I have a feeling she's going to explode a lot quicker than I would have imagined.

Her hips undulate on my face, rubbing faster and faster as my lips and tongue work her pussy. She could suffocate me with this cunt and I would die a happy man.  Latching onto her swollen bud, I suck gently as I run a finger up and down between her pussy lips before gently easing inside of her tight little hole.  She lets out a low moan, then works herself even more as I pump my digit in and out of her greedy hole. I can feel her muscles ripple around my thick finger so I nibble lightly on her clit before batting it with my tongue, my finger finding that rough patch of skin inside her and gently massaging.

My little wife doesn't scream her orgasm. Instead, she comes on a long, guttural groan, her head thrown back as her release coats my hand, dripping down onto the covers, leaving a wet patch that I want to beat my chest about. I did that. I made my gorgeous little wife come all over my face and I want to do it every day for the rest of our lives.

I release my suction on her, and slowly pump my finger, wanting to bring her down gently as she clamps her legs together, little tremors running through her body, her whimpers and her breaths slowing.

"Holy fuck Gus, that was, fuck." I stand from my kneeling position at the side of the bed and go to lie with her, but my wife has other ideas. She stops me leaning over her with her foot on my chest, pushing me back gently.

"My turn now," she smirks up at me as she eases herself off the bed and onto her knees in front of me.

"Babe, you don't have to. We can just relax for a moment."

She shakes her head back and forth, pushing my t-shirt up my abs. I take the hint and pull it off, throwing it somewhere, anywhere, in the room behind me.

I gaze down at her and my chest gets tight. Her large green eyes stare up at me, still slightly unfocused from her orgasm. Her cheeks are flushed and her big tits are heaving.  She's fucking gorgeous, and she is mine.

She runs her tiny hands up and down my thighs, moving them closer and closer to my cock that is leaking like a faucet. I cup her face in my hands, then slide them back into her hair, gathering it up in my fist so I can get an unobstructed view of her. The little minx smirks up at me before leaning forward, her wet pink tongue pushing through her plump lips, but instead of making contact with my aching cock, she drops her face down to lick and suckle my balls.

"Ana, fuck," I growl down at her. She pulls back slightly, peeking up at me once more before leaning forward and licking from the base of my cock to my tip, wiggling her tongue on the head before she grips my cock, her hand pumping me twice, swirling her tongue around my knob, licking up all the pre-cum leaking out. She moans at the taste, pulling back to lick her lips before diving on my cock, taking me right to the back of her throat. The movement so sudden I let out a yelp that turns into a groan that comes directly from my chest.

I make shallow pumps with my hips as I slide in and out of her mouth, and I'm trying really fucking hard not to come. This woman is worshiping my dick, saliva dripping out around her lips, using it as lubrication as she runs her hand up and down the part of my shaft that isn't nestled in the back of her throat. I can feel the tingle in my spine and I use her fisted hair to pull her off of me. I am not coming in my wife's throat. Not tonight.

# Chapter 11

Ana

I feel a gentle tug on my hair as Gus pulls me off his long, thick, hard cock. I think we can all agree dicks aren't that great looking, but fuck me sideways with an arm full of deck chairs. Gus owns the prettiest cock I have ever seen. Long, thick, and the type of cock they would model vibrators and dildos on.

"Get your little ass on the bed now," Gus growls at me and I can see in his eyes he's about this close to losing it completely, which causes heat to pool between my thighs because I've only ever seen Gus in complete control. I want to watch that control snap. I want to watch him come undone.

Smirking up at him, I run my forearm across my face, wiping away the spit and pre-cum that I'm sure is all over my lips and cheeks. I turn toward the bed before looking at him over my shoulder, placing first my right knee on the bed, then leaning forward on my hands before bringing my left knee up. I wiggle my arse in the air and a yelp escapes me when his large hand lands on my arse cheek with a loud crack. Before I can say anything I feel his tongue lick a stripe where I can still feel the heat of his hand, before he rubs my skin tenderly, his other hand joining my other cheek, then I feel him pull them open, his spit hitting my pussy from behind.

"Fuck yes, look at this little wet pussy, all needy for me." He uses his fingers to massage my lips, spreading wetness around, opening me up with his fingers. "I need to get this little hole ready for my fat cock, because once I get in there, I will not be going easy on you, little wife. Tell me that's what you want."

I moan at his touch and his filthy words, nodding my head with vigor until I feel his hand slap my pussy.

"Tell me what you want, Ana. I want to hear your words. I want to hear you beg for my cock and my cum." I let out a whimper because everything is too good, too much, and I want it all.

"Yes Gus, I want your cock and your cum. Please, please don't tease me," I glance over my shoulder and I see a smirk growing on his handsome face. He makes eye contact with me and I watch as he lets a trail of saliva drip out of his mouth, gasping when it hits my pucker.

"Good girl" and with those words he places the head of his cock at my entrance and in one movement pushes deep into me, not stopping until his hips hit my arse, his balls bouncing off my clit. A long, low groan rents the air, and I'm not sure if it was Gus or me.

His hands grip my hips tight, and I'm sure I'm going to have his finger marks on me in the morning. I don't care. I want everything this man has to give.

He pumps slowly, in and out, snapping his hips so he can hit me deeper and deeper. His hands run up and down my curves, massaging my back, caressing me everywhere. Whispers of how beautiful I am, how amazing I am as a woman, how he's so fucking lucking to be inside me breaks through the pleasure I'm feeling, heightening the whole experience, all my senses drowning in this man. But it's not enough. I need him to lose control. And I want to watch when it happens. When he pulls back his hips, I crawl forward, breaking our connection.

He goes to grab my ankle to bring me back, but I grab his hand and pull him toward me for a deep kiss before I use my body weight to pull him down on the bed, spinning at the last minute so he's flat on his back and I'm leaning over him.

"What's your plan, baby?" Gus smiles up at me, and I can't help but smile back as I straddle him, picking up his cock in my hand to hold his length upright. I place the head of his cock at my opening and lower myself until I'm stuffed full of Gus. This position going deeper than anything I've ever felt.

My eyes close of their own volition and I have to fight to open them so I can see Gus. He has his head thrown back, the cords of his neck on show as he groans when I tighten my pelvic floor muscles. I place my hands on either side of his head and start rocking, faster and harder until my arse is slapping down onto the tops of Gus's thighs, my pussy making obscene sounds, Gus's hands tightening on my hips, helping guide me.

He's close, I know he is, so I lean back, plant my feet on either side of his hips and bounce, his cock shuttling in and out of me, bringing me dangerously close to my peak.

I look at Gus to see his jaw clenching. "Fuck baby, fuck you gotta cum. I can't hold it."

Neither can I so at his words I slam down on his cock and grind my clit on him, my orgasm crashing through me as I feel a wave of wetness pulse through me.

Gus bands his arm around my back, pulling my chest to his,

the other hand gripping my arse hard as he plants his feet and fucks up into me hard and fast before a growl rips through his chest and I feel his release fill me up. Pulse after pulse of Gus's cock sends little shocks through my core and my body and I can't think of anywhere I would rather be than being held by Gus; my cheek pressed against his chest hair as he runs his hands through my hair, whispering sweet nothings to me.

## Gus

I wake up with a start, and see three shadowy figures standing at the foot of my bed, backlit by the security lights that beam outside my window. I drop my head back onto my pillow with a huff, a low growl emanating from my chest.

"We'll meet you outside," Jules' voice murmurs in the dark, and the two big bastard shadows followed by a short one leave what I thought was my private space. Fucking siblings.

Lifting my head off the pillow, I look to my left to see Ana's beautiful face relaxed in slumber, her plump lips slightly parted as soft breaths leave her. I roll out of bed, making sure to pull the covers higher over my wife so she doesn't get a chill. I pull on my sweats and gently creep out of the room before walking through the rest of my house on a damn warpath, storming through my open front door and out onto the porch.

"What the fuck do you three want? It's the middle of the night!" I whisper shout at their three smug bastard faces.

"We just wanted to make sure everything is going well, and to warn you we love Ana, so don't fuck this up." Tav says, the other two nodding in agreement.

"And this shit couldn't wait until the morning?"

"Wellll, it kinda could, but I was keen to do it now because you three did it to Rhodie when we first boned. So you set the precedent. You only have yourself to blame." With that, Dayz shakes her head sadly and pats me on the shoulder before heading off to her own home, her Ugg boots softly padding down the path. I drop my chin to my chest and hope like hell when I look up Dumb and Dumber have gone home, too. I tilt my head back up - no such luck.

"Look, I really, really like Ana. More than like her. There is no way I'm going to fucking hurt her. But if, for some reason, I do, unintentionally, of course, I grant you both permission to kick my ass. Good?"

Jules and Tav share a glance before both tipping their chins at me.

"I'll hold you to that." Jules smirks at me.

"Awesome, do that. Now get the hell off my porch." I head back into my home, gently closing the front door before tip-toeing back into our room. I head to my side of the bed when Ana's sleepy voice calls out.

"Was that your family just now?"

I let out a sigh before sitting on my side of the bed. "You hear all that?" I watch a smile slowly grow on her face, her eyes still closed.

"Mmmmmhmmm" She cracks an eye open, takes one look at my face and then laughs before she sits up, holding the covers to her chest, hiding those magnificent tits from me. She snaps her fingers in my face and I shoot my gaze up to meet her green eyes, narrowed in my direction.

"Eyes up here, lover boy,"

"Aw, but they're just so fucking beautiful. I want to kiss them

-" I lean forward, hovering my lips just out of her reach before I press a gentle kiss to the swell of her breast above the covers. "- and lick them -" I lick down the valley of her cleavage, her hand holding the covers up, dropping to my lap, allowing me to lick across one plump mound. I'm about to draw her nipple into my mouth when a loud grumble comes from further down. My eyes shoot to hers, holding them for a beat before we both burst into laughter. Ana flopping back onto the bed, me leaning over her, burying my face in her stomach, as giggles ripple through us.

This. This is what I love about my relationship with Ana. We can have moments of such intensity because of work or danger or pent up sexual tension, and then moments of lightness that I've never really experienced with anyone before.

"Whoops, soz about that big man, but we skipped dinner, remember?"

"No, we didn't. I definitely remember eating you for my dinner." I lift my head from where it's been resting comfortably on her soft stomach and waggle my eyebrows. Yeah, ok, I know it's a cheesy line, and so does Ana because she just rolls those beautiful green eyes of hers and pushes me back with a hand to my forehead so she can sit up.

"We can resume what you were about to do with the girls after I eat the takeout that's still sitting on the bench ok?,"

"Fine.  But only if you eat naked.  I watch to watch these beauties while I chow down on crab rangoons," I cup her breasts in my hands and brush my thumbs lightly over her tight nipples, drawing a moan from her lips at the same time her stomach grumbles again.

"Ok, come on, wife, let me feed you. Naked."

I watch as she squints her eyes, lips pursed before she nods her head. "Deal."

We settle at the kitchen island, Ana perched on the barstool but only after she placed a towel down.

"Have you ever sat on your couch naked before?"

My head shoots up at this. "No way. That's leather! Leather is too cold, or too sweaty. Why's that?" I watch as her cheeks pinken some.

"Um, nothing, just wondering."

I frown at her for a moment before my stomach reminds me it needs sustenance if I'm going to rock my wife's world again. Yes, I did just say that. We dig into our respective meals, sharing here and there in comfortable silence.

"Ok, Mr. Tombs. We have some time on our hands. Let's play a round of 20 questions. Quick fire way to get to know each other. I mean, we know each other pretty well -"

"I'd say very well after having my tongue in your -" I'm cut off by her throwing a shrimp at me. It lands on my chest before sliding down my chest hair at a glacial rate. My eyes shoot to hers and she lets out a snort.

"As I was saying, we know each other pretty well, but we don't know the simple stuff. Like, what's your favorite color?"

I scoop the shrimp off my chest and pop it into my mouth. "Ok. It's green. It used to be blue, but now it's green." Specifically, the moss green of her eyes. "What's yours?"

"Orange. Who did you lose your virginity to and how did it happen?"

I choke a little on my food and thump my chest to get it all down. "Jesus, that was a jump!"

The little minx smirks at me before circling her hands in the air in a motion for me to hurry up.

"Ok, so it was the cliche prom night, in the best hotel room I could afford, which meant it was pretty shitty. We were both virgins, both super nervous, and I didn't know that you could take a girls virginity with your fingers so when I got her ready and saw the blood on my hand I freaked out a little," I look across the counter and see Ana has her lips pulled between her teeth, her face red. I let out a little sigh and carry on. "Anyway, she said it was nothing and we could keep going, but I had lost my erection because of the whole blood thing, so she offered to give me a hand job, which did the trick. But I'm sure she also took two layers of skin with her."

Ana's laugh fills the room, and she slaps her little hand on the countertop, her jiggling tits mesmerizing me momentarily.

"So I get hard, fumble to put on the condom, and learn the hard way that I was a two pump chump." I shake my head sadly as she bursts into another fit of giggles. I'm never described as the funny man in the family, so I love how much I can make Ana laugh. "Ok, ok, not that bad. Your turn. But no details, because I'll want to go back in time and beat his ass." She rolls her eyes at me before composing herself.

"It wasn't nearly as exciting as your story, or memorable really. So, in New Zealand, the legal drinking age is 18, but, I mean, obviously we drink earlier than that. So, I was 16. It was just before my dad passed, and I had told my parents I was staying at a friend's house. Instead, I was getting white girl wasted in a field with my three friends and some older guys that we thought were sooooo cool." I nod, wanting her to continue, picturing a young, carefree Ana. "Anyway, the guy I liked was a drummer in a local band, so clearly he was peak hotness. He also had a couple of tattoos that his friend and bandmate had done. He was tall, AIDs thin, had a scraggly goatee and a floppy fringe. And he also thought he was god's gift to women. We had some very lackluster foreplay, where he rubbed my left fanny flap way too long, finger blasted me and turned out to be a one pump chump, so at least you were better than that." She snorts.

"Hold up!" I place my finger over her lips, stopping her from talking. Her wide eyes turn from shock to a frown.

"Fanny flap? What do you mean? I don't get it. What did he do to your butt?" I remove my finger from her lips.

"What? What the hell are you talking about?"

"What do you mean by fanny flap?"

"Fanny flap, you know, pussy lip?" I stare at this woman like she's been beamed down to earth.

"No, I don't know. Here a fanny is your butt."

Her eyebrows fly to her hairline before she squints at me. "Wow. I, I don't know what to say. No wonder Tuesday looked confused when I told her I was having 'fanny flutters' about you."

We stare at each other for a beat before the laughter overtakes us once more.

# Chapter 12

Gus

"Shit, shit, shit." I can hear the rumble of my brother's footsteps coming down the hall and I'm not in the mood for their crazy. I could contemplate hiding, but the last time I tried, Dayz caught me and they still invaded my office, not giving any fucks about interrupting my work day. I have a feeling that's what they're about to do again.

"Well, well, well, if it isn't Sir Fucks-a-Lot," Tav comes through the door first, a shit-eating grin on his face. A deep sigh leaves my body as I watch him take a seat across from me, Jules silently following behind and Dayz walking across to the opposite corner of my office to put down her laptop and her ridiculously large drink bottle.

"Bit thirsty there, Dayz?"

Her eyes roll, "Rhodie bought me the viral Stanley drink bottle, and it's a nice gift so I have to drink water now. The only downside is the size. Although on the upside, I have surprised myself at how powerful my pee flow is, like a racehorse. Maybe when I need to go, you guys can stand outside the bathroom door and listen in. I'm telling you, it's super impressive." She finishes her sentence by taking a long sip of her water and then smacks her lips.

"Um, thanks for the invite, Dayz, but I'll have to decline. I'm sure I'll be busy at 3pm," Tav says, politely turning our sister down.

"Oh, well, here's the thing. Since I've been using this, I've had to bump up my scheduled toilet breaks. I'll let you know the new schedule." Tav gives me wide eyes and I just smirk back. Fuck him. I'm not making an excuse for him. He can just go listen to our baby sister's toilet breaks, as requested.

"Anyway, let's get back on track. What did you get up to last night, big brother?" Tav places his hand on his chin, eyes squinting as if he's thinking really hard.

"Oh, pick me!" Jules has his hand up, an evil grin on his face.

"Yes, Jules? Do you know what August Michael Tombs was up to last night?"

"Well, Tav, I believe he was busy vigorously giving it to his wife many times over the course of the evening." Tav nods his head up and down and I roll my eyes.

"Do you two dicks have anything helpful, or, oh I don't know, work related to say to me? If not, you can both fuck off and let me work."

Tav's smile grows across his face, "Now, why the hell would we do that? Look, big brother, we're happy for you. Proud even if Ana's noises were anything to go by." He wags his eyebrows at me and I snort when the stapler I throw at his smug bastard face hits him in the forehead.

"Argh you motherfucker!"

"That's gonna leave a mark," Dayz blandly says from across the room, her eyes not even leaving her laptop screen. She has three older brothers, she knows the drill.

"I have a date later on, you dick!" Tav bitches, rubbing his forehead. Jules reaches his fist out to me to bump.

"Speaking of, is that who you've been texting lately? I've noticed you've been a little distracted."

He glares at me before answering. "Not that it's any of your business, but yes, I am going on a date with the woman I've been chatting to and no, I'm not going to tell you nosey bastards anything just yet."

"But you can wake me up in the middle of the night to tell me you all love Ana and then come in here and give me shit about her? That's a bit two-faced, isn't it?" I watch as my brother goes red before he lets out a breath.

"Fine! She's a nice lady who's been through the wringer, and she doesn't need my asshole siblings getting in her face. She's not fully on board with what we have, but when she is, I'll let you know."

Jules flicks a side eye at our brother before looking back at me with a frown. I give him a tiny nod while Tav picks at his pants, letting him know I'm on board with whatever he has to do to find out about this mystery woman. We may give each other shit, but a woman who has "been through the wringer" and is reluctant to get on board with Tav, by far the nicest of us all, obviously has a history that we should probably know about.

"Well, I'm glad that you've found someone that makes you happy. She does make you happy, yeah?" Tav's eyes shoot to mine and he smiles and nods. He's what Ana calls a Golden Retriever, and I definitely see it now that she's pointed it out. Although she also said that I was a Boxer dog, protective of family but sometimes not the brightest. She laughed her ass off after she came up with that, too.

"She does. She just has a lot of shit going on from her past and she has kids she has to be mindful of. But we'll get there." I watch as a blush covers his cheeks. I think my baby brother has fallen in love. Goddamn. Another one bites the dust.

And then there's Jules, looking bored out of his mind.

"Well, now that you've given me shit about my sex life, you could probably go back to your own offices and maybe do some work? Unless you have something work-related you need to talk about?"

"I've just dropped off a box of those military grade smart watches to Marx," Tav pipes up.

"The ones with the ear buds?"

Tav nods at me. Those things are a good piece of equipment. In a pinch, you just release the earbuds from the watch, pop them in and you're ready for comms.

"Yeah, after yesterday's drive by, he wanted the brothers to all be open for comms as soon as shit went down. Charged him family discount and put through a new order for our guys,"

I nod at him, happy with that. Having Dayz and Wire with eyes on and being able to communicate with us will make us work smoother together if we find ourselves in that situation again.

"Good work Tav. That'll tighten up the MC operations. Anything else?"

My brothers look at each other, then turn to look at Dayz, then back to me before shrugging.

"We have an update on Tony Manero?" Tav asks, clearly knowing that we don't. He just doesn't want to get back to work. I know their tactics.

"Nope. I've run facial recognition software and nothing,"

Dayz offers.

"Wait, since when do we have facial recognition software?" I ask the room.

"Since I did that most recent job for the FBI, I told them to pay me in software. It's gonna come in real handy," Dayz says with a blinding smile, making her look like a kid in a candy store.

"Nice score, little sis" Tav puts his hand up for a non contact high five and Dayz waves at him. She'll get it one day.

"What do we think of that new Nomad MC?" Jules asks.

The new Nomad MC is a concern. We've only just had things kind of settle down from the last lot of shit we found ourselves in.

"I think it's a worry. If Hammer is Prez, then his first hit is going to be his old MC. Who is now an ally of Devil's Rose MC which means we too, have skin in the game," I nod my head toward Dayz. "We also don't know who the hell else he's been recruiting. The Bratva have shipments going missing so it could all be connected." I run my fingers through my hair. Ana and I spoke about this after one particularly vigorous sex session early this morning.

Dayz nods from her little position in the corner.

"It's definitely connected. I just have to find out how. No word from Lexi, and Katya is looking into dark web rumblings. Although from looking at the Nomad MC, none of them look clever enough to have email addresses, let alone be doing business on the dark web," Lexi and Katya are Roman's daughter and ex-wife, respectively. Lexi is currently in Russia taking over her grandfather's legal and illegal businesses, while Katya is a dark web hacker.

Where our lives used to be all about running our security

business and keeping civilians safe, it's now also about keeping our wider MC family safe and rubbing shoulders with criminals. Jesus, I'm even married to the interim head of the Russian Mafia.

Life is fucking mental sometimes, but I'm not complaining. The crazy connections we've made since Dayz dropped us into this world led to me marrying the woman of my dreams. Hell, she's even better than my dreams. Just picturing her spread out on my bed, thick thighs wide open, her tight little hole waiting for me to sink into her wet heat. Shit, I'm getting worked up, and it's not a good look with my brothers sitting across from me.

"Right, you gotta go. I need to get home and get dinner on for my wife. I'm surprising her tonight,"

"Shit, I thought you liked the woman! You can't feed her stuff you've cooked. You'll be a widower before the night is over" Tav laughs as he stands, then tips my pen holder over. Jules stands next to him and messes up my papers, while I hit out on their hands with my paperweight. It's like playing Whack-A-Mole, but the moles are big bastards with shitty attitudes. Dayz stands behind them watching while she sucks on her straw, making that god awful sound.

"That's it! Fuck off the lot of you!" In a move that seems choreographed, all three throw their heads back and cackle before all trying to walk through the doorway together, getting stuck before Dayz breaks through first, and then Jules and Tav wrestle into the hallway.

Kids, the lot of 'em.

## Ana

I mull over the information that Ivan gave me as I swing from side to side in my office chair. Spinning one way has me looking out the large windows into Roman's meticulously manicured garden, the other way has me looking directly at a God awful tapestry of two dudes wrestling a bull. Sometimes rich folk have no taste.

I'm going to have to make yet another call to Roman about Ivan's findings. Hammer has been a busy little MC Pres with his shitty new nomads. Not only has he been recruiting MC members, but he's also bought out some of our lower-level junior employees. Young men that we gave menial Bratva jobs to until they could prove themselves to the outfit. It turns out they would rather be paid off by another big bad.

I do some yoga breathing that I learned off of a YouTube video because, let's face it, I'm not much of a yoga girl, but that breathing stuff is the shit. I find my center and think about our next steps. On the one hand, I'm glad that none of them are family. It'll make it easier for Ivan to deal with them. On the other hand, they're just young men who were looking for something. A living, a family perhaps, and unfortunately they got greedy, and they chose wrong. We'll have to act swiftly to shut this down. The last thing we want is to have some two bit criminals taking over our turf, or worse still, impersonating Bartashev Bratva.

I let out a big sigh, stretching my arms over my head and feel the aches and pains. Some of them from being sat at my desk going over plans with Ivan. However, most are from my activities with Gus.

Last night was...everything. I have never experienced that level of soul deep connection with another human.

*Gus.*

My thighs clench instinctively at the thought of him kissing me, touching me, fucking me. There were times where I didn't know where Gus ended and I began. Heat pools between my thighs and I'm surprised that my vajeen is ready to go again. I would have thought she would need a break after the four times we did it throughout the night, but she's proving me wrong. Shit, so did Gus. The man has remarkable recovery. I really need to get this shit done and dusted so I can head home to my hunk of a man.

"That is the look of a well-fucked woman," my head snaps toward the voice to see Roman leaning against the doorjamb with a smirk on his face.

"Roman! Argh you're back!" I jump up out of my desk chair, squealing as I rush toward my friend and throw my arms around him. We embrace and rock side to side for a moment before Sasha's deep voice cuts in.

"Ok, Ok, my turn" I release Roman and then I'm engulfed by Sasha's massive body.

"Oh. My. God, why didn't you tell me you were coming back?! You sneaky zasranets!" I slap both of them with a mock frown on my face.

"Well, my wee married Kiwi, Kovalev has been quiet and behaving himself, with a little firm guidance of course," Roman gives me his signature Bad Guy smirk. Kovalev was running the skin trade here. Thankfully Roman stepped in, strong armed him back to Russia and somehow got him back on the straight and narrow. Well, the straight and narrow for a criminal.

"What about Lexi-Lou?"

Roman's smirk breaks out into a grin as he shakes his head. No one calls her that but me.

"Lexi is now in charge of her grandfather's businesses and I was at a loose end and missing home." I wrap my arm around him in a side hug and take a deep breath.

"Well, you came home at the perfect time. We have shit going down."

Sasha rolls his eyes, muttering "there's always shit going down". Roman and I grin at each other.

"And you two love it all too much. I never thought when I brought the little Kiwi stray home -" "Hey!" He dodges me as I try to slap him on the shoulder, "-that you would turn her into a total criminal mastermind, babe," Sasha says in mock sadness.

"I'm the secretary, dammit!"

Sasha just gives me a bored look with his eyebrow raised. He's good at that. Probably because he does it to Roman on an almost hourly basis.

"Right, Pinky and the Brain, I'm jet lagged to fuckery. I'm going to have a nap in that posturepedic bed in our luxurious room in our fantastic home that I missed." He drops a kiss on the top of my head, and one on Roman's cheek before wandering off.

"Homesick much?"

Roman rolls his eyes at me. "He would not stop bitching the whole time we were away. I think I've spoiled him too much. He can't handle the simplicity of Russia anymore."

I snort and then cover it with a cough. "Yeah, the simplicity of that luxury penthouse, or was it the country mansion that did him in?"

He gives me a droll look and I smirk as I move my junk back

to my desk and dust off any chocolate crumbs I may have left on Roman's before letting him sit where he belongs. Thank god. As much as I love my friend and my job, I am over being the boss.

"So chica, tell me what's going on."

I raise an eyebrow at him. "Chica?"

"I'm trying something new, and it seems it is not working."

I let out a snort. "Not at all."

He lets out a sigh before sobering up again. "Ok, tell me everything"

"How much time do you have?"

"Well, with Sasha down for a little nap, I have all the time in the world for my favorite secretary. So spill, and I mean everything. Starting with August Tombs." He waggles his brows at me, and I can't help but laugh. It's so good to have my friend back.

"Well, you know we got married and since then, it's been a bit of a whirlwind. For one, there's the court mandated counseling we've been going to -"

"Bor-ing! Get to the good stuff! What's he like in bed?" Roman leans over his desk, resting his head in his hands, looking at me with a goofy grin. I look around furtively for I don't know what. I mean, I'm in my office with my bestie.

"Its fucking amazing. He's fucking amazing." I cover my face in my hands and squeal a little, my feet making pitter patter sounds as they run on the spot under my desk.

"I knew it," I hear Roman sigh out.

"Hey! Keep your hands and eyes and everything else to yourself! That's my husband!" I point a finger at him. Not that he would do anything to hurt me, I know that. But he is a known flirt when he wants to be.

"Yeah, yeah, I'll keep my mitts to myself. But, if he ever expresses an interest...." I throw a chocolate bar at his face while he laughs hysterically back at me. I missed this girl talk with my bestie.

"I'm glad to see you happy, Ana. You deserve the world, and that man can give it to you," I smile at Roman, his black hair styled perfectly even after the long flight.

"Thanks, I'm starting to believe it too."

A smacking sound rings out as he claps his hands once, giving me a serious look.

"Ok, enough mushy stuff. Let's figure out what the fuck is going on with our shipments."

# Chapter 13



I'm staring at three pots that all look fit to overflow any minute now. I curse the food network for leading me to believe I can cook a whole damn meal without supervision. I know I'm a grown ass man, but my cooking is hit and miss. Which isn't a problem when you live alone, you just eat the shit you made and move on with your life.

But I want to surprise Ana. I want to woo her with my amazing cooking skills and show her I want to look after her. I think aside from her mom, who lives half a world away, she's had to look after herself, and I want that to be my job. I want to have dinner on the table for her when she comes home from the office after a long day. I want her to relax as I take care of her. I want to be able to cook for her when she's busy feeding our babies, when we have them. I want it all with her.

"Holy shit, why's it so steamy in here? And why the fuck does it smell so bad?" Swinging around I see Pops standing in the doorway, the V of his knit sweater pulled up over the bottom half of his face. I look at the spatula in my hand and contemplate hitting him with it, but then I remember he's elderly and slightly nuts so he wouldn't think twice about fighting dirty.

"I'm trying to cook a nice meal for Ana. She's working late tonight, so I thought I'd take care of dinner." Pops eyes up everything on the stove and the mess on the countertops before gazing back at me with a bushy eyebrow raised.

"Riiiiight. Have you ever thought that this isn't your strong suit and maybe you should have outsourced?"

Rolling my eyes at him, I turn to the stove to turn down the heat on some of the overflowing pans.

"No. I want her to eat something I made."

"Do you want her to have the shits too? Cos I feel like this is where it's headed, son."

"Look, if you have nothing nice to stay, go home. I've already had to deal with your other grandchildren pissing me off at work."

"You're a grumpy fucker, you know that? Anyway, I'm not here for a pleasant visit, because you'd be the last person I'd see for that. I'm actually here because your mother-in-law has arrived and I'm guessing Ana forgot all about her."

With that he turns and with a flourish escorts a small, brown woman with a deceptively youthful face, and shoulder length curly black hair into the kitchen. I can feel my eyes are fucking huge in my face as I stand here, in an apron with naked tits and hairy pussy on the front that Tav gave me for Christmas; pots bubbling like crazy behind me and a spatula in my hand.

"Oh, shit! Fuck! Sorry, shit, I mean, hello! It's so nice to meet you! I'm so sorry one of us didn't come to collect you, if I had have known-"

"Bah, *Kei te Pai*, it's no worries. I mean, I wasn't supposed to be here until next week, but then an earlier flight came up and I thought 'Bugger it!' I'd surprise you. Tadaaa!" With this, her face breaks out into a huge grin as she chuckles and waves jazz hands at me.

My eyes slide to Pops and then do a double take as I see he's gazing down at her with a twinkle in his eye. No, no way is that happening. Pops has to be at least 15 years older than this woman. Not to mention he's Pops, and I can't guarantee that he's going to be on his best behavior. I was meant to sit the whole family down at Wednesday family dinner and warn them to not be their usual selves. Looks like it's too late for that now.

"Oh, well, call me surprised! Shi- I mean, shoot, I'm Gus" I throw the spatula somewhere and step forward with my hand outstretched, but Ana's mom has a different idea. She draws me in for a hug, her deceptively strong arms wrapping around me and holding me tight, like only a mother can.

It's been a long time since I had a hug like this. She pulls back and grips my biceps while she looks me over. I stand a little straighter to impress her and hope like hell she didn't hear mine and Pops' conversation.

"I'm Deborah, but you can call me Debs. Or Deborah. Doesn't worry me either way." Her eyes take in the mess of my kitchen before looking up at me, a twinkle in them. "So, Gus, what are you cooking us for dinner?"

I let out a huff, my shoulders sagging as I detail my failures so far. I can tell she wants to laugh, her lips pursed, the soft curve of her cheeks making her eyes look squinty.

"It was meant to be cannelloni, but, well," I wave my arm at the mess, ignoring Pops' exclamation of "what the fuck?" when I said "cannelloni".

"What time is my baby home?" Debs asks, her eyes wide as

she looks around.

"She won't be home until 6ish, so I have two hours to perfect this."

She glances around again before giving me a look that says "not a chance, buddy."

"Look, that is just enough time for me to teach you how to make fish and chips. New Zealand delicacy. I'll write a list of things you'll need. You pop out and get them while I clean this up and Pops keeps me company." She looks at Pops, who has a broad smile on his face. She turns to look back at the mess I've made and Pops catches my eye when he tips his head toward Debs and then waggles his eyebrows. Oh, fuck no.

"Pops, maybe you can help me with Deb's luggage?" With that, I grab him by the bicep and drag him through my front door.

"Back soon, sweetheart," he yells on his way out, the tinkle of Debs' laughter following us out the door.

"Listen here you, I will not, I repeat, will not allow you to woo Ana's mom. Got me? She's only here for a visit, and the last thing I need is you all over her." He gives me his fake innocent face.

"Who, me? I can't help it if she finds me irresistible," he smirks up at me and then tries to look over my shoulder to get another glimpse of her.

"Jesus, Pops, you're old as hell. Sexual relations at your age could cause a heart attack!"

"Ah well, son, if she dies, she dies. I can't help it if she has a weak heart and I have the famous Tombs prowess."

He pats me on the arm harder than he needs to and swans back into my house, leaving me speechless on the front porch. I run my fingers through my hair a couple of times to calm down. I swear to God this family will be the end of me. Not the MC, not the Bratva, not some random dude watching me. It'll be this family that takes me out through stress.

I take a couple of deep breaths, then look down at Debs' luggage, pick it up and deliver it to the spare bedroom. I step back into the kitchen and marvel at how, in the two minutes since I left her in there, it is now under control and tidy. That's mom power right there.

"OK, Debs, do you have the grocery list for me?"

"Sure do Gus, here it is. Be a good boy and pick that stuff up while I wash and chip the potatoes. Then when you get back, I'll show you how to put it all together, yeah?"

I nod my head and thank fuck I've gotten so used to Ana speaking that I actually understand what her mother is saying. Her accent is thicker than Ana's and if I'm honest, I think I've only understood half of what's going on because she talks so fast. What I do know is that I'm off to the grocery store and I will be buying and learning how to cook fish. I better get extra in case I fuck it up.

## Ana

Bursting through the front door of our house with mine and Roman's meeting running through my head, I kick my shoes off in the small entryway and look around the open-plan kitchen living area. There's something delicious emanating from that direction and my stomach lets out a growl.

"Gus? Are you home?"

A muffled noise coming from the bedroom has me freezing next to Gus's manly leather couch. I'm certain I heard a female voice. This is the exact situation women find themselves in when their marriages have gone wrong.

I feel physically ill. My stomach has dropped straight out of my arse, and my fists are clenching at my sides. I knew at some stage this was going to be too good to be true. Taking a deep breath, I realize there are two ways to go about this. I can just walk straight out that door never to look back and thank God or whoever else is in charge that I walked out before this got too serious; before I lost my heart.

Or, I can be the bad bitch I know I am, walk straight into that room with my head held high and ask the man that only this morning wrung orgasm after orgasm out of my body, what the fuck is going on. I decide to be the bad bitch, so I storm toward the spare room, about ready to kick the door in when my body freezes, coming to an abrupt halt.

"Mum?"

Mum and Gus are sitting on the bed in the spare room, Mum showing Gus something on her tablet. Her head snaps up at my voice before she chucks the tablet at Gus, hitting him in that fine package of his, and then she throws herself at me, her arms wrapping around me in one of her strong hugs.

"My baby girl!" She rocks me side to side, pulling back to squish my face between her hands, covering me in her kisses.

Laughing, I try to pull my face out of her hands so I can lean back and look at her. At 67 years old, she's looking a little older than the last time I saw her, but she's still the most youthful 67-year-old I've ever seen. Her hair, still predominantly black in soft ringlets around her face, her wide smile and twinkling eyes, has mine misting over.

"It's so good to see you, Mama." I hug her once more, reveling in her familiar smell and her softness, before I push her back quickly and with more force than I intended. "Hang on, what the hell are you doing here? You weren't supposed to be here until next week! Did I get my dates wrong?"

She laughs and shakes her head. "Nah, I just heard there was an earlier flight, so I figured I'd hop on that and surprise the hell outta ya. You should have seen Gus's face!" She cackles and I join her, knowing full well Gus would have had a coronary and shit his pants at the same time.

"Well, I will leave you ladies to catch up and I'll get the fish on" He kisses me on the nose, then looks at Mum and winks. We both watch as he walks out the door before I spin back around.

"What was that? What are you two scheming?" I ask the woman I trust with my life, jabbing my finger into her shoulder.

"Never you mind" Mum boops my nose and then pulls me down on the bed.

"I can't believe you're here! Like how? Why?" I squeeze Mum's hand in mine.

"Well, like I said. An earlier flight came up, and I thought 'bugger it!'. I've spent my life in New Zealand so it was time for an adventure, and whoowee! What an adventure! On the way here, I made the Uber man take me to Walmart for a look. That place is massive! And everyone has guns! Just like hanging off their pants!" Her eyes go wide and I throw my head back to laugh. I have to admit, that was one thing that surprised me, too.

"It's like the TV, huh?" I say as I smile at the look on her face. She bobs her head up and down a few times before she pulls her hand from mine and waves both of them about.

"Anyway, enough about me. I wanna know EVERYTHING.

Start talking babe and leave nothing out when it comes to that tall glass of water. Holy shitballs! Did you see how hot he is? And clearly it runs in the family because Pops, phew!" Mum fans herself and I stare at her, speechless. "Oh, don't tell me you haven't noticed." She points her stubby little finger at me.

"No, I haven't noticed, because he's a pensioner! Mum, he's like, 80 years old!"

"And aging like a fine wine, if you ask me."

"Oh. My. God." I whisper out, closing my eyes so I don't get any mental images. "But, but, what about Dad?"

She gives me a sad smile and pats me gently on the leg. "Your dad was the love of my life, but he wouldn't want me to wallow. He'd want me to live. And I've been alone long enough to know that I would like a little company." She gifts me with another sad smile and I feel terrible bringing Dad up. She's a vibrant woman who deserves all the happiness in the world.

"I'm sorry Mum. It just feels like yesterday that we lost him."

"I know, baby, but it's been almost 20 years. And it's not like I haven't been on a date here and there. It's just, I'm on this adventure, so you know, who knows what type of trouble I could get into on this wee holiday of mine?" She smiles at me, a wee twinkle in her eye. I should be more worried. I mean, she just mentioned trouble and we all know Pops is that with a glaring, neon lit capital T.

"You're not worried that maybe Pops is too old for you?" Yes, good work Ana, try to put her off with the whole age thing. I mean, I want my mum to be happy and have a good time, but I don't want to give Gus a heart attack. Or myself, for that matter. Pops is certified crazy, I'm sure of it. Unfortunately, mum seems to have taken a shine to the man and Debs Taylor is not a woman to change her mind once it's been made up.

"Too old for what? To chat with and enjoy each other's company? 13 years isn't that big a gap Ana. Sheesh, you need to be a little more open-minded." She rolls her eyes at me before placing her soft hand around mine and jiggling it.

"OK, now back to you. How is married life with Gorgeous Gus going?" With a grin, she throws herself back on the bed until she's sprawled on the pillows, waiting with raised eyebrows. I let out a massive sigh before throwing myself down next to her.

"How long have you been holding on to that little nickname?"

She snorts "Since I met the man. I mean, you're a stunning woman, Ana, but you've always only ever gone out with losers. Pasty looking men with no practical or common sense, so I wasn't really holding out much hope for this one."

"Hey! I didn't go out with losers!"

"Ah, yeah you did. You know you did. And you also know why you did it." She raises her brow at me.

"I went out with them because I liked them. They were nice guys."

Rolling her eyes, she points my direction "You went out with them so that when they inevitably left to 'find themselves' or road trip with their band, or go back to their wives-" I cringe a little at that one, "- you wouldn't be heartbroken. Gus though, he's a dangerous one. He's everything you would want in a husband." She grins at me.

"Hmmmph," I grunt out, feeling a little like a teenager again.

"Oh, don't be a baby. You know it's true." She nudges me with her elbow before continuing. "I've only spent a couple of hours with him, but I like him. He's solid. Safe. And he loves you -"

"Ah bah bah bah" I slap my hand over her mouth to stop her going down that line of thought, her eyes smiling mirthfully over the top of my hand. "Nope. We are not going there. It's only been about a month, month and a half max. There is no love there. We are just two people who are friends and who like each other –"

"– and sleep together –" Mum's muffled voice adds from underneath my hand that is still across her mouth.

"– NO! Well, yes, but we're not talking about that. Ever. Got me?" I stare into her large brown eyes that twinkle with laughter as she nods her head up and down. I take my hand off her mouth, but not before she gives me a quick lick, my hand shooting back as if she's burned me.

"Ewwww! You're a child, you know that?"

"You love me," she smiles sweetly before patting my cheek. "Come on. Let's go see how much trouble Gus has gotten into and we can continue catching up."

A huge smile splits my face, and I grab Mum's hand to pull her to standing. We hold hands, swinging them as we walk down the hall, both coming to a stop to quietly watch Gus in the kitchen. He's in low-slung jeans and a plain gray tee. His hair is an absolute mess from where he must have been running his fingers through it. I watch as his flour covered hand comes up and runs through the strands before he quickly pulls it back, looks at it like it has all the answers in the world. He curses under his breath, then heads to the sink to wash his hands again. I love seeing him like this, all flustered. For as long as I've known him, which admittedly isn't that long, his moods seem to be fairly standard. Serious, grumpy, impatient, in total control or frustrated. This side of Gus, this unsure, flustered man, tugs at my heartstrings because I know this is all because he wants to impress my mum. Who, let's face it, is already impressed that he's nothing like my previous boyfriends. He's at the sink muttering away to himself before his eyes come up and catch sight of me and Mum.

"Ladies! Um, hi, dinner is looking good, everything is under control so if you want to go back to relaxing and, uh, chatting, I can call you in when this is all done," he looks flustered as hell but he tries to casually gesture behind him as if he does, in fact, have everything under control. I side eye Mum while she side eyes me back, then gives me a grin.

"Gus, you've been slaving in here since before I arrived. Why don't you and Ana pull up a seat at the counter and keep me company while I'll take over for a little bit, hmm? Just relax, you've both had big days at work." She heads over to Gus and then bumps him out of the way with her large hips.

"Wait, you aren't tired or jet lagged?" She's the only mum I've got. I don't want her running herself ragged. Instead, she waves a dismissive hand at me and then points to the bar stool across from where she's standing for me to sit.

"Nah. I actually arrived yesterday. Booked into that fancy hotel in town to sleep it off and then I spent today watching people at Walmart."

"Wow, when she goes on holiday, the girl goes wild," I say, rolling my eyes at her. Mum quickly grabs the tea towel off the counter, spins it with shocking speed, and flicks me with it. She nods her head in satisfaction when I yelp, an evil smile on her round face.

"Babe, your mom is awesome," Gus whispers in my ear before dropping a kiss on my neck, causing a shiver to go through me.

"Yes, yes she is."

# Chapter 14

Gus

"Be nice." Ana's breath tickles my ear. Turning to look into her wide green eyes, she makes them even larger before she darts them to the intruders at our table. I should have known that these fuckers were going to descend. Like sharks sense blood, they would have sensed the motherly vibes and delicious smells emanating from my home and instead of leaving us alone, like normal people, they gatecrashed and hung around until Debs in her infinite kindness invited them to eat with us. Bastards.

Shit, even Rhodie is here, and he doesn't even live here. Although I guess I can cut him some slack because, unlike the others, he wouldn't have sensed food. He would have sensed Dayz. I glare at all of them around the table. A small hand lands on my thigh, rubbing in gentle circles, and I feel myself relax.

"It's ok babe. Mum loves this. When I was a kid, we always had loads of people at home. Mum's a feeder. That's her love language."

Looking around the table, I feel like Debs Taylor herself is the love language. Tav and Jules are hanging off her every word and have been since they set the table and she called them both "good boys". It's been years since we've been called that, so I can appreciate the endorphin boost her words gave them. She called me her "good boy" earlier and I swear it was like my mom was right there. Even Dayz is taken with Debs. I know this because she's spent the best part of dinner info dumping all the things she knows about Rose Grove and Texas. If Dayz likes you, she'll info dump, and Debs, bless her, has not only listened to Dayz, but she's asked questions, genuinely interested in what my unusual little sister has to say, and that has Dayz lit up.

But, as cozy as this all is, it's my wayward grandfather I have to keep an eye on. I've caught that horny old bastard making moony eyes at Debs twice now, and instead of being embarrassed he instead looked me dead in the eye, raised his bushy brow and rubbed the side of his nose with his middle finger.

"Babe, maybe you could stop giving Pops the stink eye?" Ana murmurs as she leans into me.

"No. He's playing a dangerous game, babe. All these fuckers are. They need to leave and find their own mothers-in-law and leave mine the hell alone," I growl out. Ana's head snaps around to look at me, her eyebrows pinched in, and I have a feeling she's about to let me have it, but her face softens and she smiles before patting me on the cheek.

"August Tombs, are you jealous? Do you want my mum for yourself for a little bit?"

I can feel the annoyed look on my face, and I could lie, but she's my wife, and I promised in our very basic vows that I would always tell her the truth. Which thinking about it now seems ironic given that they were vows for a fake marriage, but whatever.

"Yes. I want Debs to myself. And you, of course," I shoot my eyes to her so she knows I don't just want her for her mom. She smirks up at me before popping a 'chip' into her mouth.

"Mmmhmmm,"

"So, Debs, what are your plans while you're here?" Tav asks, leaning back in his seat, patting his stomach a couple of times. Of the three of us, Tav is the leanest. Not that that's saying much as we are all over 6 feet tall and broad.

"Well, Tav, I have a list of things I want to do and experience while I'm here." I watch as my family all leans a little closer to hear what she's going to say. Much like I am hypnotized by her daughter, it would seem my crackpot family is hypnotized by her.

"Well baby," All sets of eyes shoot to Pops, who just fucking called Ana's mom "baby". "Let's hear what ya got, and I'll see what I can do about making all your dreams come true," he gives her a wink and I watch as all three pairs of my siblings' eyes look at me with varying degrees of shock and disgust. Darting my eyes to Debs, I see she has a blush covering her cheeks. Jesus Christ.

"Well, Mum, tell us what's on it, and we'll ALL see what we can do to help you tick things off the list," Ana says, getting this show back on the road while I run my hands through my hair for the one millionth time since this dinner began.

"Ok! It's in my suitcase, lemme just run and get it," Debs jumps up from the table and hustles down the hall into her room.

I tap gently on the table, getting all eyes on me before I whisper yell, "Listen up fuckers, that woman is my mother-in-law. Get your own. Pops, you better not even think about doing anything with that woman. You keep your mitts off,"

"Yeah Pops! I mean, shit, that woman is a goddamn angel and I will not have you sullying her goodness!" I stare at Tav after his outrageous comment before agreeing with him.

"Yeah, actually, what Tav said. I swear to god old man I will put you in a home if you screw this up," Pops sits back in his chair, arms crossed over his chest, a smirk and an evil look in his eye.

"Oh, don't you worry. There's only one type of screwing I'm planning,"

Jule's chair scrapes against my tiles as he stands abruptly, but Tav grabs him and wrestles him back down into his chair, Jules glaring at Pops and doing the international sign for "I'm watching you".

"What the hell is happening? Why are you all acting so damn crazy? It's just my mum, guys. She's a normal lady," Ana says, looking around the table as if we have all lost our minds. Funny, because I'm not sure if we all really had them, anyway.

"That woman isn't just 'a mum'," Dayz says, copying Ana's accent perfectly. "She's awesome. And the only mom we've had around in years. So, I think it's safe to say that we want to keep her. I say we sit her down for a talk about her future and present her with a written invitation to stay. Then I vote that we formally make a start on the immigration paperwork,"

Everyone at the table nods while Ana opens her mouth before closing it again, a look of pure confusion on her face. Before she can call the Tombs family out or call the local mental health emergency hotline, Debs comes rushing back in, waving her list, plopping herself back down into her chair.

"Soz guys, it was at the bottom of my suitcase." She rolls her eyes good-naturedly before putting her little reading glasses on.

"Ok. So first off, ride a motorcycle,"

"Done. I have mine right outside and I would be happy to take you for a spin, ma'am," I turn to stare at Rhodie knowing full well that A) only an Ol lady rides behind her man and B) he has never used those well-bred manners around us before.

"What? I have manners, I'm not a caveman," He shrugs, and then snatches his hand off the top of the table when Pops raps his knuckles with his bread knife.

"She aint on the back of your bike, shit stain. She only rides on mine." He nods decisively at Debs, who beams back at him. Fucking hell. That's all I need. My elderly grandfather on his vintage Harley with Ana's mom on the back. There's a burning feeling in my chest and I'm not sure if it's panic or heartburn. I might need an antacid.

"Done! Ok, I also have - visit In-n-Out Burger, eat one of those massive steaks in a restaurant that'll take my picture and put it on the wall, go to a rodeo and see if they'll let me rope something, buy a cowboy hat and boots and shoot a gun,"

"Done." Jules slaps his hand on the table as everyone nods their heads and smiles like looney people, while Debs lets out a small shriek and jiggles in her seat.

Ana's head comes to a rest on my shoulder and I look down at her, raising my brow when she smiles up at me.

"I mean, they're all nuts. She'll fit right in with them."

Yeah babe, that's what I'm worried about.

## Ana

"*Na Khui!*" My head snaps up as Roman throws his cell phone at the wall, and thankfully, it bounces off rather than smashing into a million pieces. I can tell by the look on his face whatever it is isn't good, hence the Russian "fucking hell" he just yelled out.

Staring at my friend and boss, I watch as he squints at the wall and wait for him to enlighten me. There's no point in asking just yet. I know his mind is going a million miles an hour. When he's like this, he reminds me of Gus and Marx a little, and it's no wonder that when the shit hit the fan with Kraykowski, all three men worked together to find and neutralize the threats we were all facing. It looks like we may all be working together again sooner than we all thought.

"Another fucking shipment tampered with. Get Ivan here now. We obviously still have rats in the house. I need them brought to me so I can make an example of them." I nod and flick Ivan a quick message.

"Surely Hammer can't have bought that much loyalty within our ranks? I mean, the last lot were errand boys. But shipments? That's above their pay grade." I ponder out loud as I twist back and forth in my spinny chair. It doesn't make any sense, unless our lower-level men are a hell of a lot sneakier than we give them credit for.

Roman runs a hand down his face before huffing, "I have to think that we have a fucking sneaky rat, because thinking otherwise would mean one of my trusted men has betrayed me, and I can't go down that track just yet."

I nod, knowing that it's not an option. Not just for the safety of the Family, but also because I can't even fathom that some of the best men I know, men like Ivan, may not be who I think they are. My phone buzzes and I check the notification from Ivan.

"Ivan will be here in 20. He's at the warehouse now checking on the rest of the containers that got dropped off," Roman nods at me, picks his phone up off the ground from where it landed, checks it over before sitting back in his chair and looking at me thoughtfully.

"Why are you even here? I mean, your mom has been in town for what, a week now and you've hardly taken any time off. Go home, I'll deal with shit here and I'll let you know if I find anything out. Take the rest of the week." I give him an exasperated look before pointing out that, actually, he needs me.

"Um, I'm here because it's my job to be here? Who the hell else is going to keep you calm and do all the shit you don't want to do?"

He rolls his eyes. "Yeah, yeah, what would I do without you? I'll just tell Sasha to get his sexy, lazy ass up and help me. I'll be fine. Go." He waves his hands in a shooing motion. "Besides, I heard that today is the day that Mama Debs gets her shooting lesson." He grins at me, and I let out a groan as I bang my head on my desk a couple of times.

"Ugh, don't remind me! Gus has been having a conniption about the whole thing since it was suggested at dinner that first night Mum was here. He's been trying to put the crew off, but Mum is as bad as the rest of the Tombs family."

Roman lets out a snort. "Well, they are welcome to come here. I have a range out back."

"Thanks Ro, but it's already organized with the MC. Marx is

having a BBQ to welcome Mum and farewell Flack, who's well enough to be transported home. Gus also said their shooting range was top of the line, so less likely for any of his family to 'fuck it up'." I let out a snort when I remember Gus's words. I mean, he's going overboard on safety, but I know it's making sure Mum is safe. Which makes my heart melt that the big, hard man is trying to take care of my mother in this way.

"It may be top of the line, but I bet it's not as pretty as mine," Roman sniffs out, and I can't help but roll my eyes and chuckle at him.

"Of course not, theirs is all utilitarian. So ugly,"

He flips me the bird before asking, "Why the fuck are you still here?"

"Fine, fine, I'm going. You can sit here all alone working and I'll be out there having a wonderful time watching my very sexy husband try to keep everyone safe while Mum and Pops shoot guns." I let out a happy sigh, as it's something to look forward to before I grab my purse, throw it over my shoulder, and walk behind Roman's desk to drop a kiss on his cheek.

"Thanks Ro, have I told you lately how much I love you?"

"Yes, but I'm sure I can handle hearing it one more time."

"I love you, bestie. Take care of business and if you need me, let me know. We have another warehouse shipment coming in two days. Call me if you want me to stop by and check it over."

"Yes, yes, now shoo! Oh, I love you too. Fuck off!" I throw my head back and laugh on my way out of our office, and through Roman and Sasha's country home.

Heading out, I get into my car, which thankfully had the key battery replaced, as well as a full clean and service to get all the kimchi out. No matter how delicious that stuff is, no girl wants to turn up places smelling like spicy cabbage. Settling behind the wheel, I chuck my bag on the seat next to me and get comfortable. Roman's place is around half an hour outside of Rose Grove, closer to the next town over and in the opposite direction of the MC clubhouse. That means it's live car concert time. I crank up Dua Lipa and marvel at how when the music is this loud, me and her almost sound exactly the same. I really need to drive Gus somewhere so he can get first row seats to the Ana Lipa show. I'm snorting at how damn funny I am when I notice a black SUV following behind me. There's a single male driver and I make a note to take a few turns here and there once I hit Rose Grove town. Thus far, they've stayed fairly far behind, so they could just be a traveler like me, heading into town.

I hit the outskirts of Rose Grove and decide to test my theory. Instead of driving in a direct route to the clubhouse, I take a couple of tight turns around some of Rose Grove's sleepy streets before gunning it on the road that heads through the main shopping center. Cutting through a carpark I scream into an alley where I wait and watch the car drive past. Interesting. With all this Hammer vs Death Riders crap and the Bratva losing shipments, it's safe to say that perhaps Gus and I aren't as paranoid as we think.

I wait a few moments and contemplate calling Gus, but figure I'll be there soon enough, so I'll just let him know a bit later on. If I tell him now, he'll be all over my arse for not calling him immediately. I gaze out the windscreen and note the same car drives past once more, obviously backtracking to find me. I take this as a good sign to get outta dodge so I make my way to the main road, then onto DRMC.

Pulling up to the gates, the prospect waves me in. I have no idea his name but he's familiar and friendly so I wave my thanks as I roll in and park up next to two Tombs Security SUVs and Pops haphazardly parked pickup.

The car park is full of motorcycles, the usual DRMC ones, and another 4 parked closely together, so I gather they must belong to the Death Riders. I'm glad that Flack is feeling well enough to go home. It was touch and go for a while there when his wound site got infected, but Switch got that all under control. I've not spent a lot of time with Flack, just a wee visit when I popped in to see Dayz and Remy, but he's a nice enough man. Although I'm guessing he kinda has to be given that his daughter is the sweetest, softest person I've ever met, and he raised her. I twist in my seat and reach for the hiking boots I threw into the backseat this morning. I'm currently in my favorite outfit - forest green silk blouse, black leggings and heels, but knowing the shooting range is out the back of the clubhouse, I don't want to be traipsing out there in my good Jimmy Choos or anything.

I slip them off and toss them in the back seat, putting on socks and pulling on my boots. I gather the gun that Gus said I have to carry at all times, rolling my eyes as I slip it into my bag, throw my door open and immediately hear a commotion. Listening a beat longer, I recognise that racket as the sweet, sweet sound of the Tombs family.

Walking through the door, I come to a stop in the common room. Pops and Gus are having a heated conversion whilst Marx is standing between them, massive arms crossed over his barrel chest. I also swear I can see a hint of a smile under his full beard. Dayz is sitting on Rhodie's lap watching the show, Jules is in the corner with Fox and Nitro, each with a club girl on their knee and Mum is flitting around the room handing out cookies.

"What's going on?" I ask Tav, who is munching on a cookie.

"Gus thinks the gun Pops got your mom is too powerful. He's worried the kick back will hurt her." He shrugs and finishes his cookie in two bites before waving to Mum and giving her the puppy dog eyes. I watch as she rolls her eyes and then smiles indulgently at him. It seems these men, the Tombs family, hell, even the MC family, are mine and Mum's happy place. I haven't seen her this happy in years, and I don't think I've felt this feeling of belonging in a long time either. Everything is just... easy.

Well, when everyone agrees and isn't yelling, of course.

"Mum, what do you think?" At the sound of my voice, Gus's head whips toward me, the scowl on his face disappearing as a smile splits his face. He stomps over to me and leans down to give me a kiss. He pulls away, before thinking better of it and dropping two more soft, sweet kisses to my lips.

"I missed you, baby." He whispers.

I pat his chest and snuggle into him as he pulls me into his side, turning to look back into the room.

"Well, hello to you daughter of mine. As for your question, I'm sure I can handle it. Thank you Gus, for your concern. But they don't breed us wussy in New Zealand. And now that we're all here, let's go shoot some shit!" Mum lets out a whoop as the MC men from both clubs all laugh and stomp their big boots, winding her up even more. She has her hands in the air, raising the roof so to speak, and I watch Marx roll his eyes and shake his head before whistling to get everyone's attention.

"Right you fuc-" his eyes dart towards Mum who grins up at him "- I mean, everyone, let's get this shit set up and help Debs tick another thing off her list," More yelling ensues and we head out the back to the shooting range.

Mum gets all suited up in her safety gear, Gus, Tav and Jules all helping her out while Dayz gives mum a couple of tips. Pops is there with her, making sure the gun is safe and ready to go. In no time, Gus and his siblings step out and away from the shooting gallery, heading to wait with the rest of us who are watching.

Gus comes up behind me, pulling my back to his front and dropping a kiss to that sensitive spot where my neck meets my shoulder. I tip my head slightly so he has better access. Closing my eyes, I just revel in the feeling of being in Gus's arms. I haven't told him I love him yet. There's no way I'm saying it first, not until I know how he feels. If I say it, I might jinx this whole thing. Or I'll say it and he'll be taken from me. I'm not having that. Not yet. It's too perfect at the moment. I want to hold on to it with both hands a little longer before shit hits the fan.

Pops helps Mum line things up, gives her a wee pat on the arse that I'm choosing to ignore, before giving her a countdown. She squeezes the trigger three times fast and we watch as she hits the man shaped paper target in the heart three times.

"Holy shit, your mom just got three kill shots," Gus whispers as the crowd goes wild. The whole Tombs family are out here watching, as are Marx, Rider, Rhodie, Savage, Dex and a few other brothers I recognize but don't know by name yet; so almost a dozen people are celebrating for mum. She's pumping her arms up and down with a huge grin on her face.

She checks the gun before lining up again, this time shooting three headshots.

"Holy fuck, how is she doing that?" Tav asks, eyes wide. I clear my throat and speak loud enough to be heard over the clapping,

"She bow hunts at home." All of a sudden ... crickets. A dozen eyes all turn to look at me, then back to mum then back at me.

"Um, what?" Rider asks, blinking a few times as if he can't comprehend what I've just said.

"At home, she's an award-winning bow hunter. She hunts all sorts of things, but mainly deer. Dad fished, Mum liked bow hunting. She's never used a gun before, though. Her dad never let her and then neither did my dad. Said she couldn't be trusted with it. Besides, she's lethal enough with a bow." I shrug and walk over to Mum and hug her.

"Did you see that baby!? Ha! Screw your grandfather and your father. I told them I would be awesome with a gun!" I laugh at her before giving her a big kiss and wrapping her up in my arms again, dancing side to side with her as she's still fizzing over with excitement.

"Yup, you showed them Mama!" I pull back from Mum and then I turn to look around for Pops, who's on one knee in front of her, his hands on his heart.

"My god babe, would you marry me?" Mum throws her head back and cackles before pulling him to standing.

"Get up, you silly old fool. You're too old to be on the ground," she pulls him up, laces her fingers with his and kisses him on the cheek. I swear I see the old man swoon.

We turn and head toward the clubhouse, the show over for the meantime when something kicks the dirt up at my feet, dust puffing up. A few more hit nearby and my confusion clears when Marx bellows.

"Shooter!"

# Chapter 15

Gus

I head straight for Ana and throw myself at her, making sure she's safe. Whoever is shooting at us is a poor shot, as they haven't landed any. Either way, it's imperative that we make it back into the safety of the clubhouse.

Looking around, trying to find my family members, I see Pops has his gun out. He's covering Debs. Rhodie has Dayz covered and Jules and Tav are dotted about with their weapons drawn too. The MC brothers who came to watch the show are positioned around the shooting range and in various other places, everyone wired and alert to where the threat is coming from.

A whistle pierces the air and all our eyes dart to Marx. He raises one hand in the air, his finger pointed up, then circles it, meaning it's time for us to all get the hell outta here. I glance at Ana, who stares at me with her wide green eyes and gives me a decisive head nod. We take off running toward the clubhouse, the MC brothers both out here and the ones that stayed behind in the clubhouse offering cover fire for those of us who are out in the open.

Fox and Nitro are standing in the doorway, covering us as Ana and I burst through. Fox grabbing Ana's hand and pulling her behind him whilst not taking his eyes off of what's happening outside. We hustle out of the doorway to make room for everyone else who has made it to safety and before long we are all in the common room, huffing, puffing and pissed as fuck.

"Why is it every time you Death Riders turn up, shit hits the fan?" Marx growls out before he tugs on his beard a couple of times. Savage is looking at least a little apologetic.

"I'm sick of this shit. We're taking these fuckers out. Wire, SitRep now!" Marx bellows out, pounding a fist on the table in case someone was dumb enough to not be paying attention. Wire materializes from out of nowhere, his ever present laptop balanced on his forearm, the fingers on his other hand flying over the keys.

"Looks like Hammers crew. We got a group of them coming in hot on bikes. I'd say ETA is around 1 minute. Nothing to the back of the property that I can see, other than the one sniper stationed out there."

"How many?" Savage asks.

Wire flicks through a couple of screens that show CCTV footage from the main road and various other parts of the compound.

"I'd say around 20 of 'em. They're splitting off into groups,"

"Fuck" Marx and Savage both curse out at the same time. It's amazing how in sync these two are.

"Shit, they're surrounding us, so we have to be smart. Everyone tool up. Brothers, outside in formation, ready for anything. Tombs, take point wherever you think we need it." I give Marx a chin lift as Tav, Jules, Pops, Debs and Ana gather around me.

"Me, Dayz and Remy will have eyes on and keep you all updated. Make sure you all have your ear pieces in, it's what they're for." Wire shouts out. Dayz darts off toward Switch's room where Flack has been staying. Remy has not left her father's side since he was shot. He may feel well enough to head home now, but being one of the older members means that his healing has taken longer than expected and he's still needing a lot of rest.

The brothers all fiddle with their comms watches, putting their earpieces in, and it's nice to know that even the Death Riders took advantage of the tech as well. It's going to be the edge we need to fuck over these nomads. I watch as the MC brothers filter out of the common room, heading in different directions. My family is waiting for my instruction, Ana grabbing my hand and standing next to me, ready for anything and everything.

"Ooohhhh, are we gonna have a shootout? Yussss!" Debs pumps her fist a couple of times and, as disturbed as I am by her enthusiasm, I'm also glad that this woman isn't panicking, or hell, even phased by what's happening. A definite bonus is that she can shoot like a goddamn sharp shooter as well. I take a breath and then bark out my orders.

"Jules, with Tav on the roof," I see Pops open his mouth, but I cut him off before he can argue with me. "Need you on the ground level with the rifle. You choose your cover. Got it?" Pops' mouth slams shut, and he gives me a nod. Crazy old coot surely didn't think I was going to send him up on the roof at his age. I watch as Debs follows him and I go to open my mouth, but before anything can come out, Ana covers it with her hand, shaking her head. She stares up at me, her eyebrows raised.

"Let her help. She'll be fine," I nod. There's no time for me to wrangle the woman back in.

Looking down at my wife, I take note that she's not in heels today.

"Changed into boots. Didn't want to trudge to the shooting range in heels," she shrugs at me.

"You're not sitting this one out, are you?"

"Not a fucking chance, Tombs,"

I let out a long sigh, "Didn't think so,"

She pecks me on the lips before asking, "Where do you want me?" I want her safe at home, but we all know that's not happening.

"I want you in that tree on the fence line by the gate. I'll cover you from the ground." A smile splits her face and she tip-toes up to press a quick peck on my lips. Little does she know I did this for her safety. That tree is the least likely place to be hit, but it puts her in on the action. Gunshots split the air and me and my tiny wife step out of the clubhouse hand in hand.

## Remy

"Remy! You're with Wire and me. We need eyes on. That douchey Nomad MC is coming in hot!"

What? Jumping up from Dad's bedside, I give his hand a quick squeeze before I run out of the room behind Tuesday, or Chewy, as the men call her. She throws the door open to Wire's room and I'm hit with his spicy, smoky scent. Butterflies flap in my stomach, but his scent always soothes me.

Wire is not only incredibly lovely, and an amazing teacher, but he is also very beautiful. Today he has his hair tucked up into his beanie, but a few times since I've been here he's worn his long curls out. I've wanted to touch them, but that's incredibly personal and we aren't those types of friends.

Chewy takes up her station and Wire breaks eye contact with his screens to turn and smile before pointing at the station he arranged for me. I take a seat, about to ask Wire if he has a picture of all our security cameras, but great minds must think alike because he hits a couple of keys and within moments the large screen above us flicks to life, showing us all the brothers have their comms on. We can see all their locations and their movements as well as live feeds from all the security cameras around the compound. It's very impressive how many they have. Back home at the Death Riders compound, we only have four, one on each corner. Here, you can see almost every part of the land Devil's Rose MC own. I'm sure that's because of Chewy and her security business.

"Remy, you all good to monitor the front gate, parking lot and treeline?" I nod my head and then remember Wire and Chewy both have their eyes glued to their screens so they wouldn't have seen me.

"Yes, yup. I can do that."

"You'll need to warn brothers through comms too, so make sure you use your firm voice, ok?" Wire looks at me with a kind smile on his face, encouraging me.

"Yes, I can definitely do this. I've got this, guys."

"Of course you do, you're a bad bitch!" Chewy holds out her knuckles for me to bump, not moving her eyes from the large screen. I gently bump my fist against her little one and it makes me smile.

"Gus, if Ana is being posted in the tree, tell her to get her ass in there now. These nomads are coming in hot, ETA 20 seconds max." Chewy barks down her headset and I make a note to use that type of voice. It's time I put my big girl panties on and be confident.

Devils Rose and Death Riders MC's need me.

# Chapter 16

Gus

The roar of motorcycles tears through the warm Texas air and it's deja vous all over again. These nomad fuckers really need to get a new MO. From where me and Ana are stationed, we have the perfect view of the bikes bearing down on us, although because we are slightly off to the side, we are out of any direct line of fire. Well, we would be if these fuckers were any good at shooting. There are errant bullets flying around as a row of men pull up in front of the clubhouse, firing at anything they can point their guns at. Looking at the number of men in front of us, I feel as if we have a pretty good chance. The fact the nomads split off into smaller groups helps. I'd rather me and Ana face 6 guys than 60 or however many of the bastards there are.

"These guys are just firing willy nilly! It's bloody nuts!" Ana yells down at me from her perch.

"Just take out as many as you can, or at the very least, see if you can wing them."

"No way, buddy. We're outnumbered. We gotta even the

odds by taking these guys outta the game permanently." A smirk tugs at my lips at how fucking sassy my little wife is, and how little she cares about the law.

"Tav, Jules, 3 to the West" Dayz's voice rings out over comms, and turning I see all three men in the west fall backward. I was right, the fuckers have us surrounded.

"Gus? You have one on foot coming toward you along the fence line. Thank you." I smile at how polite Remy is while I shoot the guy she warned me about.

"Fox, Nitro, Judge, one each for you, coming in from the southern end. Back of compound." Wire calls. I have to admit, the way all three of the hackers are doing an excellent job at comms, I'm thinking I might have to ask them to cover some of our more dangerous jobs.

The next moments are a blur of voices telling us to shoot left, right, north, south. Gunfire is ringing out from every angle, bodies of men that aren't our brothers hitting the dirt. I even hear a heavily accented "Yahoo I got the bastard! This is the best holiday everrrrr!" yelled out in the distance.

A shout from above me rings out but before I can look up I flinch and a burning sensation spreads through my upper arm, like I've been stung by the biggest fucking bee in the world. Something falls from the tree and then I'm on my back in the dust. When I raise my head, Ana is on top of me, arm outstretched, firing at a fucker none of us saw coming. She spins to face the clubhouse, her black hair whipping around her.

"I need help! Gus is hit!" I watch as instead of checking me over, she goes back to her job, lining up shots and taking them. She's like a fucking Valkyrie, all focus and fire, and if I wasn't already in love with her, I would be now.

"Fuck! We have you both covered Ana." Tav's voice comes through the comms "How bad is it? If he can get to the clubhouse, we'll lay down cover fire."

"Ana? Stay where you are! You have two coming your way. Tav and Jules, cover from the roof, Tank, can you cover Ana and Gus from the ground? Thank you." I know it's not the time, but I let out a chuckle. Remy sounds like a fucking airport announcer.

I glance down at my arm as the burning gets more intense. It's only a graze, so I have no idea why the hell it hurts so fucking bad. Tav's been grazed before and never acted like this.

Pounding coming from somewhere above my head sounds out before two massive boots come to a rest on either side of my head and Tank looks down at me quickly before shuffling to the side, kneeling next to Ana and whispering something in her ear.

"Get back fucker! She's mine!" I grit out before letting my head fall back onto the ground for a moment. I take a deep breath to center myself again then raise my head up in time to see Ana and Tank fire in unison, both gunmen they were aiming at losing their guns and some of their fingers. Tank murmurs something into his comms and in no time I see the two young prospects gather up the fingerless, screaming nomads and drag them into the compound.

"You two alright? Who needed medical assistance?" Tank's impossibly deep voice grits out. Fuck, I wish I had that voice. I'd be Barry White-ing my way through life.

"Gus! He's been hit. Take him to Switch, I'll cover you," Ana barks out and then turns back to fire more shots at a couple of nomads that are still fighting rather than running like they should be.

Tank looks down at me with his brow raised in question, but I grit my teeth and shake my head.

"It's a graze man, I'll be fine," I'm dizzy as fuck and my throat feels itchy and tight, but I'm not about to tell the man that. I'm more than pissed that instead of protecting my wife, my family, fuck, even my friends, I'm lying on the fucking ground like a pussy.

Ana kneels beside me. I hear her huff a breath and then mutter to herself in her mother's language. I let the sound of her sweet voice wash over me as I listen to the happenings around me. The gunfire slows until it sounds like only one guy left. His wild gunfire stops abruptly the moment after I hear Pops' rifle ring out.

"Yippee, yee hoo motherfucker!" Pops' voice yells out before a groan comes from the roof.

"It's yippee kay aye, motherfucker!"

"It's whatever the fuck I want it to be, dickhead," Pops yells back and I bury my face in my wife's hair and chuckle into it, holding her to me with my good hand. She shakes me off, turning to me with wild eyes.

"Shit, Tank, Gus doesn't look good," A growl leaves my body when Ana puts pressure on my arm. It hurts like a motherfucker, so I grab both her hands, holding them in one of mine.

"It's ok. I'm pretty sure it's a graze. I'm fine, baby, just fine. Thank you for having my back." I gently kiss her, reveling in the feeling of her lush lips on mine.

"I'll always have your back, Gus, like now. You need help." She looks up at Tank, who curses and then does something I don't care about. All I care about is my wife, who is gazing down at me with fear in her eyes.

## Ana

Gus's eyes roll back and his head thuds against the ground.

"Fuck!  I've never seen someone faint after being grazed before," Tank says, looking down at Gus with a squinty eye. I feel for Gus's pulse, which races beneath my fingertips. Something is definitely not right.

"His pulse is racing, we need to get him inside," I get to my feet and try to pull up Gus, however the man is a beast at the best of times, tall and broad with tightly packed muscle. Out to it he's dead weight that I have little chance in hell of moving.

Footsteps make their way toward me and, looking up, I see Tav and Jules sprinting toward us.

"Switch is getting his shit ready. Jules, Tav, get Gus inside now!  The coast is clear.  Tank, provide cover just in case" Dayz speaks calmly yet quickly into all our comms and I watch helplessly as the Tombs brothers pick up Gus as if he weighs nothing.  Tank wraps his incredibly weighty arm around my shoulders and we hustle into the common room where Tav and Jules have dumped Gus on the table.

"Shit! What's wrong with the boy? It only looks like a graze on the upper arm. Has he been hit elsewhere?" Pops barks out, concern marring his tanned, wrinkled face. Switch runs a knife through the front of Gus's henley, ripping the material from his body, looking for wounds and finding none other than the bullet wound to his upper left arm. The tension in the room is suffocating. Men vibrating with anger or worry. Jules and

Tav stand solemnly on either side of Pops, Dayz in Rhodie's arms with a blank stare on her face. There's no teasing or quips from them, no incessant chatter, the unease causing my body to shake.

I can feel the panic pressing down on me like a crashing wave. I knew this was too good to last. My breaths are coming fast and I need to get a grip on myself before I completely lose it. A warm hand wraps around my shaking one and I turn to see my mum's warm eyes twinkle back at me. Not a worry in the world.

"He'll be fine, *e hine*, my girl. Trust these men. I do." She gives me an emphatic nod and her gaze drifts back to my husband's body on the same table I've sat at for dinner. Switch frowns down at Gus for a moment, rubbing on Gus's bare chest.

"Ana, does his chest always look like this?" I step on shaky legs to stand beside Switch, before looking at Gus's chest. Frowning, I get closer for a better look before jerking back.

"Is that a rash? I've never seen it before. He didn't have it this morning." A rattling sound coming from Gus punctuates my words.

"Fuck! I know what's wrong with him. Wait here!" Switch booms out. If I thought Marx had a loud voice, it's nothing on this guy. He thunders down the hall to his room, clinic, whatever you want to call it. I grab a hold of Gus's large hand in mine and caress the back of it, helping to not only anchor myself, but hopefully him, too.

Pounding on the floorboards heralds Switch's return and we all watch as he pulls the cap off of a pen-like thing and stabs it into Gus's thigh.

"Um, Switch, he's fucked up his arm, not his leg, son." Pops says, slowly, as if Switch is an idiot.

"It's an epipen. He's having an anaphylactic reaction to being shot. It's super fucking rare and I've only seen it once before on the battlefield. I'm guessing he hasn't been hit before?"

We all look at each other, eyes wide, in silence before Tav sputters, "Wait, wait, wait. Are you telling us he's allergic to being shot? No one is allergic to that!" He bursts into a fit of laughter, much of which I'm sure is brought on by relief, but even to my ears, it sounds absolutely insane. Looking to Switch to see if he's taking the piss, he just shrugs his broad shoulders at me.

"What can I say? It's rare, but there are people that have allergies to gunshot residue. I'm guessing Gus is probably used to having a rash after firing his weapon given he uses a gun in his job, but being shot would have the residue on the inside of his body, causing a stronger reaction. Most just end up with hives or a rash. Only rarely do they end up with swollen throat, and anaphylaxis," Switch looks back down at his patient and when Gus's eyes flutter open my shaky legs give out, Mum having to hold me upright for a moment before a strong steady hand takes hold of my arm and some of my weight. Half turning my head, I see Jules looking down at me, his eyebrows pinched before he mumbles in his monotone voice,

"He's ok, girl. He's ok. Fucking ridiculous being allergic to a gunshot wound, but he's alive."

I nod up at him in thanks, and someone shoves a chair into the back of my legs. I sit heavily, one hand still wrapped in Gus's, while I gently brush his hair back with my other hand.

"What the fuck happened? I feel like I'm having a heart attack and my arm is on fire," his voice croaks out. He also has a slight lisp, which has my eyebrows making out with my hairline as I look at Switch who murmurs quietly "Swollen tongue" as he goes about disinfecting the bullet graze.

"You fucking got grazed by a bullet, had an allergic reaction that knocked your big ass out, giving us all fucking heart attacks! Doc, after you patch his big ass up, I'll need you to check my blood pressure and maybe up my meds. Jesus Christ, kid! An allergic reaction? Really? Must come from your mother's side. I'd never pass on that bullshit. I've been shot three times in my life and do you see my tongue swelling up? Christ on a bike." I roll my lips between my teeth and we all watch as Pops stomps to the bar, demanding their hard stuff straight from the bottle.

Chuckles break out around me as the tension eases some now that we all know Gus is fine. There weren't any other casualties on our side, not that you can count this as one. The nomads fucked with the wrong people today.

"Switch, patch up Gus. Everyone else, we're gonna have to help the prospects with body clear up. Does anyone know where Hammer's headquarters are? Be nice to send his trash back to him," Marx looks around the room, but everyone is drawing a blank. Until now, I think we all thought it was a Death Riders' problem. Well, that was before he started recruiting Bratva men. But by bringing this fight to DRMC, it looks like it's us against them and we have a lack of knowledge about how many men he actually has, what exactly he wants from us, and where the hell to find him.

"Fuck. Fine. Chewy, you got any idea how to get rid of a bunch of bodies?" A stool scrapes along the floor and Pops hotfoots it over to Dayz, their heads together frantically whispering before her head pops up.

"Leave it with us, big man! Just pile the bodies by the

Chamber of Secrets and we'll deal with it later." Dayz gives him a grin and the thumbs up as the four Death Riders all exchange wary looks with each other.

"Gus, you all good to sit up? Do it slowly, so you don't get a head rush from the adrenaline I just gave you." Gus nods and slowly rolls into a sitting position on the table before swinging his legs to the side. Hopping off the table he tugs me to standing, dropping a kiss on my lips then taking my seat and pulling me into his lap.

"No, hell no! You were just shot. You don't need my big arse on you. Let me go!" I shake my head at him and try very gently to fight his hold on me, but his grip is too strong and I don't want to hurt him, so I give up with a huff. He presses his lips to my temple, inhaling my scent before dropping a kiss just below my ear and whispering, "Thank you, baby. I just need to feel you in my arms. I need you to ground me." I let out a breath and watch as men wander back and forth, busying themselves.

I'm feeling all over the place, the adrenaline of what we just went through fading fast. My body feels bone tired, limbs heavy, and an ache behind my eyes coming on. I'm also feeling incredibly unsettled. When I thought there was something really wrong with Gus, I thought this was it. The moment the other shoe dropped. In the heat of the moment, I didn't have the time to think it all through, but now? As I sit in his arms? Yeah, I don't think I can handle the heartache of losing him. This whole thing is a mess and I'm exhausted. I close my eyes for a moment and it must have been longer than I thought because when I open them, everyone is gathering in the common room. Marx's shrill whistle rents the air, drawing the attention to him.

"Ok fuckers. This is the second time we've been attacked

in our own house and I dont know about you, but I've had e-fucking-nough of it. Savage, this seems like your shit you brought to our doorstep, so I hope you have a fucking idea on how to fix it." Marx shoots daggers at the other man, who does not seem the least bit concerned.

"Fuck man, I would if I could, but this only fucking happens when we're in Rose Grove." He shrugs his shoulders and looks at Dex, who nods in agreement. Everyone is quiet as that sinks in. Gazing across the room, I see Dayz in her favorite spot, perched on Rhodie's knee, squishing her lip.

"So, you've never been attacked at home?" Dayz asks abruptly, cutting Marx off. He just rolls his eyes and gestures for her to carry on.

Savage shakes his head. "The only time it's happened is when we're here."

Dayz nods absently and I can see her lips moving, but nothing coming out. She spins her head in my direction before asking,

"Are your shipments still being messed with?"

"Yup. We thought we nipped it in the bud when we found the men that were being paid off by Hammer, but we had another shipment arrive today that was all messed up. Roman is tightening up security. We have another shipment coming in two days that Savage and Dex are transporting and neither of us can afford for it to be missing any product," and by product, I mean guns, or drugs. These men and my mum know the drill, so I know I don't have to hide anything or mince words. DRMC is an ally of the Bratva and, by extension, so are the Death Riders.

"Verrrry interesting." She squints and makes a motion with her hand as if she's stroking an imaginary beard. I see Savage raise a brow at Dex before they both shrug and quietly wait for whatever genius stuff Dayz is going to come up with.

While all this is happening, somehow my mother has baked bloody bickies, or cookies, as these guys call them. She's going around delivering them and giving the men little shoulder squeezes or pats on the back. I should be more concerned by how easily she's slipped into this lifestyle, but she seems happy and we have bigger things to worry about, so I'll deal with that later. Much later.

"Right, so we can assume Hammer is after you because you cut him from his own club. His men only attack us when you guys are here and I would imagine that's because DRMC and Death Riders are now allies. If he takes out both clubs, that gives him control of a larger territory and the ability to move anything he likes. The question is, why fuck with the Bratva and how the hell did he get in there in the first place?"

Everyone looks at me, and I shrug.

"We have no idea either. Most men in the Bartashev Bratva are born into it. Only very few get invited in, and they start out the lowest of the low. The shit Hammer is pulling off, messing with shipments, that's information only higher ups know. I can't imagine anyone breaking the Bratva bond to deal with Hammer."

Dayz squints at Savage for a moment.

"Last time shit went down, you said that Flack had been getting paranoid. That's why he wanted Remy here?"

"Yeah. He's been antsy since we put Hammer out. Obviously, whatever he knows is fucking true and not just his paranoid musings." Dayz nods once and then leaves the room, leaving us all hanging.

"I fucking hate when she does that," Rider says to no one in particular. "Just leaves you hanging, no explanation at all."

"Chewy said you may need our input." Remy's voice a quiet whisper in the room. Rider jumps as she's standing closest to him and he hadn't even noticed her and her father were there. Although I have no idea how he missed Flack, the man, like all the other men around here, is huge.

"Fuck! You need a bell, girl." He says, his large hand splayed across his chest.

"Sorry 'bout that," she whispers out. She looks around the room, her bangs always slightly in her eyes. From what I know of her, she's spent her whole life in the MC, although she is completely different from what most people raised in an MC are like if Marx, Rhodie and Rider are anything to go by.

"Thanks Remy, Flack." Marx nods at them both. "Savage said you had an idea shit was going South with Hammer. Was that before or after you kicked him out?" Marx says in a slightly softer voice than usual. I notice that this is something the men do when Remy is around. She brings softness out in people.

"It wasn't Dad. It was me. I was doing the digging and feeding it back to him."

We watch as she pulls her shoulders back and raises her head to look at Marx and then Savage.

"I–I don't have all the information yet, but with Wire and Chewys' help, I will. And I will kill the man that put that effing bullet in my dad."

"Good girl," Flack says at the same time as me and Dayz do. The men look a little taken aback by her words, which is funny in itself given that she said 'effing' instead of fuck, but they still back her up by banging their fists on any available surface.

"What do you know so far, Rem?" Savage asks her.

She blows out a breath. "You know when I was a kid I liked to read in quiet places?"

Savage cringes before saying, "I'll never be able to forget that time I was newly patched and a club girl took me into the pantry to give me oral. Next thing, I feel a small hand tap me on the ass and your little voice saying 'Excuse me, Mr. Savage, can I please get out of here?'"

We all laugh while Remy turns bright red. "Well, I guess I never really grew out of the habit."

"What do you know?" Marx asks, his voice still quieter than usual. It's nice, but also a little unnerving.

"I never really paid too much attention cos it was always club business, so I stayed out of it. But before the stuff with Kraykowski, I overheard Hammer. Speaking Russian." She looks at me before darting her gaze back to Savage.

"How do you know it was Russian?"

She stares at him for a moment before answering. "Because it sounds a lot like when Dex talks to his mom," All the eyes in the clubhouse shoot to Dex.

"Both my parents are Russian immigrants. All above board." He grits out. Savage places a hand on his shoulder as Marx eyes him slightly before giving him a chin lift. We all know the Tombs ran prelim background checks on the men before they became allies, and nothing was flagged, but it seems like an unusual coincidence. Especially with all the other stuff going on.

Remy continues talking, "No one ever notices me around the club, it's just how it is. Hammer was the same. I told my dad, and he said he'd keep an eye on him."

"When was this?"

"Hmm, around a month before the Kraykowski thing."

"Weren't you already Pres by that time Savage?" Marx says

"We were in the transition then. Flack was the one who led

the charge in getting Hammer to step down,"

"No wonder you got your ass shot," Pops pipes up, tipping his chin at Flack, who just grins back. Pops' eyes then dart to Remy "Oh, sorry girl" She smiles sweetly at him, crinkles her nose and shrugs.

"Ok, so I think we agree Hammer is fucking with us all, MC and Bratva. Around the time Remy is talking about there were three Russians at play. Roman was running the Bratva here, Ushakov was pulling strings from Russia, and Kovalev was in the skin trade. Savage, your MC under Hammer's leadership were still 1 percenters, although you never traded in skin, so if he was headed down that track he could have been in business with either of them way back then, and Roman, along with the rest of us, shut it all down. That could explain why he has a hard on for us," Dayz says, looking around the room at everyone who had a role to play.

"Motherfucker. We should have just taken him out," Savage moans as he runs a hand down his face.

"We need to find who he's working with. How does he know when you guys are on a run?" Dayz looks to the Death Riders, who look at each other before muttering "Fuck" under their breaths.

"And it makes sense that he's the one that placed a man on you, Gus and Ana," Gus stiffens for a moment, his arms banding around me even tighter as I'm still perched on the poor guy's knee. Soaking up all he has to give me before this comes crashing down.

"And Ana, we need to find out who his contact is in the Bratva. Once we find this shit out, we may actually have a chance to take the fight to him for a change."

That's the problem, though. If he's working with one of the

Bratva, I don't think I'll want to know.

# Chapter 17

Gus

After the other night's excitement, things have been pretty tense at home. Well, not for anyone else in our family. Debs and Pops get on like a house on fire and my siblings seem to spend a lot of time over at Pops' hanging out with her. Debs' excuse was that the newlyweds needed more time to be alone, but all that's doing is making it glaringly obvious that Ana is pulling away.

I don't know what I did to fuck things up, but I can feel that shit just isn't right at the moment. I'm hoping it's just the stress of what happened and the awful task her and Roman have of trying to weed out whoever is working with Hammer, but I can't help but wonder what I've done and how I get my wife back.

"Oh babe, don't forget we have another appointment with Marta today at 5. Want me to pick you up?" I gaze at her across the countertop from me, perched on a stool eating her breakfast while I stand and drink my coffee, leaning on the other counter.

"I don't even know why we have to keep doing this. Now that

Roman is back, surely we don't need to keep up the counseling and stuff?"

The fuck she just say? If she thinks that I'm letting her go now that Roman is back, she's got another thing coming. Obviously, I'm going to have to sugarcoat this because if I say that to her directly, she's going to lose her shit at me.

"Come on, babe, it's our last one. May as well see it through and get signed off." I shrug like it's not a big deal and turn to rinse out my cup, feeling her eyes boring into me.

"Ok. I'll meet you there. Afterwards, I need to check in on that shipment for Roman. He's going to be busy with Sasha around that time." I turn to look at her and her face looks tight. Raising an eyebrow, she smiles thinly and bobs her head.

"Shit, babe, I'm sorry. Anyone you're close to?"

She blows out a breath. "No, these three are kinda new. It still doesn't make sense how they know top level intel, but I'm sure Roman will work it out." She picks up her plate and cup and carries them to where I'm standing. She rinses them both before putting them in the dishwasher. She stands next to me for a beat before she turns her beautiful face up to mine, stares into my eyes, tiptoes up and drops a soft kiss to the corner of my mouth. I want to grab her thick hips in my hands, hold her to me and plunder her mouth with my tongue, but I let her go. Giving her the space she so clearly wants, and maybe needs.

I watch her leave, picking up her purse, looking at me once more over her shoulder before she opens the door and walks through. Fuck. I don't know what I've done or what I need to do, but this can't be the end. I won't let it be. I need her in my life. I need her like the air I breathe.

"She's worried you're going to leave her," Debs' soft lilting voice says as she steps up to lean a hip against the counter.

"I'd never leave her. I love her. I'm so desperately in love with her. Surely she knows that?" She smiles up at me and places her small, soft hand on my cheek, much like my mom used to when she was alive.

"Oh, baby. Ana has had people come and go her whole life. People that she loved and should have loved her. So, you loving her and her knowing it in her bones are two different things. Think, tama, when did she start to pull away?" She stares up at me with her dark eyes glittering in her brown face.

"She's been like this since the other night,"

"Since you were shot, yeah?"

Realization dawns on me. She's been pulling away since the shootout, but why? It's not the first time we've been in situations like that. Debs must see the confusion on my face, because she pats me on my cheek.

"Ah, Gus, losing you doesn't just mean you walking away." She raises her brows at me, waiting for the penny to drop. Fuck. Now I get it. "She comes across as someone who rolls with the punches because she keeps herself separate from everyone and everything. She does it so it won't hurt so bad when it's not there anymore." Debs sighs long and low. "Her putting space between you is her getting ready to run. It helps her feel in control. My baby has always struggled with loss and disappointment, each one chipping away at her. But with you, Gus? She's afraid she'll lose her soul if you're taken from her. She's scared, Gus. Show her that there's nothing to be afraid of. And maybe try not to get shot again, *ne*?" With that, she pulls me into her arms and holds me.

* * *

I've spent the bulk of the day in my office coming up with ways to show Ana that she's safe with me and I've been getting nowhere. I have no idea who the fuck to turn to. I can't ask Debs again because she's already counting on me to do my best to ease the hurt in Ana's heart. Pops is kinda crazy and besides, he's busy ticking more things off Debs' ever growing list. Every time we get one thing ticked off, another crazy idea pops up.

Shit. Shit. Shit. Leaning my elbows on the desk I run my fingers through my hair before tapping the alert button on my watch and wait for my siblings to respond, which takes all of around 0.7 seconds before footsteps thump in the hallway, getting louder the closer they come.

"Yo, you alerted us?" Tav says as he arrives first, just before Jules does. Dayz and surprisingly Rhodie bring in the rear.

"Rhodie, pleasant surprise," I give him a chin lift as he wanders over to Dayz's spot at the table in the corner.

"Yeah, I stopped by to bring Chewy a snack. She's busy working on that shit for the CIA, figured she would forget to eat." he shrugs as if it's no big deal, but it is. The way he treats my sister is better than anyone we could have ever imagined for her.

"Thanks man," Jules says in response, before turning his gaze back to me. Leaning back in my chair, I clear my throat, fiddle with my tie, and just let it all out.

"I need help, guys. Ana is pulling away. She's afraid that she's going to lose me, and I need to convince her I'm here to stay." I release this all on a breath and raise my eyes to look at four confused faces.

"Ok. And why does she think she's going to lose you, brother? What the hell did you do?" Jules growls out. All four pairs of eyes stare at me, waiting for my answer.

"I didn't do anything! The foster system did."

"Huh?" Tav asks, confusion screwing up his face.

"Ana was in care as a kid. Every time she got close to someone, she was moved on, or they were adopted out, or, with her foster dad, he died. She's always waiting for people to leave or be taken from her." I see realization dawn on their faces. Well, not Dayz. She still seems slightly confused but I know Rhodie will explain it all to her later.

"Did this all come on after you got shot?" Rhodie's gruff voice asks from across the room.

Before I can answer, Tav starts snorting and scoffing "He was hardly shot. He was grazed and then he pussied out because he's 'allergic'." Tav says this last word in the girliest voice he can muster up, then grunts when I throw my pen at his face.

"Yes, Rhodie, she's been pulling away for the past couple of days. Trying to put space between us. How do I convince her I'm not fucking going anywhere without going all caveman on her ass? Because you know if I do that, she'll kick me in the balls and then run anyway."

Glancing across the desk, Jules stares me down.

"So, this fake marriage, you want it to be real then?"

"Jules, this marriage is real. I went into it knowing that Ana is who I want as my wife. I want to have a family with her. It's all real. To me, it's always been real." He gives me a nod, then darts his eyes away to look around the room at the contemplative looks on Tav and Dayz's faces. Hopefully, they're coming up with a plan because I'm at a loss here.

"Chewy mentioned that you've been seeing a couple's counselor?" I nod at Rhodie's question, not sure where he's heading with this.

"Yeah, court mandated, to prove we're in an actual relationship."

"Ok, and couples' counselors help counsel couples, right?"

"Yeah. It's their job."

"Soooooooo," He circles his hands at me like I should know what the hell his point is. He frowns, looks down at Dayz, then toward my desk where both Jules and Tav are turned toward him, and I'm looking directly at him.

"Come on you guys, I'm pretty sure you're not all autistic." He takes another look at Dayz and then glances at Jules' blank face, "Ok, I'm pretty sure at least 50% you aren't autistic." He looks around again before kissing Dayz on the head, sighing into her curls before looking at me.

"Use. The. Couples. Counselor. To. Counsel. You." He grinds out in his rough voice that always sounds like he smokes 3 packs a day, even though I've never seen the man smoke anything.

"Holy shit, that's a great idea. Nice work Rhodie." Tav holds his hand up in a long distance high five and almost keels over in delight when Rhodie mimes high fiving him back. "Holy fucking shit! He did it!" He points at Dayz "That's how you do it Dayz!" She just smiles at our idiotic brother before looking up at Rhodie like he hung the moon. Shit, I may also be looking at him like that too, because that idea is going to help save my marriage.

"Ok, sorry to have to kick you all out, but I gotta get outta here. I've got counseling to get to," I rush out of my office, cheers go up along with Dayz yelling good luck at me. Hopefully, I won't need it.

## Ana

Yet again I find myself sat in Marta's not so welcoming office, pressed up against my giant husband on the small leather loveseat. I'm sure this woman is just forcing couples to leave here happy in the hopes they never have to sit on this thing again. I mean, if I were in an unhappy marriage, the last thing I'd want to do is plaster myself up against my husband and talk to this woman, and yet here we are, once again.

"So, how have you been getting on?" Marta doesn't even raise her eyes at us as she reads through the last session's notes. I side eye Gus a little to see if he's going to start the ball rolling. He looks up at the ceiling and I see him swallow a couple of times, so I guess it's up to me. I plaster a smile on my face and make sure I sound extra cheery so we can get out of here quick.

"It's been going really well! My mother is visiting from New Zealand and Gus's family has really taken a shine to her. We've all been really busy showing her the sights and things. Isn't that right Gus?"

I turn to look at him expectantly and then furrow my brows as I see he's looking a little sweaty.

"Ah, babe, are you ok?" I ask him, darting my eyes all over his face as he tries to avoid my gaze.

"Um, no, I'm not Ok. Marta, I was wondering if we might work a little on communication while we're here?" He takes a breath and lets it out slowly. I have no idea what the hell is going on. "Ana has been pulling away from me the past few days, and I'm having trouble communicating with her about it." Those chocolate brown eyes dart towards me, and for the first time I notice how wound up and worried he looks. "I, I think Ana is dealing with some pretty big abandonment issues and I'm not sure how to navigate them." His gaze comes back to mine, and where I can see he looks apologetic and maybe even a little sadness in those beautiful eyes, I'm sure he can see daggers in mine.

"Interesting. Would you care to add anything, Ana? I know we have touched on your past before, but do you think you're pulling away? Do you think you may have unresolved issues from your childhood?"

Marta looks at me over her glasses and I can feel the discomfort working its way up my body. My leg muscles feel as if they're all tensed up, my stomach is twisting and I'm overheating. It's like I've been hurtled back in time, to all the times I had to sit with caseworkers trying to figure out why I refused to bond with people. Why I refused to make friends at the different homes I went to, why I would refuse any type of comfort from the many carers I had until I landed with Mick and Debs. It's all too familiar a feeling and I don't like it. I close my eyes for a moment and remind myself that I'm not that little girl anymore. Taking a deep breath, I let it out, and lick my lips as my panicked mouth breathing has made them feel dry.

"Um, sorry, I don't understand. Can I please get you to repeat that question?" I side-eye Gus, who is now turned toward me as if he, too, is as invested in this question as Marta.

"I was just asking if you think you are pulling away. In terms of your childhood trauma, of losing loved ones and, as a result, having difficulty forming close bonds with people, do you think that is having any effect on your marriage with Gus? Gus mentioned that there's been a bit of distance between you two recently." She asks me, her brows raised, her beady eyes staring me down. What the fuck, Gus? Way to go, buddy. We will definitely be having words about this later on.

"I would have to say no. I've grown a lot since then, and I have created a family of sorts with my very close friends that I have made here in America. I would say the distance Gus has been feeling of late has probably got more to do with the fact that I am very busy at work. As is he. We are both working on large caseloads at the moment." I shoot daggers at him, squinting, so he really knows I'm pissed. The coward just looks the other way, running his fingers through the softest goddamn hair I've ever had the pleasure to touch. Damn his brilliant hair.

"Gus, do you believe Ana has put her trauma behind her and is giving her all to this relationship?"

He clears his traitorous throat. "I think she thinks she has, but I feel like there's maybe a little more she has to work through. It feels like she's always waiting for something bad to happen, and that she always has one foot out the door."

I turn fully this time to glare directly at him, watching his giant body try to shrink back into the corner of the love seat. I take a deep breath to center myself and remind myself that we are here purely to prove that our fake marriage is real. We have lied every other time we've been here, so why the hell are we psychoanalyzing me all of a sudden? Shit, I'm sure Gus has some childhood trauma he needs to work through too, but you don't see me bringing that up. Nope, it's time to get back to the program, which is where I tell this woman what she wants to hear, and then we go on our merry way.

I turn to make eye contact with Marta, "Ok, well maybe I have a little further to go in getting over my past, but I'm sure with Gus's help, I should be able to get there." I place my hand on Gus's and fight the urge to squeeze the life out of it while I plaster a smile on my face and hope that Marta buys this shit. She has every other time.

"Gus, how do you feel about this? Do you think you can help Ana work towards getting to a place where she feels as if she's safe and settled and happy? Whether that is within this relationship or not?"

I glance at Gus, who is looking at me, studying me almost. He swallows before he answers roughly, "Of course. I will do everything in my power to help Ana work through her fear." He holds my gaze as he speaks, as if making me a promise. But it's a promise that I'm too angry to even think about right now.

She peers at us over her glasses before nodding. "Very well. I'm glad you admitted there's more work to do, Ana. That's what people who come to see me often forget. We are all works of art, and sometimes we need a little extra work here and there to complete the masterpiece. I'm happy with how you work within your relationship and the ability of both of you to be thoughtful and mindful of each other." I watch as she writes something down on that infernal notepad of hers. "I told you both last session that this was going to be the last time I meet with you, however considering what we've spoken about this session, I feel the need for one more catch up. I would also like to point out that I am more than a couple's counselor. Ana, if you ever feel like your childhood is affecting you in ways that you cannot work through on your own or with Gus's help, then please, don't hesitate getting in touch with me. Until then, keep supporting each other and loving each other. I'll see you next week. Same time." She gives us a nod before popping up out of her chair, walking over to the door and holding it open for us as we hold hands and wish her well.

We hold hands until we get out in the elevator where I drop his like a hot potato.

"What the actual fuck Gus?!" He at least has the decency to look a little embarrassed.

"I didn't mean for it to go like that. It's just, I don't like the distance you're putting between us and I thought maybe counseling would help?" His shoulders are up around his ears, his eyebrows pulled together, looking like a little kid who got caught graffiting cocks everywhere. I drop my chin to my chest, close my eyes, and let out a sigh. I'm not doing this here. I know what he wants and I just can't give it to him. Not at the moment. I'm in love with him but I don't know what I would do if I lost him. The other night was too close. It brought our whole world crashing down on me, and I need to decide if what we have is worth risking my heart and soul for. Can I survive taking a chance, or is it better for me to cut ties and move on without him?

The lift hits the car parking level; the doors sliding open.

"Look, I have to go check this shipment. I'll talk to you later, ok?"

"Do you want me to come wi-" Gus's alert goes off on his watch and I stare at his handsome face as he frowns down at it.

"You better go. I'll be fine. I'm only checking to make sure it's all there. Savage and Dex will be there as they're transporting this shipment. It's that new deal between Death Riders and Roman that Marx set up. I'll be covered. Go." I lean up and give him a soft kiss on the lips I love so much and I head to my car. I need to get this shit out of the way, clear my head, and put Gus out of his misery, one way or another.

# Chapter 18

Gus

Iwatch as the love of my life walks away and I curse my damn siblings. This shit better be important if they've used our emergency alert. I check my phone and Dayz's message says to meet them at DRMC, in the Rev Room. Hopefully, she's busted the fuck out of this case. The quicker we can get this shit dealt with, the quicker I can get back to my wife. I unlock my SUV, pull myself in and start her up, cranking my radio loud to drown out the voices in my head telling me I've lost Ana for good. Speeding out of the garage, I head directly for the compound. It's only a short drive, but it's long enough for me to worry not only about my relationship but about the safety of my wife. There's a bad feeling in my gut. It eases somewhat as I pass Savage and Dex heading the opposite direction, both of them giving me a finger wave on their way past.

Pulling into the MC compound, I frown at the Tombs vehicles, including Pops' badly parked pickup truck in the carpark. Bypassing the clubhouse and common room, I head directly to where Dayz wanted me. Stepping into the surprisingly cheery torture chamber, the scent of fresh linen assaults me.

"Ugh, shit, why does it smell like a laundromat in here?"

"Dayz has upgraded the space with an infuser to make the place smell less like piss," Jules blandly informs me.

"Isn't it like a thousand times better? This place is really becoming quite homey." Dayz says as she swans around in her coveralls, although I notice she's sans goggles at the moment. Swinging my gaze toward the center of the room, I do a double take when I notice a man sitting there, although it's easy to not notice him at all. Everything about him is beige. Beige suit, beige tie, beige skin.

"Um, who the fuck is this and where the fuck did you get him from?" I step closer, trying to think where I've seen him before.

"This, my large, grumpy brother, is Tony Manero." My head whips back toward the man who already has a dark patch on the front of his pants where he's pissed himself even though he isn't really looking all that worse for wear. Yet.

"Pops and Debs happened upon him earlier today," My head spins towards the pair, who are sitting on a couch along the wall. Dayz really has gone to town in this space. Pops smirks at me while Debs waves.

"Explain to me how you two 'happened upon him'?" My eyebrow raises of its own accord. I need answers. Ana and I have both been stalked by this guy, but never close enough to take him down. And if I'm being honest, we've had bigger things to worry about than some creep watching us. I won't say he's harmless, but he hasn't tried anything yet, so I was going to wait and see how it all played out.

"Well, me and Pops were going to drop off some baking at

the office, and Pops pointed out that you and Ana have had a stalker for a while now. It wasn't hard to figure out it was this guy." She shrugs like that explains it all.

"Pops? Anything to add?" He rolls his eyes at me, sassy old coot.

"Yeah, yeah. We saw him, Debs worked her magic on him, asking if he could help her fix her tyre, acting all foreign and dumb like. He gets out of his car, goes to help and WHAM! I throw a sheepskin seat cover over his head, spin him until he's super disoriented and then me and Debs throw him in the trunk, et Voila! Tony Manero." I should be surprised, shocked even, that these two pulled this off. But I'm not.

"Wait, what's up with the sheepskin seat cover?" Tav asks, perplexed.

"That's all I had. What do you think I drive about with damn pillowcases in my car? Use your goddamn melon kid. Fucksakes!" I watch as Debs runs her hand through Pops' hair and pets him like a cat, the grumpy old fucker calming down immediately. She catches me watching them and she gifts me with a wink and smile. Shaking my head, I turn back to Tony Manero, who has been crying quietly during this entire exchange.

"Please, what do you want from me? I'll give you anything, please!" Tony snivels out. I turn to my family, noticing Marx and Wire have also arrived, rounding out our little party.

"Yeah, he's been like this the whole time. I don't know where Hammer is getting these guys from but this guy is fucking soft," Pops spits out in disgust. I mean, he's not wrong. For a guy who's been causing headaches for us and snooping where he shouldn't be, I thought he'd be a little tougher than this. Dayz hasn't even done anything to him yet, instead letting me question him.

"What do we want?" I echo his question. "We want to know why the fuck you've been following us all over the state. Who sent you?" I grab a seat from the corner of the room, dragging it closer to where he's tied to the bright yellow metal chair over the grate in the floor. I place my chair across from him, close enough so that when I sit down, my knees touch his, causing him to flinch.

"Wh-who sent me?" He sputters out, fear etched on his face. The dark patch growing larger by the second.

"Are you deaf? Who do you work for? The Nomad MC, the Bratva, somebody else?" I lean back in my chair, watching him closely as Dayz hums in the background, the sound of tools being arranged on her rolling work table. Tony's eyes are enormous as he watches her go about her business. I kick him in the shin to get it back on track, causing him to jump and then cry.

"NO! No, no, I-I contract for the government,"

"Which government? US or Russia?" Marx barks out.

"W-What?" His head swings towards Marx before abruptly twisting back to look at me as Dayz leans over and slaps him, causing him to sob.

"Which. Government?" Even I can hear the impatient growl in my voice.

"US! I-I work for immigration!" Wait, what?! I also am pretty certain I hear Ana's mum whisper "Whoopsy"

"I'm an investigator. They sent me out to watch you, make sure this marriage is real."

"Why wouldn't it be? He loves her. He's loved her since he met her. He's just stuffy sometimes, and I bet he hasn't told her to her face yet, but he's definitely planning on doing that,"

Dayz helpfully info dumps.

"Wait, you haven't told her you loved her yet? What the hell, kid? No wonder she's been ignoring your big ass. Jesus, have I taught you nothing?" My head very, very slowly turns until I'm glaring at Pops. Not that he gives a shit, he gives it straight back.

"For fuck's sake. What the hell are you lot - " Marx growls, waving his finger around, pointing at anyone with the Tombs surname, including Debs, who just smiles and waves at him. "Gonna do about this fuck up? Sort it out and get him off my property." He storms through the door and I'm wondering if I have any antacids I could lend him. God knows he probably needs them. Looking back at our hostage, I can't quite help but ask what's been getting to me since we first got a fix on this guy.

"Is Tony Manero your real name?" He sighs deeply, in between snivels.

"Yeah. My mom saw the movie when she was a teen, loved it. When she got pregnant with me, she thought Tony was a good name." He shrugs, "Anyone who's ever seen the movie gives me shit about it."

"Yeah, I bet that sucks," Tav agrees with him, like they're old buddies, whilst untying the poor fucker from the chair.

"Ok dude, what'll it take to get you to forget allllll about this and give Gus and Ana an excellent report? Got any debt we could cancel for you?" Dayz asks, gesturing to Wire and herself. Tony blinks up at them, eyes so fucking wide I'm amazed they're still in his head.

"Y-you can do that?" He asks in amazement, looking back and forth between the two of them, rubbing his free hands down his thighs, wincing when he feels the wet patch, his cheeks growing pink before Dayz draws his attention again.

"Of course we can do that. We're like Liam Neeson. We have a particular set of skills." She blows on her nails and rubs them on her chest. I turn to look back at our poor victim and I can't believe that he looks as if he's really fucking taking this into consideration.

"Um, i–if you could, I guess that'd be great. I have a massive student loan. If you could get rid of that, it'd make things so much easier. I'll be able to save up to get out of my mom's basement." We all cringe a little at this.

"Sure thing, dude. We'll cancel the debt. I'll even bank over that hefty refund the IRS owes you." He nods with wild eyes before confusion crosses his face.

"Wait, the IRS doesn't owe me a refund."

"Sure they do," Wire says with a wink. Tony's mouth opens in an "o" shape before he snaps it shut and nods.

Dayz taps away at her laptop that she's balanced on the stainless steel table. Wire is on the other side of her with his laptop working away as well. Both laptops surrounded by gnarly looking metal tools and some dentistry equipment.

"It's all done buddy. Debt wiped and refund put through to your primary account. I've taken the liberty to bank a portion of that over to your baby mama to sort that pesky child support back pay you owe her. I'm sure it'll be enough for her to let you visit again."

"Wait, how do you know I'm not allowed to visit?" Dayz gives him a terrifying smile, wandering to stand beside us before she leans in really close to whisper in his ear.

"I know everything."

Tony Manero's eyes grow wide and he lets out a little "meep".

"Will that be enough to not mention this to anyone, or do we need to visit you again?"

"Lady, and um, you, big computer guy, thank you very much for what you just did for me. And I mean no offense, but I never want to see any of you people ever again."

"Fair enough. Consider it done." She slaps him on the back and Tav helps the poor man to his feet.

"Come on, I'll drive you back to your car." He looks down at Tony's trousers. "Dayz, better grab me a small tarp for my seat," Tony turns bright red, but follows Tav out of the room as best he can.

"Right, babe, you wanna drop me home?" Dayz asks Rhodie, who smiles indulgently at her "Of course, baby."

"Gus, you good with clean up?" As if she even has to ask. I'm always on cleanup duty, although this one will be easy. Bit of bleach to get rid of Tony's DNA and a tidy up and it'll be back to rights. I nod and watch as the others all leave to get drinks at the MC bar. I could use the solitude for a moment.


## Ana


I'm still pissed at Gus after that bullshit ambush at counseling, but there's nothing I can do apart from put it out of my mind and concentrate on the job at hand. Get to the warehouse, check the shipment is all there, and hand it over to Savage and Dex.

I pull up next to our warehouse and note that there doesn't seem to be a guard near the entrance door. I'm not overly worried and just shrug it off, figuring they're on their rounds. We always have two guards on duty, one in front, one in back, and every 15 minutes they do a quick perimeter walk.

Instead of wasting time waiting for them, I let myself in using the passcode. Another thing that alerts me to the fact that whoever is messing with us has inside knowledge. The only way into the warehouse is with a code, one that updates every 27 hours, just to be tricky. You try to get in any other way and security gets flagged immediately. Not just the two on duty, but pretty much any Bratva in a 20-mile radius.

Letting myself in, I come to a stop when I hear voices. Now shit's getting really fucking weird. The shipment should have been dropped directly into the warehouse by the delivery truck, then locked up tight. I'm meant to be the next person to come into contact with it, not whoever the hell is talking.

Sneaking further into the building and thanking my lucky stars that I changed into my flat boots for this, I soundlessly move to crouch behind a stack of boxes, trying to recognize whoever is talking. The voice is gently accented, although whoever they are talking to must be a native English speaker, otherwise they'd be talking in Russian.

"*Da*, we want these three boxes loaded up. Leave the guns, we're after the drugs. The girls will transport them the rest of the way."

Girls? What girls? Rustling and banging comes from the direction of the voices and I know that I'm severely unprepared for this. In my tizzy after counseling, I've left my gun in the car, although it's not like I'd be keen to get into any sort of altercation with these guys alone. I'm going to need backup. Doing a quick mental check, I go through who the hell to call.

Savage and Dex are meeting me, but I got here ahead of them so I could check everything first. Meaning they could be anywhere from 10 to 30 minutes away. I could call Roman, but he's in interrogation at the moment, and I know for a fact he doesn't answer his phone when he's in the zone. The Tombs fam called Gus in, so obviously they have some shit going on. Scrolling through my contacts, I pull up Ivan. He has never let me down. Anytime I've needed him, he's been there, at my back.

*Ana: Warehouse. Two unknowns moving out three boxes of goods. Need backup ASAP.*

*Ivan: 2 minutes little underboss.*

I let out a breath I didn't even know I was holding and edge closer still to see if I recognize either man. One of them looks vaguely familiar, yet again a newer, junior member. The man he's working with is wearing a leather vest much like the MC members wear, so there's no doubt in my mind that he must be another of Hammer's men. How many men has Hammer recruited? We cut a swathe through a number of them the other night, more men than DRMC has. Hammer must have been on a massive recruitment drive.

I'm distracted by a gentle buzz in my pocket, but before I can check it, I hear a gun go off. Taking a breath, I peek around the boxes I'm hidden behind and see the young Bratva kid on the ground, gunshot to his chest. I don't feel upset at a fallen comrade or anything, not with him being some type of traitor, but it makes my stomach drop looking at how young he is. He had a life ahead of him and he made the wrong choice. I would say a long life ahead of him, but men who join the Bratva know the risks.

I shuffle back a little and hit something that I know wasn't behind me 2 minutes ago. Sucking in a breath, I freeze in place when a large hand lands on my shoulder, and then another wraps around my mouth from behind.

"It's me, little underboss," is whispered in my ear, and I let the fear and tension ease out of my body.

"We have to get going. I got the rat, but the other guy escaped. Possibly for backup. We need to move." I nod up at my friend. His dark brows pulled down low, his eyes darting around to find the best means to slip out undetected.

He reaches his hand out and I slip my hand in his, letting him pull me behind him toward the big roller doors rather than the front door or even the side.

"Are you sure about this? We'll have to hit the roller doors and that'll give us away," I hiss at his giant back as I'm dragged in his wake. Ivan is over a foot taller than I am, so I trot to keep up with his steps. I peek around his large body and see that in a moment we will step out from behind the rows and rows of shipment boxes, into an empty space at the center of the warehouse, a space where we will be in the open, with nowhere to hide.

Ivan frowns down at me, his jaw ticking before giving me a nod, and we make a move. We step into the space and a slow clap echoes through the warehouse. Standing in the middle of the warehouse is Roman. When the hell did he get here?

"Ivan, a surprise to see you here, *drook.*"

Ivan drops my hand, instead moving to rest his large hand on the back of my neck, much like Gus does, but where Gus does it affectionately, Ivan doing it feels wrong.

"Did you think I'd never find out, *brat?* Did you think all those young street urchins you recruited would keep your secrets?" Roman is unmoving, his dead eyes staring at Ivan, unblinking. I have no idea what he's talking about, but surely he can't think that Ivan had something to do with what's going on? I frown at Roman, who hasn't even looked my way, too busy with this stare down. Tipping my head sideways, I flinch slightly when

Ivan's grip tightens. From the corner of my eye, I can see Ivan's cheeks pushed up, a smile on his face.

"Well done, Pakhan. You finally figured something out, huh? Who was it that gave the game away?"

If I didn't know Roman so well, I would think that he was unbothered by Ivan's goading. But I do know him well, and I can see the tension in his jaw as he gives a shrug.

"You may have thought that I had no idea what was happening in my house, Ivan, but I've always known we've had a rat. I just didn't know it was such a big rat," Roman smirks, then reaches his hand forward toward me,

"Come Ana," Ivan's hand tightens around my neck almost uncomfortably before he pushes me forward. I stumble to catch my footing before turning to look at the man who I thought was my protector, my friend.

"Ivan? What the hell? Tell me Roman has it wrong, it's not you. It can't be!" I stare into Ivan's dark eyes, flicking my eyes between both of his, and seeing nothing. No remorse, no guilt. "You're my friend!"

Ivan's rich laugh that I always liked fills the warehouse, before he snaps his gaze to mine, a bitter smile on his face.

"I thought you'd be used to this by now. People moving on without you. Leaving, betraying, ditching you. That's what happens to you, isn't it? People use little Ana to fill a need - friend, employee, daughter, wife. And then they move on with their lives to find something better, or die."

I stand there in the middle of the warehouse, unable to move, blinking my eyes to keep the tears at bay, my heart thudding so hard in my chest that I can hear it. I feel sick and betrayed and angry and so very hurt that it takes my breath away. He's right though, isn't he?

I feel a large hand wrap around mine and looking down; I recognize Roman's pinky ring as he tugs me back toward him, my feet moving without me telling them to. I have no control over anything other than my spiraling thoughts.

"Ivan?" Turning to the voice, I see Savage and Dex standing side by side. I don't even remember hearing their bikes or seeing them arrive. The noise in my head clears enough for me to notice the similarities between Dex and Ivan now they're standing only a few feet from each other.

"Ah, little brother! How is my father and your whore mother?" Ivan grits out, seeming to take glee in the murderous look on Dex's face. "I wondered when I'd see you again. I had thought it would be sooner than this. At your funeral, perhaps? But yebat, you Death Riders are a lot harder to kill than you look."

Dex turns an unnatural shade of red. He takes a step forward but freezes in his tracks once Roman bursts into laughter, then halts.

"I remember when you first arrived on the Bratva's doorstep. Crying to my father about your sad life. How daddy didn't want you now he had a son with his new wife. But it wasn't your father that refused to let you visit him, it was your whore mother. A woman who opened her legs for all the Bratva men. So my father took you in, and you pledged your loyalty."

"My mother did what she did to survive after his mother took her place!" Ivan yells, spittle flying. "And I may have pledged my loyalty, but that was to your father. Not the soft faggot who took his place. A man too fucking dumb to see what's in front of him."

"I don't know about that brat. I did put a stop to Kovalev's business both here and in the motherland," Roman replies, in an almost bored tone.

"Did you, though?" A sick smile grows on Ivan's face until I can see his pointy incisors.

What the actual fuck? This is not the man I know. This is not my friend, this is some imposter. I still can't make sense of anything that is going on.

"What was your plan? Work alongside Hammer, making big money doing despicable things? Try to get rid of your brother because you're pissed you never got to see your dad? What the hell Ivan?" My voice is high pitched by the time I finish my sentence, I'm not sure if it's panic or hysteria.

"My plan is to destroy you all. And you, in your naivety and 'friendship', helped me more than you'll ever know." He says so simply, and I just can't anymore. I turn my back on him and catch Roman's eye. His brows furrow when he sees my face, his lips thin before he tips his chin, indicating I get out of here. When I don't move, his gaze lifts to Savage, standing a little way behind me, gun trained on Ivan.

"Savage, get your man to take Ana to her car, please." A simple nod and Dex steps forward, not before spitting at Ivan on the way past, Ivan wiping his little brother's saliva off his face with his sleeve, laughing like this is all a joke. Dex gently wraps a hand around my bicep and leads me out to my car.

"Hey, you all good to drive? Do you need me to follow you?" I shake my head, then look at the man. Knowing what I know now, I can see why he was so familiar to me. He's a leaner, darker version of Ivan. "Ok. Well, um, you get on now and don't listen to what he said. He's always had a fucking nasty way with words." He huffs and shrugs his shoulders, suddenly looking like a little boy.

"Um, are you ok? I mean, it's not everyday you find out your brother is working to kill you."

He gives me a sad smile. "It's not the first time he's tried." The shock must show on my face because he gives me a sympathetic smile before taking my key fob from me, unlocking my door and giving me a gentle push to get in. "Are you sure you don't want me to follow you home?"

"No, I'll be good. Thanks, Dex." I give him a weak smile, shut my door, take a deep breath and start the engine. He bangs twice on the car roof, making me jump before he gives me a finger salute, and I drive away from the warehouse, and my friend. Even thinking about Ivan makes the tears prickle my eyes, my throat getting thick. I grip the steering wheel tight to stop my hands from shaking, but my chest is pounding with pain as I think about his words. His words, that I should be used to this. My entire life has been people moving on. People leaving me. People using me and then finding a better kid, or a better shag, or a better girlfriend. My breathing is coming in pants as I pull into Gus's driveway and I need to get the fuck out of here. I need to get away, just head up into the woods and take stock of everything. Yes, I know I could go to Gus or Mum, but I need to be alone right now. I just need to go.

I rush inside, not even bothering to turn on all the lights. I run straight to the garage to grab some of my outdoor gear, taking it out to my car and shoving it in the trunk before heading back inside to mine and Gus's room to pack some clothes. I stand in the doorway, breathing in the scent of Gus, before I shake it off, take my bag out of the walk-in-wardrobe and throw in the clothes I'll need before taking one last look at our room, closing the door behind me. Walking into the kitchen, I contemplate leaving Gus a note. But what the hell would I say? Thinking better of it, I take my bag and step out onto the porch.

"What are you doing?"

Tuesday's voice makes me jump, my hand coming to my chest as my heart thunders. I do a quick mental check of my panties to make sure I didn't wet or shit them.

"Jesus Dayz! What the fuck!? You almost scared me to death! What the hell are you doing?" I squint at her in the low light.

"I'm just asking what you're doing," she shrugs at me.

"Just packing for a trip is all," I answer her, trying to dodge her gaze, which is unusually laser focussed on me.

"You're leaving, aren't you?" I drop my head and let out a breath before looking at my sister-in-law.

"What makes you think that?"

She lets out a sigh before flopping down on the porch steps, shaking her head side to side. "Ana, a lot of people underestimate me. Don't be one of them."

Frowning at her, I cough to clear the thickness in my throat. "What do you mean?"

"You think I can't see what's going on? You've enjoyed my family, but you've always kept a little bit of distance from everyone. Especially from Gus. I thought that was just a quirk of yours, but it's not. It's you not wanting to be friends or family with anyone. Not really. Why?"

She stares at me with her unnerving gaze before it flits off to something over my shoulder.

I move toward where she's sitting and take a seat on the steps with her, but down a step and right up in the corner. I know she's not much a fan of touching people other than her family and Rhodie.

"You know I grew up in care, yeah?" she nods and then motions for me to continue.

"When you never know where you're going to be from one

night to the next, it makes it hard to make friends. Will they be there tomorrow? Will my foster parents? I guess it's just easier to not get attached. And if you do, you leave before they can leave you."

"That makes sense. Leave and hurt them first rather than let them hurt you." She nods and goes to stand.

"Wait! That's not what I'm doing!"

"Sure it is." She gives another emphatic nod.

I clear my throat, looking at the dimming sky. "Tonight I found out who betrayed the Bratva. I–it was Ivan. My friend. Except he wasn't my friend. And that hurt Dayz. I don't want to be hurt anymore. By anyone. I'm leaving to stop myself from being hurt."

"And hurting Gus and the rest of us at the same time."

"No! That's not what I'm–"

"Yeah it is. It's ok. I get it. But I have a question."

My shoulders slump. I never thought about hurting anyone. I look up at Tuesday, her wide whiskey eyes staring down at me.

"Why, if you have a chance at having love and a family, would you run away from it?"

I swallow loudly, open my mouth and no words come out. I don't know what to say. When she puts it that way, it doesn't make any sense.

Tuesday lets out an impatient sigh before sitting down again. "When I was a kid, no one liked me."

"I'm sure that's not–"

"It's true. For show and tell, I'd do full presentations about the Bermuda Triangle. Anyway, I share my birthday with Gus. Every year we would have a party and I would get sick of Gus's friends always taking up all the seats. One year, I asked my mom if I could have my party on a different day, so I could invite kids from my class. She kept putting me off but, in the end, she relented. My birthday came, and no one came to my party. My mom made a big thing out of maybe putting the wrong date on the invites, but I knew it was because I had no friends. I thought a party would help me make them, but it didn't. So, when I ended up at the MC and they liked me, I had a real chance at making friends, and there was nothing that was going to stop me from grabbing that opportunity with both hands. I now have two best friends AND an ol man. If I had gone back to hanging out by myself and doing what I always did, I wouldn't have everything that I have now."

I look at Tuesday as she stares into my eyes, as if she needs to communicate her message without words, even though her words hit the bullseye. She raises her eyebrows before her gaze flits away again.

"Thank you, Tuesday." I stand and walk to my car, removing some things I had packed.

"Shit, I didn't think that was going to work." Tuesday's comment pulls a chuckle from me. "So, you're staying then?" I turn to look at the quirky, loving woman on my steps.

"I'm not leaving. But I do need to spend a weekend in nature to think and center myself again."

I can see her thinking about this before she nods abruptly. "Yes. Nature is your version of my closet. I will make sure Gus is ok while you're away. I'll tell him it's only for a short time and you will be back."

She stands and strides toward her cabin with purpose before tripping and then spinning back to me.

"I would miss you if you left. So, maybe don't do that."

"Thank you, Dayz." She tilts her head at me, a slight pinch

between her brows, before shrugging, then turns to head into her cabin, gently closing the bright yellow door behind her.

## Gus

I know I should head home, and I will, just not right now. I need to figure out a way to fix things with Ana, and I have nothing. What I do have is a beer in front of me, sitting on the bartop of the DRMC clubhouse, dripping in condensation and I havent taken one sip. Instead I have picked the bulk of the label off and left it in little pieces on the bartop.

"Ok. I get why the fuck your brothers are still here. Jules is with Fox and Nitro, doing whatever debauched shit they get up to. Tav is, well, I actually never know why Tav is here." Marx looks thoughtful for a moment.

"I just put it down to being the youngest. He doesn't do well alone. And I think he enjoys spending time with guys who don't rag on him like me and Jules do." I shrug.

"I thought Chewy's the youngest?"

"She is. I mean, I love my baby sister, more than anything, but we all know she doesn't fit into the usual birth order psychology."

"Or any other psychology, for that matter," I hear Marx mumble out. I snort under my breath. He may grumble about Dayz, but I know for a fact he loves her like a little sister.

"Anyway, that still doesn't answer my question. Why the hell is your big ass sitting at my bar looking like someone kicked your puppy?" Marx rasps out. I let out a sigh, running my hand over my face.

"Ana –"

"Ah, say no more. She's skittish, that one." Marx taps twice on the bar and a beer magically appears.

"How did you know?" He takes a pull of his beer, raising his thick dark eyebrow at me like I'm an idiot, before swallowing and thumping his beer down on the bar.

"You can smell it on her. Yeah, she comes across as in control, efficient, take no shit. But, if you look past that, there's a little girl always waiting for the other shoe to drop."

"And that, Marx, is the problem. How do I convince her that short of dying, I'll always be with her? I can't imagine being anywhere else."

He looks thoughtful for a moment, then the front door bangs open and both of us swivel to see Roman standing in the doorway, fixing his cufflinks, oddly flanked by Savage and Dex. He looks up at us with a bored look on his face before stepping into the room.

"Ah, just the gentlemen I needed to see."

"Ah, fuck. If this prick has turned up, we got bigger problems than I thought." Marx grumbles out before hefting his bulk off his bar stool and tipping his head toward church, instead of his office, although given the size of Marx, myself, Roman, Savage and Dex, his office may have been a little closer than we all would have liked. I mean, I get along well with these guys, but I don't want to share a leather couch pressed up against any of them.

"Take a seat and tell me what new shit storm is about to hit." Marx gestures at us as he flops down into the Pres chair at the head of the table.

I watch Roman look around at us all before his eyes land on me for a beat too long before he turns back to Marx.

"As we all know, Hammer has been quite the thorn in our sides, what with trying to kill you all." Roman waves his hand toward us all and I see Marx's jaw clench beneath his impressive beard. "And fucking with my shipments, which until this evening was a minor annoyance that I could handle."

"What happened this evening? Wait, where the fuck is Ana? She was meant to meet you two there," I point at Savage and Dex.

"Ana is safe, Gus. I sent her home before anything big went down," Roman says, holding my eye contact. He's a scary bastard and I'm never too sure whether you can truly trust him, but I know he loves Ana and if he says she's safe, then I know I can take his word for it. I give him a nod to continue. "This evening it was brought to my attention that two greedy motherfuckers struck up a friendship of sorts to destroy us all." He rests his hands on the table, fingers spread, the knuckles crusted over with blood.

"So you found your rat then?" I ask him, knowing that Ana will be relieved.

"I did. It was a big fucking rat with no loyalty and a hatred for my marriage." Roman is a cold-hearted bastard. I know this. He's the type of man that you don't want to meet in a dark alley. Whoever the rat is, hurt him. Not physically, but I'm guessing they're close, trusted. And whatever was said about Roman's marriage to Sasha has hit a sore point with him. Fuck. I don't really want to know, but if it's someone high up, Ana will be devastated.

"Who?" I lean forward and notice that my breath has hitched, waiting for Roman to answer. Surprisingly, it's Dex that breaks the silence.

"Ivan," My heads whips to look at him, fuck. This is bad.

"Ivan? Ana's friend? That big, dark-haired bastard? He always struck me as pretty solid. Why the fuck would he buddy up with Hammer?" Marx asks the room, as confused as I am.

Savage and Dex share a look that doesn't go unnoticed by Marx, who leans forward, glaring at the pair.

Dex clears his throat. "Ivan is my estranged brother. He's 10 years older than me. We share the same father, different mothers. He's hated me my whole life. Tried killing me on a couple of occasions when I was a kid, and then about 20 years ago he just up and left. Haven't seen or heard from him since. Until tonight."

"Well, fuck,"

Roman nods in agreement. "Exactly what I thought."

"So, what? Hammer and Ivan form an alliance. Hammer gets rid of the Death Riders, taking out DRMC in the process. Then Ivan pays him in drugs and weapons from your stocks?" Marx asks, leaning back in his chair. "Doesn't sound like it's worth the trouble on Hammer's end. Especially with the number of nomads we've gotten rid of."

"That alone isn't. But when I clipped Kovalev's wings, and we shut down his skin trade, it would seem that Hammer and Ivan stepped in to take over the gap in the market."

"That's not all," Savage speaks up, his fists clenching and unclenching. "The girls they're selling, they're making them smuggle Roman's drugs inside their bodies."

I expect a big show of anger from Marx. Usually, he'd yell or throw something. Instead, he drops his chin to his chest, rubbing his hands over his face a couple of times while cursing under his breath.

"How do we put a stop to this?" He looks at the men around the table, waiting for someone, anyone, to have a plan.

"Ivan has been dispatched already. We only need to deal with Hammer and his MC." Roman says, his face as stoic as ever, not giving away the fact that this evening he killed one of his most trusted men.

Dex clears his throat. "I'd also like to try to find as many of those girls as we can. I know it'll be a fucking impossible task, but I have to undo the shit my brother has done to them."

Marx nods his head in agreement. "Fuck yes. Goes without saying. You'll have Wire, Chewy and Remy at your disposal."

"You have Tombs Security as well. Whatever you need that may help, let us know." I let all the men know, because shit, this isn't something any of us can let slide.

Roman stands as he claps his hands together. "I will clean my house of Ivan's filth, and my scientists will track all traces of my drugs. Perhaps we'll be able to get a lock on where some of these girls may be. Thank you men, I knew this would be a beneficial meeting." Without a word or even a look back, he exits church, whistling as if he doesn't have a care in the world.

"I really hate that guy," Marx says to no one in particular, causing us to chuckle.

"Ok, there's not a lot we can do right at this minute. Savage, you and your men head home to your families. I'll let Wire and Chewy know what we're looking for. Let's agree to both work on finding that Hammer motherfucker. I'm looking forward to handing his ass over to Chewy, if I'm being honest."

"She's a scary woman," Savage says, before darting his eyes at me "No offense man,"

"None taken. You haven't even seen her at her worst. Or best. Although there's not much in it either way." Savage lets out a snort before he and Dex stand to leave, fist bumping me and Marx on their way out. Marx waits until both men are out of earshot before speaking again.

"We got a lot more shit coming our way,"

"Yup."

"I know you offered your help, but if you wanna cut out on this one, you can. This time might not be like last time with Kraykowski and the rest. This time, we may have to do some nasty shit." Marx's dark eyes hold mine. I know he's giving me an out.

The shit that we went through together last time was a necessity. It involved my sister. This time ... this isn't something I'm going to walk away from. Those girls? Those are other people's sisters, daughters, wives and mothers.

"Listen man, I get it. But you need to get that earlier on in the week we were out there shooting nomads with the rest of you. Not to mention I've spent the last few years cleaning up my sisters 'messes'. I think the time to get out has long since passed."

A grin stretches across Marx's face. "Yeah, I guess you got a point there, man. I can't interest you in a patch, can I?"

I huff out a laugh. "Nah. Not for me. Ask Tav maybe, he's always liked wearing matching outfits," I throw back my head and laugh while Marx gives me the finger and tells me to "Fuck off".

"Yeah, yeah, I'm going. I've got a woman to check on. She's going to be devastated over Ivan."

He nods "Let her know we all got her back."

"Will do. Thanks, Marx."

I head out to my SUV and on the drive home think of all the things I can do to help Ana. I could call Debs, but from Pops' text to "Leave them the fuck alone" I know that it'll be less painful to just try to nut this one out myself. At the last minute,

I pull into the grocery store to pick up ice cream. Once me and my 6 flavors of ice cream are loaded up, I drive home and prepare myself for a grovel.

Pulling into my drive, I see Dayz and Rhodie sitting on my porch swing, Rhodie's long legs swaying it back and forth while Dayz's legs are swinging in the air, too short to reach the floor.

"Ah, hey guys. You know I love you both, but can you clear off my porch?"

"Nope. We are here to comfort you." Dayz says, not even looking at me.

"Um, ok. Thanks for that. I need you to comfort me. Why?"

"Oh, because Ana left. She's gone." Dayz says, shrugging her shoulders, like it's an everyday occurrence. I blink once, then twice, trying to take in what the fuck is happening.

"Dayz, I know this isn't in your wheelhouse, but can you please back up a little and tell me again what the fuck is going on?" I take a couple of deep breaths to center myself.

"Ana was upset when she came home earlier. I caught her packing up all her stuff. We had a very good chat. About feelings. Then she left."

"Not sure where she went, Gus, but maybe Roman will know. They're close." Rhodie says, and thank fuck for him because love her as I do, Dayz is goddamn useless at times.

"Yeah, good thinking. Thanks man, I'll call him now."

"Oh yeah, by. The. Way..." Dayz words start slowing and slurring a little as Rhodie drops kisses on her bare shoulder "Don't worry, I'll tell you later," It's nice they love each other but I'm not in the mood to watch them make out when my Wife is off somewhere else. I squint at Rhodie and then tip my head for them to go home.

Dialling Roman's number as I watch Rhodie pull my sister

up off the porch swing, slapping his big hand on my shoulder, squeezing it before leading Dayz back to her place.

"Ah August, I wondered when I was going to hear from you," Roman's accented voice croons down the line.

"Where is she Roman?"

"Where is who?"

Taking a deep breath, I try not to unload a barrage of curse words down the line at him, knowing full well if I did, he'd be an asshole and not tell me what I need to know.

"Where is my wife Roman? I need to make sure she's OK." I hold my breath and I'm sure I can hear Sasha in the background.

"Fine. She's staying in the small forest block I own. It's a 2 hour drive from here,"

Of course, he owns a fucking forest. Checking my watch, if I get on the road now, I'll be able to be with her before midnight.

"Thank you, Roman! I owe you o–"

"Gus? It's a 6 hour hike from the road. You'd be better off packing up tonight and walking in tomorrow when it's light. Oh, and take a tent. Knowing her, she would have taken her one-man tent. I'll send you the coordinates. Have fun, drook." I'm sure I hear the fucker snort before he hangs up on me. I look at the phone in my hand for a moment before letting out a breath and doing exactly what Roman told me to do. I ready all the shit I took camping last time, get into bed, and set the alarm for first light. Buckle up baby, I'm coming for you, and when I find you I'm going to put you over my knee and pinken that fine ass because you fucking hiked 6 hours in the dark to god knows where.

# Chapter 19

Ana

I relax into the soft cushions of the rocker, sitting on the porch of Roman's retreat, and thank the stars once again that I have such an amazing friend. And one that is filthy rich. When I took off from Gus' place last night, I called Roman. I told him I needed to use his woodland retreat to factory reset myself after all the shit that went down yesterday. Thankfully, he talked me out of doing the 6 hour hike and instead had his helicopter meet me at the small clearing where we park our cars. I mean, not that I wouldn't have been able to handle that hike in the dark, but as someone who grew up having bush survival drilled into her, night hikes are just asking for trouble.

Arriving last night meant that I could get up with the warm spring sun, and sit and clear my head on the big flat rock a short walk from Roman's log cabin. It overlooks the river that runs through the property, and listening to the sound of nature, the water trickling through, gave me a sense of peace that I desperately needed.

Last night I spent tossing and turning, kicking myself over

not seeing what was right in front of me. How could I not see that one of my closest friends, someone I could rely on through thick or thin, was a snake this whole time? My stomach was in knots as I replayed every interaction we had over and over, asking myself if maybe I listened more, or perhaps I spent more time with him, things may have been different.

But this morning, sitting on that rock with a blanket wrapped around my shoulders and a steaming hot cup of tea by my side, I realized it wasn't my fault that I didn't see his intentions or character earlier. How could I? People allow you to see what they want you to see. He hid himself from me, and worse still, from Roman.

So I sat there, waiting for the sun to climb higher in the sky and by the time the warmth reached my face I realized I could sit on that rock and wallow in the betrayal, add him to the list of people I've lost in my life and close my heart off for safekeeping, or, I could brush it off and let the feelings blow away into the wind.

And that's what I did. I had to. Because I may have lost one friend in Ivan, but I still had Jenn and every other loyal friend I've made since I've been here.

When I spoke to Roman, he told me he and Sasha had just returned from breaking the news to Jenn. As far as Jenn knows, Ivan was killed in the line of work, a single gunshot wound to the head. The funeral will be arranged after the ME releases his body, and she will need all of us to help her through this time, no matter our feelings for her husband. Which for me, will remain complicated for a little while yet.

I tip the rocker back, using my toe to push against the warm wood of Roman's porch before kicking off my Uggs and tucking my feet up underneath me, letting the movement soothe me. I may have sorted one lot of feelings out on that big, flat rock, but now I'm consumed by other feelings. Guilt for how I left last night. Guilt for turning off my phone after speaking to my mum and Roman. Guilt for not calling Gus and letting him know what was going on. How the hell am I going to make this up to him? Last night I was a bitch and then ran without a word. I know my husband. He'll be going out of his mind with worry, and it's my fault. I can only hope Dayz or Roman passed on the message that I'm only going to be away for two days, but you can never be too sure and if I turn on my phone to call him I'm certain I'll see missed calls from him and I'll feel even shittier for what I've done to the poor man. Argh!

I angrily pick at the fluff on my comfy sweatpants when a clanging noise breaks through the sounds of the bush. Looking up, I can see birds leaving one tree for another further away. I put down my fifth cup of tea in as many hours, standing and shoving my feet into my Uggs to see if I can get a better idea on what the hell is making that god awful racket.

The clanging sound seems to get louder and closer. It's clearly not an animal because there is no reason an animal would be that bloody loud in its own habitat. Twigs snapping now join the metallic sound, which is actually quite rhythmic, as if it's something swinging back and forth.

"Fuck's sake!" The expletive is growled out and my knees can't hold me up. I plop down into the rocker, my hands coming up to my mouth. I recognize that growl. My eyes are glued to the small, barely there path that cuts through the trees. Another growl breaks the silence and I watch with rapt attention as my big, handsome, growly husband steps into the clearing, wearing his ridiculously new and shiny hiking gear, a stupidly large hiking pack on his back. His metal drink bottle and cup are swinging from a side strap, knocking against each other.

My eyes devour the sight of him. Here, 6 hours from the road, through dense wood where he has obviously walked to find me. He scowls at something on his leg before he glances up, locking eyes with me. He freezes. The only thing moving is the ticking of his jaw. Judging by the look on his face, he's unsure whether he should sweep me up or tan my hide. Or both.

He stands stock still, not moving, but that's ok because I realized something when I was on that rock this morning. Gus has made all the moves in this relationship, and I've spent the whole time working out exit strategies. I convinced myself that I was going to have to walk away to keep my heart intact. But I could never do it. I love him. I am in love with my husband. And instead of being a pussy, as Pops would say, I'm going to be the badass bitch that ran the Bartashev Bratva, for an albeit short time, and I'm going to make the next move. I'm going to take what I want, consequences be damned. And what I want is August Tombs and all the crazy that comes with him.

Holding Gus's gaze, I slowly stand, stepping off the porch, one step at a time, until my feet hit the ground. We hold each other's gaze and then I'm running. My legs pump, the distance between us shrinks until I launch myself at him, and, because it's Gus and he is the most in control, dependable man I've ever met, he catches me.

# Gus

She comes flying at me, landing in my arms, exactly where she belongs. I can't even begin to describe the feelings coursing through my body. Relief that she's here, safe. The anger that she put herself at risk hiking 6 hours in the fucking dark; we will be having a conversation about that. And love. I love this woman so fucking much and even though she put me through hell the past 12 hours; she ran to me. To trust me with her heart. To catch her. The feeling of her here, in my arms, feels like heaven. Well, almost. I'd feel a lot fucking better having her in my arms if they weren't half dead thanks to straps of my pack digging into my shoulders.

"Babe, as much as I love holding you, I need to put you down and get this fucking pack off my back. And these fucking boots off my feet." She pulls back to look at me, her eyes glistening and a huge grin on her face. She loosens her grip on me and I place her on her feet before unhooking my arms and dropping the pack that holds all my camping supplies and enough snacks to last 3 weeks.

I drop it on the ground, and then for the first time take in my surroundings.

"What the fuck?!" I vaguely noticed Ana sitting on a porch, but my eyes were locked on my wife, not the fucking opulent log cabin with an entire wall of windows. "I thought you were out here camping?"

Ana turns to look at the house behind her before shrugging her shoulders. "I usually do. I packed my tent, but Roman offered me the house and a ride up here because of the late hour."

"Wait, what? A ride? So you didn't fucking hike 6 hours in the dark?" She frowns at me before answering.

"No. Roman had his helicopter pick me up in the clearing next to the car park."

"Helicopter." At this point, I'm just repeating what she's saying.

"Um, yeah. There's a helipad at the back of the house. Wait, didn't you talk to Roman? I thought that's how you would have found me?"

I stare at her for a moment and in my mind curse Roman in every swear word I know. That motherfucker.

"Roman is the one who told me where to find you. He also told me it would be best to spend last night at home and then start the 6 hour hike up here at first light. The Russian prick." I watch as humor dances in her eyes, her lips pulled between her teeth as she tries not to laugh.

She leans sideways to take a good look at my pack before straightening up and looking up at me.

"Did you bring your tent?"

I let out a long sigh, my eyes closing. "Yeah, I was planning on camping with you until you were ready to come back home."

Ana's eyes drop to our feet, before looking up at me, glittering with unshed tears. Her tiny hand reaches up and cups my cheek, allowing me to nuzzle into her.

"Oh Gus, my brave, beautiful husband." She whispers out. My eyes open and I stare down at her.

"Ana, my brave, beautiful wife," I whisper back. A tear slides down her cheek and I brush it away with my thumb. I drop my forehead to hers, breathing in her sweet scent. I then realize the more pungent smell overpowering hers would be me. I drop a quick kiss to her lips before pulling away.

"Babe, as much as I want to stand here and ravage you, I really need to get inside and take a shower. I fucking reek." She pulls back from me, throwing her head back in laughter.

"Ok, lemme show you around, then you take a shower and we will do some ravaging," she giggles as she takes my hand and pulls me along behind her up the steps and into Roman's cabin. It's fucking beautiful and tranquil and it makes me hate the guy even more that he made me hike up here. Even so, it was worth every fucking step when I saw the shock and awe in Ana's face that I was here. For her.

I stop in my tracks, tugging on her hand, pulling her to a stop. She turns to look at me and, as relieved as I am to be here, there's still some shit that needs to be taken care of.

"You ran from me, Ana. You left without a word. Do you know how much that hurt me? Do you know how worried I was? Wondering if you were coming back or if you were hurt somewhere?"

She furrows her brows, guilt written all over her face, as she dips her eyes and looks at her feet.

"Gus, I - I'm so sorry. I was all twisted up about counseling and Ivan and it was all too much." She peers up at me with those brilliant green eyes, and I know I can't hold it against her. Where her trauma has led her to run, mine has led me to hold on too tight. Maybe if we work on it together, we can meet somewhere in the middle.

"I understand baby, just next time, leave a note, yeah?" She bobs her head at me and her lips curl on the edges. "And don't think you won't be punished, Wife. I'm going to redden that ass for every time I pictured my life without you in it, for every time I sniffed your pillow trying to draw your scent into my lungs because you weren't in my arms. You owe me that much,

Ana." She brings my hand up to her lips, kissing my knuckles with her lush lips.

"I owe you much more than that," she whispers before she turns and leads me into the master bedroom. Two walls are lined with floor to ceiling windows. The view is breathtaking, and yet I'm finding it hard to tear my eyes away from Ana. She leads me into the giant ensuite and I have to admit to myself that I cannot wait to get in there and wash away 6 hours of dust, dirt, and nature. The shower takes up one entire wall with so many shower heads. I have no idea how to work them all, but Ana does, so she sets everything up for me, allowing the water to warm.

Without a word, she tugs at the bottom of my Henley, running her hands up my sides before helping me remove it and throwing it on the floor somewhere behind me. She kneels at my feet and unlaces my boots, giving me time to kick them off to the same place my shirt went. She unbuttons my pants, the ones the man sold me, made of some type of breathable material that makes an annoying "swishy" sound as I walk. She tugs them down, taking my boxers with her, ignoring my hardening cock as it points directly at her, wanting to say hello. She pulls everything down to my ankles, allowing me to step out of them and then she stands, gathers up my clothing and stops in front of me with my stinking bundle of gear in her hands. She looks at me, chewing on her bottom lip a little.

"I've turned on the massage jets. You shower, Gus, and I'll take care of this. I'll be waiting for my punishment in the bedroom," she averts her eyes, looking coy, and my dick goes from half mast to full. Well, as spectacular as this shower is, I don't think I'll be lingering, especially knowing what waits for me on the other side of the door.

I rush through washing myself, barely letting the 5000 jets massage my aching muscles. I may be city fit, but getting up at dawn, driving two hours to the clearing and then hiking 6 hours has left me tired and sore in places I didn't even know I could be. Roman, that Russian asshole, is definitely going to pay for this. Stepping out of the shower, I dry myself roughly with the towel Ana left for me, wrapping it around my waist as I step out into the bedroom, and then I freeze.

Sitting naked at the end of the bed is my wife. Her long, black hair is loose, tumbling over her shoulders, flowing down to the middle of her back. My cock is hard enough to pound nails, resting against my belly. Ana is a fucking beautiful sight that has my cock leaking like a faucet. I take two deep breaths to calm myself down. If I can't get myself under control, then this punishment will be over before it begins.

I stand in front of Ana, letting my towel drop. I draw my finger down her cheek, under her chin before tipping her face up to mine, letting her see how much I want her.

"I'm going to spank that luscious ass of yours." I hold her gaze and her eyes flutter closed before opening and staring into the depths of my soul. Fuck. Closing my eyes, I tip my head back, rolling my shoulders and breathing out, before meeting her gaze again.

"Do you have anything to say, baby?"

"I'm sorry."

I raise my brow at her. "What for?"

She gulps, "I'm sorry that I got scared and upset and I ran away from you. I'm sorry I didn't talk to you about it. I'm sorry that you were worried. I-I'm just, sorry," her voice tapers off to a whisper at the end. I kiss her softly before pulling back.

"Because you apologized so sweetly, I'm going to feed you

my cock before I spank you. Would you like that?" She bobs her head at me, holding my gaze as she slides off the bed onto her knees, licking her lips. Shit, I might be punishing myself more than I'm punishing her right now.

"Open wide and stick your tongue out." She's fucking perfect and does exactly as I say, her pink tongue sticking out, waiting for me. I pump myself twice, angling my cock head just above her, watching as I drip onto her pretty pink tongue. She makes a groaning noise at the back of her throat and I watch as she swallows what I've given her before sticking her tongue out again, eager and waiting. I decide to tease her a little, slapping her cheeks gently with my dripping dick, before slowly feeding him into her hot, wet mouth. She wraps those pretty lips around me and sucks me with so much vigor my eyes cross.

Between the suction of her mouth and her tongue working up and down my shaft, I'm worried I won't last long. I cup her gorgeous face in my hands before running my fingers back through her hair, pulling it away from her face so I have the perfect view of her, her gaze holding mine as she works my cock with her mouth. I'm shallowly thrusting my hips, I don't want to go too deep and hurt her, but that seems to be the least of her worries as she pulls off my dick, smirks up at me and then dives back on, taking me so deep that her nose nestles into the hair at the base of my cock. I let out a groan when I feel her tongue wriggling on my balls and her fingers tugging at them. I can feel the telltale tingle in my balls and the base of my back, but I'm not coming down her throat. The only place I'm coming is in her tight, pink heat.

I pull back from her, staring at her, the saliva on her face, her cheeks flushed, her eyes dazed. Fuck, my wife is going to ruin me. I sit on the edge of the bed, watching her as she wipes her drool and my pre-cum off her face.

"Stand up baby. I need you over my knee. Give me that pretty ass." She does exactly what I say, rising to her feet so gracefully before coming to stand in front of me. I stare at the cleft between her legs, her pretty pussy topped with her trimmed dark landing strip, and I see the unmistakable glistening of her folds. She places herself over my knee, the top of her body resting on the bed, her ass in the air, the tangy scent of her perfuming the room. I run my hand over her generous globes before landing two swift, firm spanks. She lets out a squeak, her ass clenching before relaxing, the pink handprints creating a burn before I rub it out.

"I'm going to spank you ten times, baby. I think that's a fair punishment, don't you?" I hear her murmured "Yes" so I land all ten blows in quick succession before kneading the burn out of her plump ass.

Using both hands, I spread her cheeks apart, looking down to see her glistening pussy peeking out from between her luscious thighs. I let a string of saliva drip out of my mouth onto her pussy, and using one hand to keep her ass spread, I massage my spit into her folds, dipping my thick finger into her, teasing her slightly before pulling back. She's so fucking wet for me and I know she's aching. But she hasn't earned my cock yet, or hell, even her orgasm. Not yet. I continue to tease, running my finger through her lips, pulsing in and out of her as she writhes in my lap, pushing her ass back at me every time I pump in.

"That's it, little wife. Take what I'm giving you. I want you to spill all over my fingers, get them nice and wet."

"Gus, I need you," she moans at me, but she's not getting what she wants just yet.

I tease her a little more, adding another finger, wriggling

them in her channel, her juices squelching at my movements. Her whines let me know she's getting close, so I pull back, running my soaking fingers around the outside of her lips, massaging her plump cheeks, letting her come down a little before diving back in and starting the teasing again. I do this over and over, whispering filthy things to her, letting her know she deserves everything I'm giving her, but she doesn't deserve to come until I say so. I twist my fingers inside her so I can rub that rough patch of skin inside her. She bucks up in my lap, ass high enough in the air for me to drop down and lick her little back hole, puckering under my attention.

"Please Gus, please let me come!" She begs, twisting in my lap so she's looking at me over her shoulder, her cheeks flushed, hair stuck to her face, eyes wild, lips parted.

She's so fucking beautiful. I lean back, wrapping one hand gently around her throat so that she's looking at me dead on, and pump my fingers brutally.

"Never again, Ana. Please, never run from me again."

Her eyes roll back a little, her mouth hanging open. I pull my fingers from her and slap her ass before shoving them back in.

"N-never. I promise." She licks her lips, and I feel her swallow before she closes her eyes. I can feel how close she is, so I bring her to the precipice of her orgasm before letting her go, lifting her off my lap, and placing her on the bed on her stomach. Swiftly I kneel over her, my knees on the outside of her legs angling my cock into her glistening hole. Holding steady at her entrance, I lean forward and growl in her ear, "Come, Ana," Then in one smooth thrust, I'm home.

# Chapter 20

Ana

His words growled in my ear along with his thick cock pushing into me has me flying apart, tipping over the edge; fireworks go off behind my eyes and my body convulses under the weight of my husband. All thought flies out of my head as Gus starts pumping into me at a blistering pace. He has his hands gripping my hips, pulling me back onto his cock as he thrusts into me, roughly fucking me harder than I've ever been fucked before and I love it. I love how he's taking his anger out on my body in the best of ways. The deliciousness of his hands on my skin, his sweat dripping on my back, him inside me. I'm consumed by Gus and it all feels so right. He pulls out of me, moves to the end of the bed, flips me to my back, grabs my ankle, and pulls me until my legs are hanging off the end.

He gives me a feral smirk before placing his hands under my knees and pushing up, folding me in half, my cunt spread wide. He slaps my pussy with his hand and then dives in, this tongue, fingers, lips devouring me. Holy fuck. I've lost the ability to speak. Only moans and grunts escape me, sounding animalistic even to my own ears. In no time at all, the pressure builds in my lower stomach and I'm worried I'm going to pee myself. I wriggle to get away, but Gus isn't having it, using his arms to pin my knees up near my shoulders. He makes a feral growling sound.

"This is your punishment. You're going to fucking take it, all of it." He stares down at me, holding my gaze. I'm panting and my head is fuzzy and I know he wants something from me, but my mind is full of cotton wool. He growls again before landing a slap on my puffy sex once more, clearing the fog from my brain.

"Please, it's too much," I gasp out. "I'm s-sorry, Gus. I won't do it again. Please, let me come!"

He makes a rumbling sound of approval before swiping his tongue from my ass to clit in one long swipe and then doubles down on his efforts. My body feels like a live wire, my chest is heaving at the sensations pinging through me. I'm panting so hard my vision is blurring and just as I'm teetering on the brink for the second time, just about to go over, he unfolds me, straightens, lines up his cock and fucks into me with such force that the damn breaks and I scream, coming all over him, wetness flowing out of me, dripping off the bed.

"Fuck yes baby, fucking drench me in your cum," Gus growls out, before his hips stutter and he lets out a long, low roar, his cock jerking inside me, setting me off again. He pumps his hips gently, moaning, gasping for breath. My legs clamped around him, trembling as my pussy keeps pulsing around him.

Oh. My. God. The release is so big, so huge that all the emotion that has been building up flows from my eyes, tears dripping down into my hair. I feel Gus gently pull himself from me, scooping me up under my arms and placing me higher up the bed until my head is resting on the pillow.

"Shhhh, shhhh baby, it's ok. I'm here and I'll always be here with you. I didn't hurt you, did I?" Gus's hands are on either side of my face, wiping my tears with his thumbs, his soothing voice breaking through all my emotions.

I gaze up at his dark brown gaze, full of worry.

"N–No, you didn't hurt me, I hurt you! I didn't mean to. I'm s–sorry Gus. I'm so sorry," I sputter out. His face softens, his eyes look all melty as he smiles softly at me before pulling me into his powerful arms, my face resting in that yummy space between his shoulder and his jaw.

"Oh baby, I'm fine. I'm good. I hurt you too, by holding on too tight and pushing when I should have given you space. I'm sorry." I lean back to frown at him.

"We can't both be sorry."

"Why not? We both made mistakes. But we know better now. I know to give you space if you need it, and you know not to run at the first sign of a problem. There. Done." He smiles down at me with such certainty that I can't help but smile back. I place my hand on the side of his face and marvel when he leans into my touch. Rubbing his stubble with my thumb, I draw his face down to mine and kiss him, pouring all my emotions and feelings into the kiss.

Gus pulls back from me, then thinks better of it before dropping a kiss to the top of my nose.

"Come on babe, we have cum all over us and in us, and I don't know about you, but I feel like I need to luxuriate in Roman's shower some more." He slaps me on the ass, then goes to jump up off the bed. Instead, a howl erupts from him and he rolls back onto the bed, writhing in pain.

"Gus! Gus, what the hell is happening? What's wrong?" I'm up and leaning over his rolling, rocking body, trying to figure out what's happening. The noises coming from him are pure agony, giving him an inability to speak and it's freaking me the hell out. Do I run and call the chopper? Do I administer first aid? His face is screwed up, all red, and he's panting as he stretches his long, shapely leg straight up in the air, flexing his toes.

"Argh, fuck! Cramp! It burns! Fuck, fuck, fuck!" I watch as his calf almost ripples before the cramping calms, Gus's breathing slowly coming back to normal. He releases a breathy sigh before flopping his arms and legs back on the bed like a starfish. With his soft dick out. While I lean over him, boobs swinging in his face, nipples pointing south and his cum leaking out of me. We are such a mess and I can't help the giggle that bubbles up in my throat. Gus turns his head toward me with a frown and a pout, like a sad little boy, and I can't help it. I absolutely lose it. It doesn't take long before Gus stops pouting, instead rolling his eyes at me, grabbing my boob and giving it a jiggle.

"Yeah, yeah, it's so funny. You hike 6 hours and not get a cramp." He pouts at me one more time before batting his lashes at me. "Can you please help me up, Wife?" I let my giggles subside, then crawl over Gus to get out on his side of the bed.

"Fuck, that's so filthy and hot," I hear him whisper, and I know it's because he's just copped an eyeful of what's leaking out of me. I slide off the bed, stand and offer him my hand, pulling him to standing, my breasts pressed against his lower chest.

"Promise me you'll always be there to help me up after a

hike?" Gus says, smiling down at me.

"Always, my love." I watch the smile slip from his face, replaced with shock and awe.

"Did you just...?"

"I did. I love you, Gus. With everything in me. And I'm not going to lie and say I'm not scared, because I am. I'm fucking terrified that something or someone will take you away from me and I'll never recover. But I'd rather have you for however long I have you for, than never have you at all." I stare into his eyes and watch as they crinkle in the corners until a grin covers his face.

"Ana, I am so fucking in love with you. When," I watch as he swallows, "When I thought I'd lost you, I went mad with grief and anger and blamed myself for wanting you so much that I'd pushed you away." He looks so sad, so I lift the hand in mine to my lips and kiss the back of his knuckles. His other hand cups my face and I lean into his warmth.

"Baby, I need you. I want to wake up with you every morning and go to sleep with you every night. I want to make a life with you, children, a dog, everything. I cannot picture my life without you in it. Nothing and no one will ever tear me away because you are the reason I breathe. It's all you Ana. Without you, there is no me." He pulls me into his chest, his hand cupping the back of my head as I let tears of relief fall. God, I love this man. I fall asleep with visions of a long live together.

## Gus

"Mmph, Gus. Babe, your phone." Small hands shove me until I roll toward the bedside table where my phone is currently jumping around. I'm exhausted after the marathon make up sessions Ana and I have been indulging in. We've been wrapped in a bubble for the past two days, but it looks like that's all coming to an end.

Marx: Enough with the honeymoon. Come and get your fucking family.

I throw my phone on the floor and cover my eyes with my forearm.

"What's wrong? Do we need to go back?"

Soft, little kisses pepper the arm covering my face, so I wrap it around my wife's shoulders and pull her in for a kiss. Morning breath be damned.

"It was Marx. I need to 'come and get my fucking family'." Ana makes a snorting noise, then cuddles closer.

"Well, we probably should head back. I told Dayz I'd be away for two days, and I have been. I don't want her to think I'm a liar."

"Wait, what do you mean you told her two days? When?"

"I saw her when I, um, ran away. I told her to look after you and I'd be back in two days." A long breath leaves me. "She didn't tell you, did she?" I can hear the amusement in Ana's voice.

"No. No, she did not." Ana laughs, then rolls away to the edge of the bed before springing up. I've never seen anyone go from asleep to fully awake and full of pep quite like she does.

"Ok, well then, I'll call Roman for a ride, then I'm going

to pack our stuff and have one last cup of tea on my rock out there." I admire her as she dresses, pulling on her soft, casual clothes. Her hair is all mussed up from the last time we made love. Slow and steady. Breathing each other in, loving each other.

"I'll get our shit ready. You call Roman, then relax baby. I got this." She grins before dancing around to my side of the bed, dropping another kiss on my lips and heading off to make her call.

Going through my bag, I pull on clothes for the first time since I got here. It's been nice spending naked time with my wife, but now it's time for revenge. I check to see where Ana is. She's outside, walking around, talking on the phone, a big smile on her face. Quietly searching the house I find the laundry, and our clothes that we never got around to washing. My hiking laundry is in there and it's exactly what I need.

Picking up my worn socks, underclothes, and t-shirt, I bring them to my nose before gagging a little. These will do nicely. Roman will learn not to fuck with a Tombs. I giggle like a little girl as I stuff my gross clothes in little hidey holes all around Roman's luxurious cabin. Take that asshole.

"Babe! How're you getting on?" Ana's voice calls out, so I run back to the master room and start throwing shit into our bags. She wanders in, leaning on the doorjamb as she watches me. "Our ride will be here in 20. Meet you on the rock when you're done?"

"Sure thing baby, I'm almost done here, anyway." She spins on her tip toes before flouncing off down the hall. It's amazing the change I can see in her. From that one small act of hiking all the way here, showing her I am all in, that I will fight for her; she's a different person. More relaxed, more open. Shit, maybe Roman did me a favour after all? I think of all my manky stuff stinking up the place.

Fuck it. He may have gotten this one thing right, but he's still a dick.

I grab our stuff and lug it out the front, following the track to the helipad where I dump it all on the ground. Gazing around me, all I can see in every direction is the large wood that Roman owns. The sounds of nature fill my senses almost to the brim. Looking back toward the house, I can see Ana on the large, flat rock, a sense of peace surrounding her. I follow the path back down, heading to my wife. Lowering myself down behind her, I pull her into the V of my legs. She leans her weight against my chest, taking my hands in hers, guiding my arms to wrap around her.

"I love you, little wife,"

"And I love you, massive husband." I let out a chuckle, then bury my nose in her hair, relishing the smell and feel of her as the sound of chopper blades gets closer.

"Time to go home, Gus."

* * *

I stand looking at the four dumbasses, and my mother-in-law, in front of me, all looking varying degrees of guilty. Well, ok, maybe only Tav and Debs do. The other three Tombs are staring at me like the assholes they are.

"Does anyone, anyone at all, want to explain to me why the hell Marx has summoned me, not so politely, to 'come and get your fucking family'," I use my fingers to indicate the exact words Marx used to describe them.

I look at them all, one by one. Tav is taking great pains to look anywhere else but at me. Debs is looking at her feet, Dayz is staring at something behind me, her head tipped like a curious dog and the other two are just looking bored.

Pinching the bridge of my nose, I take a deep breath before feeling a small, soft hand gently caressing the tense spot between my shoulders. I look down at my wife and smile. We've spent the last two days wrapped up in each other. Meaning these fuck knuckles have been left to their own devices. Which somehow meant they all decided they needed to become Marx's problem.

"You do all realize that this is an MC clubhouse? Which means it's for the MC. Not pain in the ass in-laws."

"Well, now, I like to think that we're all friends...?" Tav trails off when Marx growls at him. To any other person, that growl on its own would put a man in his place. But it would seem the Tombs are made of different stuff because even though Tav's argument dies on his lips, none of them look particularly bothered.

"Tell him what the fuck you did," Marx growls out, leaning across the dining table in the common room, glaring at the five of them lined up on the other side.

"Wellll, there was a bit of a...hmmm, how do I put it.... a bit of a kind of explosion." Tav winces out, his face screwing up the longer he speaks. I let out a breath, and I hear Ana snort behind me.

"A kind of explosion? Does anyone want to explain what the fuck kind of exploded?"

Dayz's eyes flick to mine briefly before flitting away again. "It wasn't a 'kind of' explosion. It was definitely an explosion. And it was a person. Or people."

I blink once. Then twice, trying to register her words. I turn to look at Marx, who is almost vibrating.  He's that pissed. Glaring back at my family, I put my hand into my jacket, pull out my antacids and without even looking at Marx, I offer them to him in my outstretched hand.  I wait a moment and then they're snatched out of my hand and a gruff "Thank you" is aimed my way.

"Can you run that by me again, please?"

Dayz huffs with impatience. "The nomad bodies. Me, Pops and Tav were running an experiment to get rid of them, and they exploded. Kaboom. All the insides outside. Which," she spins to look at Pops, "I've figured, must have been their diet. If they're anything like this MC, they'd have a heavy diet of beer, carbs, sugar-"

"Fuck you're right girl!  We didn't take diet into account. We figured they'd ferment like normal cadavers, but their diet of beer would have accelerated it.  Making them all pop off like corks on homebrew," Pops chuckles, shaking his head. Tav, Dayz and Pops are all leaning in to each other and I know they're gonna wanna pow wow about this new information, so I growl at them, making them stand to attention, even Pops.

"So if you three exploded someone, why the hell are you two in trouble?" I look at Jules and Debs at the end of the line.

"Um, I may have dropped a little, tiny bit of 'fun time herb' into the brownies I baked."  The others snicker under their breaths.

"Ok. And why was that a problem?"

"She didn't tell us. Remy had some, and it didn't fucking agree with her," Wire grinds out, and Debs looks his way apologetically.

"Wire, it's ok. I'm fine. They just made me feel funny for

a while," Remy places her hand on Wire's forearm, petting him gently, and now I see what Dayz was watching over my shoulder.

"Still, you should have known before eating them. You said some pretty crazy stuff," he mumbles under his breath. A pink blush covers her face, and she almost withdraws into herself. Wire murmurs something to her, and then places his hand over hers. Interesting.

"I'm so sorry, Remy, I didn't think. I should have warned you before you ate them. Sorry Marx, sorry, guys." Debs drops her eyes to her hands, and she looks so remorseful that if Marx doesn't soothe her soon, me and him are gonna have problems. Marx softens his voice when he speaks.

"It's ok Debs. You meant well. Maybe just give us all a heads up next time, yeah?"

"So you'll still let me bake for you?" She says, hope in her large, brown eyes.

"Fuck yes, you aren't getting off the hook that easy." She beams up at him before looking to Wire and Remy. Wire gives a tight smile and a nod, while Remy, the exact opposite of Wire, gives her a wide grin and a thumbs up.

"Ok, that leaves me with you, Jules. What did you do?" I brace myself. Much like Dayz, Jules doesn't mince his words. He stares at me for a beat, then exhales. Shit, it must be bad.

"I was fucking a few of the club girls with Fox and Nitro and accidentally," his eyes swing to Marx, "thrust too hard." I frown at my wife, who looks baffled as to what the problem could be.

"So, Marx is pissed because you fucked a club girl, too hard?" She asks him, looking at him in a way I do not like. Like she wants to know what type of fucker he is. He's a filthy fucker.

And she's mine. So I remedy that by covering her eyes with my hand. She giggles and then pries my fingers apart so she can see.

"It gave her a fright. She went shooting up the bed, head-butting Fox's lap with force, breaking his cock. He can't go on the run he's scheduled for. He won't be able to ride for a while." He has the decency to cringe at this, at least.

I look at Marx, and I can see his lips twitch slightly, but we have to put on a show of strength. If we don't, these assholes will run amok.

"I have no idea why the hell you even had an orgy in the middle of the fucking day. On a Tuesday. When you're meant to be working on finding those missing girls for the FBI. You," I jab my finger at him "Are going to help Dayz and Pops clean up the mess they made," I hear him mutter "What the fuck?" under his breath, but he nods before they excuse themselves to get to work.

"Wait, what about me?" Tav says, his hand in the air like he's at school and I'm his fucking teacher.

"You have a bike. You're going to do the run with Nitro. No. Fucking. Shenanigans. Got me?" He nods enthusiastically.

"Get with Nitro, he'll go over route and shit with you," Marx says, waving him off.

"And you, Debs, you're on cooking duty here for the next week. Ok?" She beams up at me like I just gave her the best present in the world before nodding and heading off into the kitchen, Ana's arm around her shoulders, their heads bent together.

"Sorry man. I just don't know what comes over them." I run my hand down my face and accept the beer the prospect hands me after Marx waves his over.

"They're like honey badgers, man. They just don't give a fuck."

We both take a long pull of our beers, sitting quietly for a moment, then Marx lets out a snort, and then a chuckle, shaking his head back and forth.

"I swear to god, when those body parts rained down on my compound, for a split second I wished I had never pulled your sister into my office that night. If we had just let her do her thing, stayed out of it, then I wouldn't have to put up with all this shit." He takes another sip before he carries on. "But then my brother wouldn't have found his person and I wouldn't have one of the best enforcers I've ever had. I mean, my brother is a scary bastard, but that tiny woman? She can get grown men to spill their guts like no one I've ever seen."

I snort, "Thanks man. I'll take that as a compliment for the Tombs family fuckups."

"Yeah, you guys are alright. You're growing on me. Like a fungus."

Ana

I follow Mum into the kitchen and we go through what's in the fridge and pantry in companionable silence for a while. We work together like a well-oiled machine, somehow deciding that lasagne is on the menu tonight, without saying a word to each other. I look at her. Her dark curls bouncing around her face as she chops and dices ingredients. I notice the gray in her hair, the crinkles around her eyes from where she smiles so much. I realize that I've been so in my head I haven't been a good daughter.

"Mum, I'm sorry I haven't been spending much time with you since you've been here,"

"Aw baby, it's ok. You're a busy girl, and you've had a lot

going on. But I have too. I've been having so much fun with this crazy family. You don't need to worry about me, girl."

"But I do! You came here to see me and you've had to make do with hanging out with Pops." She smiles at me with a twinkle in her eye.

"Trust me, it's no great hardship," Um, ok.

"Anyway baby, how are things going with Gus? Have you stopped running and decided to hold on to that man with both hands?" I roll my eyes at her and then fix her with a bored look, one that she waves off with a snort. "Well?"

"Yes, Mum. I've stopped running and I've decided to maybe do a couple of sessions with that counselor lady. I'm hoping, no, I want, to enjoy my friendships and my relationship without that worry gnawing at me." Her face softens as she puts down the knife she was using and crosses the kitchen to wrap me in a hug.

"I'm so proud of you, baby. I mean, it's taken long enough, what 20, 30 years? But you're getting there and I never thought I'd see the day."

I wipe a stray tear off my cheek and nod at her. I'm proud of myself too.

"So, Ivan's funeral is tomorrow. How do you feel about that?" She eyes me, knowing full well how close we were. And we were. But he made his decision, and it cost him his life. Yes, he was my friend and yes, we had some amazing times. I will use this time to grieve for my friend. To say goodbye to the man I knew and loved, not the man that betrayed me. I also want to support Jenn, who is still my friend. She will need all the help she can get.

"I'm going to say goodbye to the man I knew. And to offer support to Jenn. She's going to need it."

"We'll all be here for you too, babe," Gus says from where he is leaning against the doorframe of the kitchen. My stomach flutters a little when I look up at him, marveling at how he chose me, and he loves me, and he will never hurt me. Knowing that deep in my heart is heady and powerful. And freeing.

"Sorry to interrupt, but we gotta get going, babe. We got our last session with Marta,"

"Yup. And we're going to ace this one!" He holds his hand out for me and I twine my fingers with his, letting him lead me out to his SUV that still doesn't have running boards on it. He grips my hips and lifts me in like I weigh nothing.

"I love you," He whispers as he drops a kiss to my lips, then buckles my seatbelt before rounding the front, tapping a merry tune on the hood, smiling at me through the windshield. I rest my head on the headrest and smile to myself. Yup, free. Free to love this man as much as he can handle.

# Epilogue

## Gus

I pull into the MC compound, parking next to the other Tombs Security SUV, what looks to be Tav's bike, and, as per usual, Pops' pickup that is parked across two spaces.

"This better be good," Ana grumbles as I help her out of the SUV. "I'm starving and this is seriously cutting into our dinner time." I nod in agreement.

We were just leaving Roman's office with a plan to stop off for the Kung Pow chicken Ana is "dying for" when I got the alert that we were all needed. I have no idea when we stopped meeting at the office and started meeting at the clubhouse. It was insidious, much like how my family has inserted ourselves into the DRMC. I shake my head at that. It was all Dayz's fault, really. Not only is she an Ol' Lady, but, thanks to her skill set, she is now the unofficial part time enforcer of the Devil's Rose MC. Freeing Rhodie up to take his rightful place as his brother's VP. A place Marx had been holding until he could find a replacement for his brother's role. Who would have thought it was going to be a tiny neurodivergent woman?

Shaking my head, I take my wife's hand and lead her into the common room, which is looking pretty full right now. My whole family and most of the MC brothers are here, some at the bar, some sitting at the dining tables. My sister and Rhodie are on the couch, across from Pops, who seems to have commandeered a lazy boy. I tip my chin up at Marx, who is busy smirking at me across the room. Clearly he knows what's going on and it's making me tense, because it most likely has something to do with my family.

Ana plops down at the table, looking around at everyone talking and laughing with each other, the scowl on her face growing by the second. She's been a little irritable the past couple of days, but I'm putting that down to how busy she is at work. The Bratva are working overtime trying to track down their drugs.

They aren't the only ones with a lot on their plate, though. Savage's Death Riders have been having more problems with Hammer. He's been fucking with them by masquerading as them, taking some of their runs. It makes me wonder whether Savage would ever just cut loose of the Death Rider's ties and patch over to Devil's Rose MC. It seems like it would solve a lot of problems. Let Hammer have his little name and club until we all destroy him.

DRMC and my siblings have been busy working all other angles we can think of to trace the missing girls and put a stop to the auctions, but it's a little like the Hydra. You cut off one head, two more grow. There is no end to the number of despicable men wanting to rise and take the lead.

"Ok, what the hell was so important we had to come all this way? I'm missing out on my Kung Pow chicken!" Ana grumbles, just loud enough to draw attention. Tav clears his throat before stepping up to the front of the room, standing next to Marx.

"I, well, Marx has an announcement, and I wanted you all here for this." Tav smiles out at us and I frown, catching Pops' eye. We both squint at each other in confusion. Dayz is ignoring the goings on, instead choosing to play tonsil hockey with Rhodie. Jules comes out from the kitchen to help Debs pass out cookies. The woman came for a holiday but seems to have now become the full-time cook here at the clubhouse.

"Ok. Well, what is it?" Ana asks, clearly impatient. She waves her hands in the "hurry up" gesture and I trap one of her hands in mine, kissing the back of her knuckles. She melts into me, momentarily forgetting that she's hungry. And pissy.

"Ok, listen up, you fuc-" Marx's eyes dart to Debs before he clears his throat, "I mean, you folks," He looks at Debs again, who beams at him and gives him two thumbs up. Nodding, he carries on, "I would like to welcome our newest prospect to the Devil's Rose MC family, although you all know the cheeky asshole. Welcome Tav!" He whacks Tav on the back and hands him over a cut that says "Prospect" on the front.

My eyebrows fly up, a little shocked that he never mentioned anything to me. But, thinking about it for two seconds, I realize that this is the perfect place for my little brother. Tav is a golden retriever. Yes, he has us, but he's always been a soft-hearted soul who loves and needs people in his life. I'm over the moon that he's going to have so many people that have his back as fiercely as he has theirs, and the patch to go with it.

Everyone around him goes crazy. Heavy leather boots stomp, whistles ring out, the brothers and the Tombs all clap and offer our noisy congratulations and Ana ... bursts into tears.

"Um, Ana, you ok babe?" I stroke her back, unsure what the

hell is going on. The room hushes, and Tav comes over to squat in front of her.

"Hey, hey, what's wrong Kiwi Sis?" He started calling her that once we got back from Roman's cabin. Neither me nor Ana actually realized how much my family loved her and were scared she was going to run out on them too. Since everything settled down, they've all just doubled down on their love for her and for Debs. Between them and the MC, our family has grown exponentially.

"Nothing is wrong. I'm just so damned proud of you Tav. You're going to make a damned good brother because you *are* a damned good brother," she splutters out before sobbing.

"Um, thank you?" Tav says, eyeing her as he backs away before mouthing "what the fuck?" at me.

"What's wrong with her Gus? What did you do?" Dayz's accusing tone hits my ears and I spin around.

"I didn't do anything! I don't know what's wrong," I'm getting a little concerned. This isn't Ana. I sit next to her, then lift her from her chair onto my lap, wrapping her up as she continues to cry and snot all over me.

"Isn't it obvious?" Pops' voice breaks through the strained silence. I hope whatever is "obvious" to him isn't anything fucked up. But it's Pops, so you can never be too sure.

He looks around at the room of blank or slightly concerned faces.

"There are communists in the funhouse." He says with all the confidence of a man who is absolutely off his rocker. Marx raises his eyebrow at me, and I shrug. Everyone else is squinting at each other as if we're trying to solve a riddle.

"There are COMMUNISTS in the FUNHOUSE." He says again, slower this time to really drum home what he's saying. Or not saying as the case may be.

"Old man, what the hell is that meant to mean? Are you talking about the Bratva?" Marx says in his voice that sounds like he's been gargling glass.

Pops eyes him, before huffing, rubbing a hand down his face and trying once again.

"There are communists in the funhouse. Japan is attacking." What the actual fuck? "The English have landed. Granny is coming in the red car. The painters are in. Shark week, bloody Mary, the crimson wa-"

"Fuck's sake, I'm not on my period. I'm PREGNANT!" Ana yells out, stunning the old man into silence. My brain stumbles over the words she just spoke before coming online with a vengeance. I look down at her and my face may display shock, but I can feel warmth blooming in my chest at her announcement. She's looking down at her lap, her fingers twisting, avoiding my gaze. I don't know what the hell is going on around us, but all I see is her, and I need her bright green eyes on mine. Tipping her chin with my big rough finger, her eyes peek at me, glistening with tears, and I see apprehension.

"Baby, are you sure? You're having my baby?" I gently caress her cheek before dropping my hand to her soft, rounded tummy.

Holding my eyes, she nods. "I took six tests. Mum confirmed they were all positive." Her eyes dart to Debs, who has her hands clasped under her chin, a huge smile on her face. I notice that she's cuddled into the crook of Pops' arm. Pops, whose eyes are glistening with tears as well.

"Oh Ana, my little wife," I whisper, "Our love made a baby. Thank you. Thank you for taking a chance on me and making me the happiest man in the world." She beams up at me, a cheeky smile on her face.

"Thank you for fake marrying me," I swat her on the ass.

"It was real, Ana, it was always real. I love you, Wife."

"And I love you, Husband."  I sip from her lips before throwing my head back and crowing.

"We're having a baby!"

# In case you're wondering

Hei aha - no matter
Kei te pai - it's good, I'm good, all good
Kotiro - girl
Zasranets - Asshole
Brat - Brother
Drook - friend

# Thank you for reading!

Thank you so much for choosing to spend a little time with the characters I made up. What a wild ride!

If you want to know more about me or what I'm reading you can find me all over the place -

Follow me at my author page on Facebook

Friend me on Facebook

Join my group Cleo Browne's Babes

Follow me on Instagram

Keep your eyes peeled for upcoming books in the Devil's Rose MC Series, The Tombs Security Series, and a new series, because I can't just write two concurrently, The Davies Family Series - Small Town Romance set in Rose Grove. There may even be cameos from some of your fave characters.

# Cleo Browne Books

**Rhodie – Devil's Rose MC Book One**

**August – A Tombs Security + Devil's Rose MC Crossover**

Wire – Devil's Rose MC Book Two
*In progress*

Tav Devil's Rose MC Book Three
*In progress*

# About the Author

Cleo Browne is the pen name of a neurospicy geeky girl from Aotearoa New Zealand. As a child, she realized very early on that she wasn't a people person, so she would spend all her time reading and writing her own stories. These stories usually ended with the line "and then they died". As an adult, she has gotten slightly more people-y (not much) and better at not killing all her characters off when she writes.

Cleo loves to write about women who don't need a man to do their dirty work and the hot alpha men who turn to mush when they watch their women handling business.

When she's not writing romance novels about strong, curvy women and the men who adore them, she hangs out at home with her hubby, her boys, and her ancient greyhound who likes to creepily watch her write.

# Acknowledgements

First off, I'd like to thank all the wonderful readers who took a chance on a kooky little autistic woman and read my first offering, Rhodie. Without you all reading it and loving it, this book would never have happened. I would have just faded away into obscurity, never to be seen or heard from again. So, thank you. I appreciate you all.

Second, I'd like to thank my author bestie and all round good biartch Shaye Torrel. Thank you so much for talking me off the cliff when I would freak out that I didn't know what I was doing. I still don't, but at least I'm not freaking out about it. I wouldn't be here without you, chick!

Thanks to my partner PN. Without his constant words of encouragement, "I really didn't think MC books were a thing," I would never have finished this book. Thanks also go to my boys. Ronnie, for being completely disinterested, and Louis for your two hour long phone calls that would eat into my writing time. Love you guys.